## "I'm not much of a[...] shall we?"

Still laughing, Troy gave Molly his hand.

High Valley was in a party mood. And, as they swayed together, her heart caught in her throat.

"Look." Troy jerked his chin toward the sky.

Molly glanced up. "It's snowing." Fluffy flakes drifted lazily down and landed on her face and parka. The colored lights and faces in the crowd swirled together as the song changed to Thomas Rhett's "Christmas in the Country."

"Magical, isn't it?" Troy's voice was husky in her ear. She loved this song.

"Troy, I..." The music and crowd noise faded until it was only the two of them.

The softness in his eyes and gentle smile almost undid her, unlocking feelings and emotions she'd thought were gone forever.

"This is probably a mistake," she whispered.

"You and I were *never* a mistake."

Dear Reader,

*A Rancher's Return* is the final book in my The Montana Carters miniseries. Although each book stands alone, if it's your first visit to the Carter family's Tall Grass Ranch and close-knit town of High Valley, Montana, I hope you'll check out the other three books, each featuring another Carter sibling. There's also a Montana Carters short story, "Reunion at the Bluebunch Café," to read for free on Harlequin's website.

This book is Molly Carter's story. She always wanted to be a big-city nurse, and she's home in Montana on vacation, not to stay. But when she bumps into her teenage love, Troy Clayton, a onetime ranch hand turned technology entrepreneur and now ranch owner, things get complicated.

Like Molly, I once focused on having the career and life I thought I wanted without letting myself consider other options. But, also like Molly, when I learned to open my life and heart to unexpected possibilities, I found my own happily-ever-after.

I enjoy hearing from readers, so please visit my website, jengilroy.com, and message me there, where you'll also find my social media links and newsletter and blog signups.

Happy reading!

*Jen Gilroy*

# A RANCHER'S RETURN

## JEN GILROY

Harlequin

**HEARTWARMING**

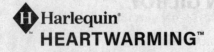

**Harlequin®**
## HEARTWARMING™

Recycling programs for this product may not exist in your area.

ISBN-13: 978-1-335-05126-4

A Rancher's Return

Copyright © 2024 by Jen Gilroy

For questions and comments about the quality of this book, please contact us at CustomerService@Harlequin.com.

TM and ® are trademarks of Harlequin Enterprises ULC.

 Harlequin Enterprises ULC
22 Adelaide St. West, 41st Floor
Toronto, Ontario M5H 4E3, Canada
www.Harlequin.com

Printed in Lithuania

**Jen Gilroy** writes sweet romance and uplifting women's fiction—warm feel-good stories to bring readers' hearts home. A Romance Writers of America Golden Heart® Award finalist and short-listed for the Romantic Novelists' Association Joan Hessayon Award, she lives in small-town Ontario, Canada, with her husband, teenage daughter and floppy-eared rescue hound. She loves reading, ice cream, ballet and paddling her purple kayak. Visit her at jengilroy.com.

**Books by Jen Gilroy**

**Harlequin Heartwarming**

*Montana Reunion*
*A Family for the Rodeo Cowboy*
*The Cowgirl Nanny*

Visit the Author Profile page at Harlequin.com.

In memory of my first literary agent, Dawn Dowdle,
founder of Blue Ridge Literary Agency,
who died suddenly, November 13, 2023.

I'm grateful to Dawn for launching my author career,
and for her support and friendship in life and writing.

# *CHAPTER ONE*

Nowadays, Molly Carter didn't belong in High Valley, Montana. Maybe she didn't belong anywhere else either, but she couldn't hide out in one of the community center's restrooms all evening. As her late dad would have said, she had to put on her game face and "fake it till you make it." With a smile on her face, if not a spring in her step, she straightened her shoulders, opened the door and made herself return to the party room.

Decorated with orange pumpkins, yellow squash, colorful fall garlands and twinkling white lights, the venue was festive. And while she'd lingered in the restroom, the spacious area had filled with people here to celebrate Molly's mom's engagement and upcoming marriage to rancher Shane Gallagher. Her mom and Shane were having a double Thanksgiving wedding with Molly's brother Bryce, the sibling nearest her in age, and his fiancée, champion barrel racer Carrie Rizzo. Although this party hadn't initially been planned for Bryce and Carrie, when they'd decided to get married at Thanksgiving as well, it, like the weddings, became a joint celebration.

Country music echoed from the sound system, and the caterer directed staff setting up buffet tables. Her mom's friends, members of a local women's group called the Sunflower Sisterhood, darted here and there, lending a hand where needed. And beneath yellow-and-white bunting festooned with hearts and their intertwined initials, the engaged couples greeted their guests.

"Hey, stranger." Molly's eldest living brother, Zach, found her at the edge of the crowd and wrapped her in a hug. "When did you get in?"

"Late this afternoon. I only had time to shower and change before coming here with Mom and Shane." Molly returned Zach's hug, breathing in frosty late-October air mixed with the crisp scent of his aftershave—one their late dad had also worn. The backs of her eyes smarted. She liked Shane and he made her mom happy, but she missed her dad and thought of him daily.

"It's good to have you back, but you look tired." As Zach studied her, Molly's cheeks warmed. Of all her family, Zach was the one who was most likely to see behind her happy facade. But since his wife, Beth, was expecting their first baby soon, Molly counted on him being too preoccupied to notice much of anything else.

Molly brushed away his concern with a light laugh. "Even though I took my time, it was a long drive." She'd packed up her studio apartment and handed over the place she'd called home for the last three years to a medical student from Kentucky, as wide-eyed and eager as Molly had once been. Then she'd made the cross-country trek from Georgia, hauling a rented trailer filled with boxes behind her old but reliable SUV. For now, she'd left the trailer by the barn at her family's ranch, but it only held her visible baggage. The rest she planned to keep hidden and pretend she was the same Molly she'd always been.

"I still wish you'd let one of us fly to Atlanta and drive back here with you. Dad would have—"

"I'm an adult." Molly stopped Zach. "I know you worry but there's no need. I hardly saw any people, and no animals bigger than a desert cottontail." But those five days alone had given her too much time to think about things she usually buried deep.

"There she is." The women of the Sunflower Sisterhood came over in a group to greet her, and Molly was enveloped in more hugs. Questions quickly followed.

"Atlanta's nice but it's great to be home. I'm taking an extended vacation to be here for the holidays, the weddings and, of course, Zach and Beth's baby." Molly gave Zach a brief smile before turning back to Rosa Cardinal, her mom's best friend who owned the local craft center. "Between graduate school and contract work, the past few years have been busy. I'm glad to have a break before starting a permanent job." That job, a clinical research position in pediatric nursing, would be waiting for her in early January and she should be thrilled about it. She *was* thrilled. Molly smiled harder as she answered more of Rosa's questions.

"Where are Beth and Ellie?" As Rosa and the others dispersed, Molly glanced at Zach before scanning the crowd for her sister-in-law and teenage niece.

"They're here somewhere." Zach's grin was resigned. "I dropped them at the door and went to park the truck, but they probably got waylaid by folks. You know how it is."

"Yeah." That was small-town life. You stopped and chatted with people even if you'd seen them the day before. "There they are." Molly waved and moved toward Beth, who was with Molly's middle brother, Cole, his wife, Melissa, and several excited kids.

There were more hugs and greetings, and Molly embraced Zach's adopted daughter, Ellie, Bryce's kids, Paisley and Cam, and Melissa's daughter, Skylar.

Although neither of them had grown up in High Valley, Beth and Melissa seemed at home here, whereas Molly was now the outsider. She'd wanted city life and she'd gotten it, but at what cost? She pushed the thought away. She was here to spend time with her family, and then she'd go back to Atlanta. She'd ignore those prickles of unease that had become increasingly insistent on her cross-country drive. She was living the life she wanted. The life she'd been planning from the time she was eight years old, the same age as her niece, Paisley.

Cole grinned and said, "Look at you, Jellybean. I hardly recognized you in that fancy dress and shoes." He picked Molly up and swung her around like he'd done when she was a kid.

"Put me down!" Molly squealed in protest. "And don't call me Jellybean either."

"Sorry, Mol." Cole lowered her gently to the ground. "I'm teasing. Even grown up, you'll always be my baby sister." His tone was apologetic. "I love you, and I'm glad you're home is all."

Molly smoothed her blond hair away from her face. "I love you too." Like their dad, her brothers were good men who set a high standard. Although she'd dated a few guys in Atlanta, they hadn't matched the ones she'd grown up with.

As Molly turned around, she stilled, and her heart gave a painful thud. *It couldn't be.* She blinked, and heat rushed to her face.

"Molly?" His voice was deeper, but she'd have recognized that rich timbre anywhere.

"Yeah. Hi, Troy." She'd also have recognized him anywhere. Troy was older, they both were, but if anything, he looked even better than he had at twenty. Tall, broad-shouldered and with the same dark brown hair and vivid blue eyes, he was also somehow bigger, with a new air of confidence and leadership. "I didn't know you were in High Valley." The last Molly had heard, he'd left the area when she'd gone to college and, unlike her, he'd never come back.

"You two already know each other?" Cole glanced between them.

"I was still living at home the summer Troy worked for us as a hand," Molly said through numb lips.

"That's great." Cole beamed, oblivious to any undercurrents. "Troy and I didn't cross paths then, but I met him a month ago at a livestock auction. He's on board as an investor for my stock contracting business. He's back in town because he bought the Bitterroot Ranch." Cole looped an arm around Molly's shoulders and gave her an affectionate squeeze before turning to Troy. "While she's here, Molly's giving me a hand with the business."

As Cole's words washed over her, Molly could barely take in what her brother was saying. Troy here? It should be impossible. But, as Cole talked on, a quick glance at Troy assured here he was all too real. So many ranch hands passed through the area, and he was just one more. At least, that was what she'd tried to make herself believe. She'd put her memories of that summer before she left for college out of her mind and heart and thought she'd succeeded.

"Good to see you again, Troy." *Liar.* He was the last person she wanted to see. "I should get going. I told my mom I'd help set out the… food." Another lie, but it was the first thing she thought of. Although she'd offered, the food and everything else tonight was taken care of. All Molly had to do was have fun—which had suddenly become a lot more complicated.

"I should head out." Troy's beard-shadowed cheeks reddened. "I only came by to drop off a set of keys. My Realtor forgot them in my car earlier. He said he'd be here tonight, and since I was coming to town I offered to drop them off. I didn't know it was a party for your mom and brother."

"No worries. Stay." Cole clapped Troy's shoulder. "There's plenty of food, and some folks will remember you and be glad to catch up."

"You'd sure be welcome." Zach echoed Cole's invitation. Like all the Carters, her brothers were hospitable. Molly usually appreciated having a welcoming family but not now.

She made her way toward her mom on shaky legs. She'd only be here a few months. She'd avoid Troy when she could, but even when they happened to cross paths, they were both adults. It would be fine.

It didn't matter how a guy like Troy had managed to buy a ranch like the Bitterroot or what he'd been up to in the past nine years. Although, her stomach churned at the memory of his stricken expression as she'd left him in the barn that night.

Back then, after that brief and secret summer romance, she'd thought pursuing anything more with Troy would be the biggest mistake of her life. But now she was older and wiser. Maybe he was the best thing that had ever happened to her. Except, she couldn't admit it because if she did, she'd have to admit other things as well.

She'd made a life in Atlanta, and it was her real life—one Troy Clayton wasn't part of.

*MOLLY CARTER*. Troy had been back in High Valley less than twenty-four hours. It figured that the one person he didn't want to see was who he'd bump into. From everything he'd heard, Molly was long gone and only returned to High Valley for occasional visits. He'd planned to slip into the community center, return the keys to his Realtor and slip out again. Instead, he'd ended up at a Carter family party with a glass of fruit punch in one hand and a plate of food in the other, being welcomed by folks he hardly remembered like he was a long-lost friend.

He ate a cheese puff and tried to pay attention to Mr. Kuntz, a white-haired man who'd owned the town's feed store before he retired.

"You hit the jackpot buying the Bitterroot Ranch." Mr. Kuntz nodded approval. "Apart from the Carters' spread, you won't find better land between here and the Canadian border. The barns are in good repair, and there's excellent breeding stock to build on."

"That's the idea." Although Troy had dreamed of owning the Bitterroot Ranch since he and his dad had milked cows there one winter, he'd only made an offer on it because the place was profitable and could become even more so. Along with investing in Cole Carter's stock contracting venture, buying the ranch was part of Troy's strategy to diversify his business interests. As a

kid on those cold early mornings in the Bitterroot's milking barn, he'd vowed that he'd take
care of his family when he grew up. He'd make
sure he and his folks and younger sister would
never have to worry about losing their home or
where their next meal came from. He'd kept that
vow and more, achieving his goals even earlier
than he'd planned.

Mr. Kuntz gestured to the crowd, where Molly
was crouched among a group of children, her
back to Troy. "Molly Carter's sure grown up into
a fine-looking woman. She reminds me of my
Theresa. My late wife was a nurse." Mr. Kuntz's
eyes got misty. "You'll need a wife and family
at the Bitterroot. How many bedrooms does that
house have? At least five, right?"

"Yeah." It had been built when most people
had large families. However, Troy wouldn't let
himself think about having a wife and family.
While he'd gotten the ranch he wanted, he'd set
the rest of his dreams aside to focus on work.
Once, he'd imagined sharing that ranch house
with Molly, and them having a family to fill
those bedrooms, but that was in the past. "I'm
happy as I am. I like my own company." The
ranch house, and the acres of land it sat on, were
an investment. He'd use the primary bedroom,
kitchen and living room and a smaller bedroom
as an office. Or maybe he'd rent the house out

and move into the bungalow that used to be grandparent accommodation.

Troy stepped aside to let a family group reach the buffet table and got a better view of Molly. Still with her back to him, she now stood in the center of a circle as the children ran around her playing some game. Her honey-blond hair fell in soft waves to her shoulders. In a navy blue dress that skimmed her knees, her outfit was simple, conservative even, but it had gauzy sleeves and a tailored look that drew his attention to her soft curves. It wasn't the clothes, though. She'd look as good in jeans and a T-shirt mucking out barn stalls. Despite time and the sting of hurt that Troy had buried deep, no other woman matched her and maybe never would.

"You can manage on your own, but why would you want to?" Mr. Kuntz's voice was wistful. "I used to joke with Theresa and the kids about my 'man cave' in the basement. But Theresa passed way too soon, only in her late thirties, and now with our kids grown and gone, having the whole house to myself gets lonely. I cook for myself and have a cleaner, but love and companionship are important." He patted Troy's arm. "I hear Molly's sticking around for a few months. You should make a move before some other fellow does."

Troy had made his move long ago. Although at first Molly had seemed as keen on him as he was about her, she'd sent him packing at the end of the summer. Wounded, Troy had made sure that kind of rejection would never happen again. Apart from his family and business partner, Pete, he didn't give his trust easily or depend on others, and kept his relationships casual. Money talked, as the saying went, and he was never sure if people liked him for himself or his bank account. And although his heartbreak over Molly had almost destroyed him, it had also made him more determined to reach his goals.

As several men drew Mr. Kuntz into a conversation about golf, Troy glanced toward the hall's exit. The speeches were over, and dancing had started. He'd already congratulated the happy couples. If he slipped out now, nobody would notice. He made it as far as the buffet table to set his plate of almost untouched food down when he heard Mr. Kuntz's booming voice.

"I appreciate the compliment, but you should ask one of the young fellows to dance, not an old geezer like me. What about Troy over there?"

Troy turned and saw Molly standing by the man's side. Her cheeks went pink when Troy caught her gaze.

"Come here, lad." Mr. Kuntz waved. "Don't be shy."

Except for Molly, Troy had never been shy with

women or anyone else. "I'm sure Molly has lots of guys wanting to dance with her." The color on her cheeks deepened to red. "Besides, I'm leaving."

"You see?" Molly's voice was choked.

"Nonsense." A gray-haired woman came around the table and looked between Molly and Troy. "The party's only just gotten started." She extended a hand to Mr. Kuntz. "Let's show the young folks how it's done, shall we, Werner?"

"But, Mrs. Shevchenko, I… You…" Molly looked around as if searching for someone to rescue her.

"I'd be delighted." Mr. Kuntz gave the woman a courtly bow and smiled at Troy. "Nina and I went to school together. We used to compete for who'd get the highest marks in math."

"I usually won." Although Nina Shevchenko's voice was smug, she gave Mr. Kuntz a warm smile. "Welcome back, Troy." She turned the full wattage of her smile on him. "I'll drop by this week with a few meals so you don't have to cook while you're getting settled. How does lasagna and chicken potpie with a batch of my sunflower cookies and chocolate brownies sound?"

"That would be great, but you don't need to—"

"It's no trouble." She waved away Troy's protest. "If you're not home, I'll leave the food in a cooler on the porch."

She and Mr. Kuntz joined the dancers, leaving Troy and Molly alone. If he was smart, he'd make his apologies and head right over to that exit. However, when it came to Molly, he'd never been smart. He held out a hand. "Shall we?"

She took it, and her smooth skin against his palm sent shivers up his spine.

"I'll only dance with you because folks are staring. I don't want to cause a scene." As they moved onto the floor with other couples, Molly kept her head bowed.

"I don't either but…" He swallowed. Of course, it was a slow dance. The romantic waltz, "Harvest Moon Heart" by Rob Georg, with lyrics about true love, was like a knife to Troy's heart.

"Congratulations on buying the Bitterroot." As she moved to the music, Molly kept a careful distance between them. "I remember you liked that ranch."

"I did." And buying it proved to himself and everyone else that Troy Clayton had made it. He wasn't the kid whose folks lost the family ranch because of two years of crop failure and his mom being laid off from her town job. He wasn't a ranch hand any longer either, with most of his meager paycheck going to help his family, or a student juggling school, loans and multiple jobs. He'd worked hard, put himself through college, paid off those loans, sacrificed to be a success and never questioned his choices. "Cole said you live in Atlanta."

"Yes." She finally raised her head, and looking into her blue eyes still about winded him. "It's a great city."

Although she didn't say it, there was a "but" there. Maybe what she hadn't said was even more important.

He nodded. "Before moving here, I was based in California, Silicon Valley, but I've been to Atlanta a few times on business."

"What kind of work do you do?" Her voice was cool, almost as if they were strangers.

"I'm a technology entrepreneur. I start companies and then, after a few years, I sell them." There was a lot more to it than that, including creativity, a savvy strategy and luck, but Troy loved building something from nothing and seeing it flourish.

"That's…great." Molly's voice hitched. "You were always interested in technical stuff. How are your folks doing? They must be really proud of you."

"They're fine. They live in San Francisco." In a condo Troy bought for them after he sold his first company. Although his folks *were* proud, sometimes he caught them looking at him with matching concerned expressions. Maybe no matter how much he achieved in business, they worried about him the same as ever, as if he'd somehow failed in life. "My parents are done with Montana winters, but they want to spend their summers here with me. When the Bitterroot came on the market, it was good timing. Real estate's an excellent investment." Maybe he'd buy his folks a house in town where they'd have a better chance to make friends and be part of things than out on his ranch.

His gaze caught Molly's again before he made himself look away. His focus was on the ranch and the climate change start-up he and his business partner had launched a few months ago. He couldn't let himself be distracted by Molly's blue eyes or looking for her sweet smile. Even if she hadn't directed that smile toward him tonight.

"A ranch is more than an 'excellent investment.' It's a place to put down roots from one generation to the next, to care for that land for the future." As Molly exhaled, her warm breath brushed Troy's cheek. "You grew up living and working on ranches. I thought… It doesn't matter. It's none of my business…" Her voice trailed away.

"It *does* matter." Guilt curled in the pit of Troy's stomach. Had he moved too far away from those roots he'd once cherished and forgotten what land and environmental stewardship meant in reality, as opposed to theory? Even at eighteen, Molly was passionate about what she believed in, and that was one of the things Troy had loved about her. If, at twenty, he'd even known what love was.

The song ended, and Molly dropped his hand. "I promised Cole I'd pitch in with his stock contracting business, and I'd never let him down. But since you've invested in his venture, I don't want it to be awkward." She hesitated. "I'd rather people didn't know...about us." She fiddled with a silver bracelet on her right wrist.

"Of course." Troy wasn't about to blab to folks that the only woman he'd ever loved had dumped him.

"Great." She slid the bangle bracelet up and down her forearm. "We can be colleagues and friends."

"No, we can't." Molly was still way too appealing, and Troy had to keep his distance. "Since I'm the biggest investor in Cole's business, as well as his partner, technically, that means I'm his boss. Yours too." He flinched. Even to his own ears, he sounded pompous.

"Oh. Of course." She backed away.

Troy mentally berated himself. He'd never been a heavy-handed boss and he wouldn't start now. However, Molly still had a way of breaking down the walls he'd put up and reaching the hurt kid deep inside. The one who was scared, vulnerable and wanted to make his mark in the world but hadn't yet figured out how. "I'm sorry. That came out wrong. I didn't mean—"

"It's fine." Her voice was brittle and her smile artificially bright. "I'm going back to Atlanta in a few months anyway. Until then, you'll do your job, and I'll do mine. For Cole, right?"

"Yeah." Troy stuffed his hands into his pockets so he wouldn't reach out to touch her, to hold her like he once had. Back then it had felt as if, with her in his arms and by his side, he could take on the world. "Cole needed extra capital. In a year or so, I'll have my investment back and more, and he'll be on his own again. I believe in him and that he'll succeed." Like he'd once believed in Molly, although it wasn't really the same thing. "I won't be the kind of boss who breathes down your neck."

"I never thought you would be. Anyway, I should...mingle." Molly's smile was so tight it was more like a grimace.

"Go on, then." Before she turned away, Troy made himself give what he hoped was a neutral, professional smile while trying to ignore the powerful rush of attraction that drew him to her.

Maybe coming back to this part of Montana

was a bad idea. But it was too late now, and Troy wasn't a quitter. He'd just have to avoid Molly for the next eight or nine weeks. How hard could it be?

# CHAPTER TWO

THE NEXT MORNING, Molly slid her empty suitcase under the bed, where the white-frilled bed skirt hid it from view, and grabbed a sweatshirt from the chest of drawers. Except for the colorful Welcome Home, Auntie Molly banner her nieces and nephew had made and hung on one wall, her bedroom at the ranch house looked the same as it always had. The view from the old casement window hadn't changed either, with land that belonged to the Tall Grass Ranch stretching as far as she could see.

Today the fields were etched with silver frost, and mist hung over the white-painted fence that encircled the horse paddock near the house. She shivered and shrugged into the sweatshirt. It was an old High Valley High School one she'd left behind when she'd gone to college and wanted everything shiny and new. Now the worn blue fleece embraced her like an old friend.

"Molly? You up?" Her mom's voice reached

her from the bottom of the stairs, as it had in those school days.

"Yeah. Coming." Not bothering to brush her hair, she pulled it into a high ponytail, left the phone that held her Atlanta life on the bedside table and took the familiar stairs with their worn runner two at a time.

From what she'd seen yesterday, the ranch house was as unchanged as her bedroom. Although her folks had simple tastes, even before her dad passed, money was tight. Apart from an occasional coat of fresh paint, her mom had "made do," as she put it. Molly's stomach lurched as she rounded the corner into the front hall with its gallery of framed family photos, where her master's degree graduation picture was front and center. Although Molly had worked part-time to pay her own way as much as she could, her mom and brothers had helped fund her education. That was likely why the stair runner and other things hadn't been replaced. Were her college costs also the reason Cole needed an investor for his stock contracting business?

"Morning, honey." From the stove, her mom greeted her with a cheery smile. Her blue eyes shone as she gave Molly a one-armed hug. "I'd have let you sleep in, but once they're done their chores the hands are reshingling the henhouse roof. I didn't want you waking up to that racket."

"I've been up for a few hours." She'd hardly slept but she couldn't tell her mom that without also telling her why. *Troy Clayton*. She turned to the coffeepot and poured herself a cup of the fragrant brew. "I unpacked my clothes, and except for a few boxes, the rest of the stuff in the trailer I rented can go in the main barn. I talked to Bryce and Cole last night. They can unload it with me later." If the biggest reminders of her Atlanta life were out of sight, maybe she could stop thinking about it.

"You don't have to store your things in a barn. I cleared space in the basement or—"

"It's fine." Molly swallowed a mouthful of the full-bodied coffee without tasting it. "With Zach, Beth and Ellie moving in here, and you moving into Carrie's place on her farm while you and Shane are building your house, you don't need my belongings taking up space."

"You're family, Molly. It'll be a pleasure having you take up whatever space you want and need." Her mom popped a plate of pancakes in the oven to warm and then came over to cup Molly's chin in her hands. "Is everything okay, sweetheart?"

"Sure. I'm tired, that's all." She manufactured a smile.

"It's no wonder. Between work, school and that long drive across the country, you need a good rest."

Except, no amount of "rest" would soothe the turmoil in Molly's heart. "I'm fine, Mom, really. What can I do?" If she kept busy, she wouldn't think about Troy or anything else. She usually grabbed breakfast on her way out the door, stuffing containers of yogurt and trail mix, a piece of fruit and maybe a muffin into a lunch bag. Here, though, her family and the ranch hands came in for breakfast, and the meal was a time to talk and get ready for the rest of the day.

"No need for you to do anything." Her mom gestured with a spatula before putting it in the dishwasher. "The table's set. Eggs, pancakes and sausages are cooked, so get some food and set yourself down in your usual place and dig in. The hands and your brothers will be in shortly."

"Are you sure? I always help. I'm not a guest." She took a plate from the stack at one end of the long farmhouse table and served herself the food her mom indicated.

"Let me spoil you a bit, all right? At least for the weekend, you're on vacation." Her mom put several slices of bread into the toaster and then filled a glass jug that had belonged to Molly's grandma with maple syrup. "Besides, I've got ranch breakfasts down to a science. After the wedding, I'll be sharing this routine with the others. It's right Zach and his family live here, but I'll miss this house and everything that comes with it."

"That's understandable but think of the wonderful new house you'll have with Shane." Her soon-to-be stepfather had emailed Molly the architect's plans and asked for her input on the bedroom with attached bath that would be hers whenever she visited.

"I know. I'm thrilled to have everything fresh and modern, but it's hard to let go of the memories." Her mom put toast on a plate and joined Molly at the table. "I remind myself that Zach, Beth, Ellie and the baby will make new memories here. Besides, this house will still be part of my life, only in a different way."

Like it would still be part of Molly's life. She took a piece of toast and buttered it. She'd certainly changed over the years, and it made sense others had as well. But it was still strange to think of coming here and having Zach and his family living in the only true home she'd ever known.

"I almost forgot to tell you. I have an appointment at the wedding dress shop for a final fitting this afternoon. You need to try on the maid of honor dresses I picked out for you, and I thought we could look at shoes."

"Fine with me." Molly picked up her fork. "I'm happy to wear whatever dress you want. It's your wedding and—" Male voices echoed outside the back door and boots stamped on the mat.

"Look who I ran into outside." Cole came into the kitchen, and his face was ruddy with cold. "Troy and I have a meeting, but chores took longer so I invited him to join us for breakfast. We can all talk together."

"We?" Molly put a hand to her unbrushed hair.

"Yeah, you, me and Troy." In his sock feet, Cole came across the kitchen and gave her a teasing grin. "Don't worry, I'll give you a few days to settle back in before hauling you out of bed at the crack of dawn to come out to the barns." He turned to Troy. "Molly's never been a morning person. Back in the day, she always tried to get assigned the late chores instead of the early ones."

"I did not. I never asked for special favors." Molly bit back the rest of her protest. She'd never wanted to be treated differently because her folks owned the ranch, but now she didn't want to sound like a teenager arguing with her brother.

"Molly always worked as hard as the rest of us." Peacemaker Zach took his seat at the head of the table in the place that had once been their dad's.

"She sure did." Cole's expression sobered as he and Troy sat across from her, and Bryce took the chair on Molly's right. "Mom says things work out in unexpected ways, and I guess they do. I'm a lucky man having the two of you on board with my business for the next while." He raised his glass of orange juice in a toast.

After a career-ending rodeo injury that could have killed him, Cole *was* lucky, and Molly didn't begrudge him the good things that had come his way. Her once footloose and fancy-free brother was settled in life, as well as work, and content in a way she'd never imagined he could be. But why, out of all the possible investors at that livestock auction, did he have to meet Troy?

As she picked up a small bowl of strawberry jam, her gaze caught Troy's. Her mouth went dry, and she got the same fluttery feeling in her stomach as the night before when they'd danced together.

"Earth to Molly. Jam, please." Bryce touched her arm.

"Of course." She fumbled with the bowl and almost dropped it. "Oops."

Bryce took the container from her. "Remember when you put jam in your hair, and it stuck up in spikes like along a dinosaur's back."

Laughter broke out around the table, and Molly gritted her teeth. "I was five. Mom said I was too little to use her strawberry shampoo so I thought her homemade strawberry jam would work."

"We all did stuff like that when we were kids." Troy's voice broke through the laughter. "My dad said he wanted to get his grandpa's watch cleaned so I decided to surprise him by taking it into the shower with me." He shook his head. "Luckily I didn't ruin it. My dad wasn't even mad. He said kids are curious and that's a good thing, although it might not always work out the right way."

"I agree," Molly's mom added, and the conversation moved on.

Molly turned to Troy, and her heart pounded. "Thanks." As the youngest in a big family and the only girl, she was used to her brothers teasing her and telling embarrassing childhood stories. However, Troy had stuck up for her, defended her even.

Warmth suffused her chest, and she tucked a loose strand of hair behind one ear. Letting herself fall for him again would be a bad idea. But right now, all she could think of was how good it felt to have him in her corner—and the attraction that still hummed between them, no matter how much she wanted to deny it.

AFTER ZACH AND Bryce returned to work with the ranch hands, Troy poured himself another cup of Joy Carter's excellent coffee and went back to the farmhouse table, where he unpacked his laptop. Nowadays, he held meetings in boardrooms, but when he and Pete had started their first company in college, it had been at a kitchen table. Sitting at the table at the Tall Grass Ranch where he'd often eaten as a hand was comfortable and reassuring, just as with buying the Bitterroot, he'd gone back to his roots.

"Sorry, what did you say?" He turned to Cole beside him with Molly still across the table, intent on a printed copy of Cole's business plan.

"I asked if you wanted to use our office in the barn or stay here." Cole shifted in his chair and worried his bottom lip.

"I'm fine talking in the kitchen as long as you are." Troy gave the other man an encouraging smile. Entrepreneurs whose companies he invested in were often nervous, but Cole seemed unusually on edge.

"Great. All this…" Cole waved at the business plan. "It's new to me. I know about animals and the basics of cash flow, profit margins and the rest, but not at this level. I never went beyond high school so…" He shrugged and flicked through his copy of the plan as if he didn't know what to do with it.

"But you're smart, and college isn't everything." Molly looked up and touched Cole's hand. "Plus nobody's as good with horses and cattle as you. Troy wouldn't have invested in your business if he didn't believe you'd be successful. Right?" Molly's tone and expression were positive, her blue eyes determined. Troy knew that despite how things had ended between them, she was counting on him not to let her brother down.

"Absolutely," he said. "With your rodeo experience, your business has a great chance of success. Apart from the money, think of me as both a mentor and an extra pair of hands." Troy shut his mouth fast. As an investor, he often mentored budding entrepreneurs, and it was a win for both of them. He protected his investment, and the business owner benefited from Troy's expertise and contacts. But offering to be an extra pair of hands went beyond giving advice. "I mean, I won't be involved on a daily basis, but you can always call me if you need to."

"Really?" Some of the tension in Cole's expression eased, and he rubbed the back of his neck.

"Of course. I'm here for you." Troy cleared his

throat and fiddled with a pen. *Never mix business with personal relationships.* He'd made that vow soon after he started out, and it had served him well. Except now, with Molly beaming at him like she was still the girl he remembered, as if he hung the moon and stars, he wanted to be more involved in Cole's venture—personally involved—than he could ever have imagined.

"Thanks, Troy. That's fantastic." Cole's voice was gruff.

"It sure is. So where do we start?" Molly looked at him expectantly.

Troy caught his breath. She and Cole had given him their trust, and he wouldn't let them down. "I want to go over a few things in the plan. I also have some suggestions for cutting costs, which should pay off in future years."

"We're all ears, aren't we, Cole?" Molly leaned toward her brother, and her eyes glowed with sisterly pride.

What would it be like to have Molly's love and support directed at him? Troy's throat went dry, and he took a mouthful of coffee.

"Sure. Whatever you say, Troy." Cole's laugh was awkward. "Boss."

*Boss.* He was the guy in charge. As Troy took Cole and Molly through the plan, highlighting strengths, weaknesses and opportunities, her steady gaze made him sweat more than the most demanding CEO ever had. "See here?" He gestured to her to come around the table to look at the chart on his laptop screen. "These are my income projections."

As she leaned in to study the screen, Molly's ponytail brushed Troy's cheek and he breathed in a scent of vanilla and some soft flower. Jasmine maybe? Jasmine used to be her favorite flower, and he'd bought her a plant for their one-month anniversary. Back then, each day with her had been a celebration. He'd fallen fast and hard—which was how it had ended between them too.

"You think by adding more fall-calving cows Cole could generate that much extra money?" Molly's blue eyes went wide.

"I do." His breath quickened. Pay attention to business, not memories, and definitely not that sweet, enticing scent that made him want things he couldn't have. As Troy explained his reasoning behind the income figures, Molly reached around him to point out other things on the chart to Cole. Her arm skimmed the top of Troy's shoulders, and his skin tingled through the thin cotton of his shirt.

"Why don't you two sit next to each other to look at the chart together?" He pushed his chair back and stood so Molly could take his seat. Troy hadn't been able to stop thinking about her since yesterday's party, and at least this way he could put some physical distance between them.

"Thanks." She gave him a brief smile before studying the screen again.

"But what about buying that bull? I also need a stallion and bucking mare." There was a worried furrow between Cole's eyebrows. "Even with upping fall calving, money will still be tight. Big Red, the bull we bought a few years ago, is for ranching. My plan is to develop a breeding program for rodeo. I want to have animals that are as skilled athletes as the cowboys and cowgirls who ride them."

"That's why you need to take a long-term view. On the next slide…" Troy reached for the keyboard at the same time as Molly did, and their fingers brushed. He took his hand away as quickly as if he'd touched something hot. "Go ahead. I suggest you lease a different bull and stallion to start. That's more cost-effective. Then you'll have enough money to buy a really good bucking mare." As Troy outlined the pros and cons of leasing versus buying stock, Cole and Molly listened intently.

"That makes sense." Cole's smile was approving. "I'm starting with a small herd, and we'd save feed if we were only using the animals for a few months of the year." Cole's smile was wry. "Beth says Big Red cost us more than he earned last winter. She already suggested renting him out to a friend for a month or so to make Big Red pay for his keep. Dad never did anything like that, but when Beth came on board she said the ranch had to change to survive."

"She's right." Molly folded her hands in her lap. Had she been as affected by that brief touch as Troy? "Because of Beth, this ranch is doing better than it has in years. And Troy's leasing idea is a good one."

"But can we find a stallion and bull to lease that are in the budget and have the right genetic makeup?" Cole rubbed a hand across his forehead. "I have contacts, sure, but they're for buying, not leasing stock."

"Between your contacts and mine, we should be able to get exactly what we need. Shane likely knows some good folks too." Troy hesitated. From the little he knew of him, Cole was independent and didn't like asking for help. A lot like him. However, there were times when people were stronger together.

His stomach rolled as he studied the back of Molly's head, her ponytail bobbing as she pointed out information on the laptop screen to Cole. She'd looked great last night dressed up for the party, but somehow she was even more attractive now. Maybe it was because in that old sweatshirt, with no makeup and tousled hair, she was more real.

"Okay, let's do it," Cole agreed, and held out his hand for Troy to shake. "You think Shane will be okay getting involved? He's a great guy, but he's marrying Mom. I don't want to take advantage. He's got money and contacts, sure, but he earned those, and he's got his own family."

"That family now includes you." Wearing outdoor clothes, Joy came back into the kitchen with a basket of eggs. "Shane wants to let you build your own operation like he did, but he also had help. You say the word and whether it's contacts, money or anything else, he'll be there for you like your own dad would have been."

Molly's breath stuttered audibly, and she got up and went to stare out the kitchen window.

"You okay?" Troy joined her as Joy and Cole talked about ranchers who might have stock available for lease.

"Sure, fine." Molly's voice was tight, and her shoulders were hunched. "It's all good. Thanks to you, Cole's bound to be a big success."

"Thanks to you too. You're great...at explaining things." Troy's stomach lurched. He'd almost said *she* was great, period. "He's lucky to have you on board." The vulnerability in her face touched a place he'd buried deep.

"It's only for a month or so." Was that relief or regret in Molly's voice?

"Yeah." Troy heard the regret in his own voice and took a step back. "Cole and I are heading out to the barns to take a look at the usable space. Are you joining us?"

"No, I'm going to town with my mom for her wedding dress fitting." As Molly turned to face him, that vulnerability was nowhere in sight, and Troy wondered if he'd imagined it.

"Of course. Have fun." Troy swallowed a lump of emotion.

He respected Cole and wanted him to succeed. Yet, as he dealt with Cole's business, being around Molly, and the unfinished business between them, was stirring up all sorts of things—and feelings—he'd trained himself to forget.

Since no good could come of any of those feelings, he'd have to try harder to keep their relationship professional.

# CHAPTER THREE

"WHAT DO YOU THINK?" Joy stood in the middle of the dress shop's private fitting area as Donna, the owner and primary seamstress, took some final measurements. In a pale blush pink that fell in soft folds to her ankles, the dress had long sleeves, a high back and a scoop neckline embellished with vintage lace. And as Joy caught a glimpse of herself in one of the long mirrors, her hands tingled, and warmth spread through her chest.

"You look beautiful, Mom." Molly moved from her seat on one of the gray velvet chairs and gave Joy a careful hug, mindful of Donna. "That dress is simple, elegant and chic. Like you."

Joy got misty-eyed. "Thanks, honey. I hardly recognize myself. It's sure a change from barn clothes."

"You also look great in barn clothes. I hope I look even half as good when I'm your age. What's your secret?" Although Molly's expression was teasing, it held a hint of sadness that put Joy's maternal radar on alert.

"No secret." Joy held pins for Donna, a woman near her age who attended the Carter family's church, and studied her daughter's bent head. "Some good genes, maybe, but if so, that's luck. Fresh country air and mostly homegrown food. The love of family and friends. I've had a simple life but mostly a happy one. No big excitement." Joy lifted an arm so Donna could snip a loose thread. "Not like you with your adventures at college and now in Atlanta." She nodded her thanks to Donna who excused herself as a bell rang in the main part of the store.

"I guess." Molly's voice was flat. "Sometimes I wonder…do you ever have regrets?" Molly sat on the chair again, and Joy perched on a matching sofa.

"About my life?" Joy kept her tone casual. Before Molly left for college, their relationship had been tense. It was natural, Joy supposed, and part of Molly's need to separate from her family, but since then, she hadn't seen her daughter often. And they'd never regained the closeness they'd shared before those years of teenage angst.

"Life, choices, you know?"

"Of course, I have regrets. I wouldn't be human if I didn't." Joy forced a light laugh. One day, she hoped she could be truly open with her daughter, but they weren't there yet. She could, however, open the door to a closer adult relationship by telling Molly a bit of what was in her heart. "Although I don't regret marrying your dad, looking back I wish I'd waited and gone to college first."

She stared at her reflection in another mirror. Now in her sixties, she was a lifetime away from the teenage bride who'd married Dennis. She barely remembered that starry-eyed girl in the enormous veil and billowy dress she'd chosen with her mom a few weeks after senior prom.

"That's why you wanted me to go to college. But you and Dad were happy, weren't you?" Molly's voice trembled.

"So happy." The backs of Joy's eyes burned. "My folks tried to talk me out of marrying so young, but I insisted." She exhaled. "Since I wanted to have a family right away, I grew up fast." At least in some ways. "If I'd known then what I know now…" She stopped. There was no use looking back. "I never imagined being a bride again at my age." She made her voice bright.

"You're a gorgeous bride, and Shane's a lucky man." Molly's smile was strained. "It's going to be a wonderful wedding. Weddings. Bryce and Carrie too."

"I didn't expect to remarry but being with Shane feels right." And they fit together in a different way than Joy had with Dennis. "You never know where life will take you. It sounds trite but it's true." Joy studied her daughter. Something was wrong but what? "Is there anyone special in your life? That ER doctor I met when I visited you seemed nice." And he'd shown unmistakable signs of being interested in Molly.

"No, I'm happily single." Despite her words, Molly's voice had a bitter note. "I went out with that ER doctor a few times, but he's not for me. For a start, his job is his life."

Wasn't Molly's job her life too? *Don't interfere.* Zach, Cole and, most recently, Bryce, had all said that to Joy, but wanting your children to find happiness with a loving partner was caring, not interference. "I'm sure the right man will come along."

Molly shrugged. "Maybe I don't want to marry. I like an independent life. I can travel, join a softball team and buy a horse."

"But what about…" Joy stopped herself from saying something that might provoke an argument. Molly was a born mother. She didn't want to forgo having a family, did she? "You can do all those things as a married woman and—"

"Yes, but I'd have to consider what my husband wanted." Another shrug. "I'm fine on my own."

Zach, Cole and Bryce had all said the same thing not so long ago. Joy put a hand to her mouth to hide a smile. Was Molly protesting too much? Had she already met the right man? There'd been something about her interactions with Troy Clayton, first at the party and then at breakfast, that had also pinged Joy's maternal radar.

"You've made a good life for yourself, sweetheart. I'm so proud of you." Joy leaned over to pat Molly's hand and tried to mask her unease. She'd sensed something between Molly and Troy the summer before Molly left for college but had convinced herself she was wrong. Molly couldn't wait to leave home and start her new city life. She'd never have considered settling down with a ranch hand. "You've achieved everything you wanted, and your future is bright."

So why didn't Molly look happier? Was she upset about Joy remarrying? She'd said she was okay with it and she seemed to like Shane, but was Molly only putting a brave face on for a situation she couldn't change?

"Don't forget my new home with Shane will be yours. I know it will seem strange at first visiting somewhere else, but you'll still be welcome with Zach and Beth at the ranch house and—"

"It's fine. Here's Donna coming back. I can't wait to try on the dresses you picked out for me. They look great in the pictures you sent. I like all the styles, but in terms of color, either the soft gray or burgundy would complement your pink. What's Rosa wearing?"

Like all Joy's kids, Molly shut down and deflected things she didn't want to talk about. However, that behavior told Joy her intuition was correct. Even if she was truly okay with Shane, Molly *was* upset about the wedding. That wasn't surprising. She'd always been a "daddy's girl," and Dennis's sudden death in a farm accident when Molly was a young teen had devastated her.

"Rosa chose burgundy for her matron of honor dress, but the two of you don't have to match." For the simple wedding she wanted, Joy had chosen both a matron and maid of honor, her best friend and her daughter, to stand up with her.

Joy manufactured a smile for Donna. While her conversation with Molly was over for now, Joy had only gotten started.

"THERE YOU GO, GIRL." In a stall at one end of the horse barn, Molly checked on Daisy-May and rubbed the Appaloosa's ears. Two days after her mom's dress fitting, and with her own silvery-gray maid of honor dress chosen and with Donna to be altered, Molly had finished unpacking and was settled back here on the ranch. It was temporary, though, and she couldn't let herself get too comfortable. "I missed you." She rested her head against Daisy-May's neck and breathed in her familiar scent. "You're my best buddy, aren't you?"

Daisy-May nickered and nosed Molly's jacket pocket.

"I already gave you a treat. Did you forget about that carrot?" Molly shook her head and left the horse's stall, closing the door behind her. She'd also missed this barn and the other horses, although none was so dear to her as gentle Daisy-May.

She glanced around the high-raftered space divided in half by a wide central aisle lined with stalls. The barn looked almost the same as before she'd left for college, but there were still subtle differences. Even since she was last home, the lighting had been upgraded and several of the stall doors had been replaced.

There were new horses as well, including Christabel, a white pony with brown spots who belonged to Cole's stepdaughter, Skylar. "You're a pretty girl." Molly admired the pony who wore a dark blue blanket personalized with her name.

"A pretty expensive girl. Cole told me about her pedigree."

At Troy's voice, Molly turned to greet him. "Skylar's dad is big in the horse world, and money isn't an issue." These days, money likely wasn't an issue for Troy either. "I didn't see you." How long had he been here? He hadn't heard her talking to Daisy-May, had he? Her face heated as she tried to remember if she'd said anything embarrassing.

"I was outside in the yard with Cole. I came in to take another look at the tack room. We've got a contractor coming later to measure for an addition."

In jeans, a dark felt cowboy hat, fleece-lined denim jacket and boots, Troy looked like a ranch hand, and Molly had to remind herself he wasn't. He was her boss. She rubbed Christabel between her ears. "It's great for Cole to have your help in expanding."

"Although you don't *always* have to spend money to make money, in Cole's case, and to get his business to the next level, he needs to invest in stock, equipment and barn space. That's where I come in."

Troy leaned against the stall and patted Christabel. His hands were well-shaped, and a faint white scar bisected his right knuckle. That summer they were together, he'd cut his hand on a rake, and Molly had bandaged it before driving him to the hospital to get stitches. She'd teased

him about being her "first patient" who wasn't
family.

"Cole's grateful to you. We all are. It was hard
for him to leave rodeo, and now with his business he has a new and positive goal." Molly made
herself focus on the present, not the past. And
definitely not on how holding Troy's hand had
once given her a sense of comfort, safety and
steadfast love.

"You're a sweetheart, Chrissie. Not stuck up
at all despite those fancy horses in your family tree."

As Troy spoke to the pony, Christabel nudged
his face, and Molly busied herself with putting
away an empty feed bucket. He'd always been
good with horses, and they responded to his
kindness and calm, gentle nature. The same
things that had once drawn Molly to him. They
still did. She stuck her hands in the pockets
of the brown barn jacket she'd grabbed from a
hook in the mudroom. "Do you have horses at
the Bitterroot?"

"Two came with the property, but I want to
buy a few more along with heritage breed cattle. I kept the ranch foreman on, along with
any hands who wanted to stay. They're man-
aging the place for me, but in time I want to
get more involved." He chuckled as Christabel
headbutted an old beach ball suspended from

a hay net. "Homemade toys are the best, aren't they, honey?"

His voice was low, and its sweetness rubbed at a wound in Molly's heart that had never truly healed. Troy was talking to Christabel, not her, and she'd given up the chance to hear him call her honey. "You should talk to Bryce. He and his kids are raising Hereford pigs. His fiancée, Carrie, is big on sustainable agriculture. She says raising traditional breeds is good for both the climate and ranch business."

"For sure." Troy rolled his shoulders, and butterflies took flight in Molly's stomach. She remembered holding on to those same shoulders as Troy lifted her like she weighed nothing. "I need more hours in the day. It's good to be busy, but I'm already pulled between ranch work and my day job. Still, I'm lucky. Not a lot of people, let alone a guy my age, have their dreams come true."

Molly's own dreams had come true too, at least in terms of work. So why did she feel so off balance? "You're busy. I should get back to the house and let you get on with your day." She shivered as a gust of wind buffeted her from the open barn door.

"Wait." Troy's blue gaze caught Molly's and held. "Look, I just wanted to say… I hope life's been good. I only ever wanted the best for you. Back then and now."

"My life's great." She hugged herself in the bulky jacket. "I've got an amazing job lined up in Atlanta starting in January, and I'm sharing a condo with a nursing friend while I save to buy a place of my own. Like you, I'm lucky. I had a dream, and I went for it like I planned."

Still Troy didn't look away. "No regrets, then?"

The same question Molly had asked her mom but was afraid to examine for herself. "Everybody has regrets. Like my last haircut." She tried to joke and tugged at the choppy ends of her hair. "It's been a few months but I'm still growing out these layers."

"Your hair is…it's fine." Troy hesitated and something that might have been admiration sparked in his eyes. "If you have time, Cole could use your input."

"Sure. On what?" If Cole needed something, why hadn't he asked her himself?

"It's a bit…awkward." Troy walked beside Molly to the barn door. "Cole's fantastic with livestock and everybody likes him, but when it comes to keeping track of details, he's…" He shook his head.

"Organizationally challenged?" Molly laughed, and what had briefly felt akin to intimacy between them vanished like morning mist. "That's my brother. He says everything he needs to know is in his head, but that would be a problem in business."

"Exactly." Troy's deep laugh blended with her higher-pitched one. "I don't want Cole to think I'm checking up on him, but if you could help him get on top of paperwork and scheduling, it would make things easier for all of us. I remember you worked closely with your mom to manage the ranch business, and you were good at it. So now, with Cole, if you could get a few things back on track by saying you want to lighten his load, I'd appreciate it."

"No problem." Although Molly had never wanted to stay on the ranch, she'd loved the business part of agricultural life. After her dad's death, Molly and her mom had shared a lot of that work, so she understood how to help Cole. And since she also understood her brother, she knew how to offer that help without overstepping and annoying him. Although she'd offered to support Cole with the business, so far he'd been the one asking her to pitch in with specific tasks. She didn't want him to think she was interfering or taking over. "Leave it with me. I'll get things sorted out, and Cole won't ever know you talked to me."

"Great." As they reached the barnyard, Troy

rubbed a hand across the back of his neck. "I want Cole to succeed, and he's learning he needs to ask for help but…"

"Sometimes he can be his own worst enemy." Molly finished Troy's sentence like she used to do. "It's a Carter male trait. My dad was the same but in this generation we're doing things differently. Zach and Beth, Cole and Melissa and now Bryce and Carrie, work as a team with my mom. This ranch is a real family effort and that includes Cole's stock contracting business."

Molly hugged herself again as the cold wind swirled around the yard and cut through her jacket. Nobody had asked if she wanted to be part of the family business officially, and she hadn't offered. She shouldn't feel left out because she'd always said ranch life wasn't for her. So where had that unexpected sense of loss come from?

"Auntie Molly." Paisley and her brother, Cam, ran around the side of the barn followed by their stepcousin Skylar. All three kids wore parkas, hats and mittens and reminded Molly of herself at that age. "Grandma said you were out here. I wanted to ask if… Oh, sorry, Mr. Troy." As Paisley skidded to a stop, she almost collided with Troy, and he held out a hand to stop her from falling.

"No problem, and you can forget the mister, it's Troy," he said as Molly hugged her nieces and nephew.

"The school bus just dropped you off?" Molly asked as the kids crowded around her talking about their day. Their excited chatter warmed her inside and out.

Cam tucked one mittened hand into hers. "Grandma's looking after us until Daddy, Carrie and Aunt Melissa finish work. Can you play cars with me?"

"And do wedding hairstyles with me and Skylar?" Paisley's expression was hopeful.

"But I want cars and—"

"I want to do hair *and* make cookies," Skylar interjected.

"That's a lot of things," Molly said to forestall an argument. "I love spending time with you guys, but you still have barn chores, remember? I'll pitch in so they'll go faster." She glanced toward the ranch house where her mom waved from the back deck.

"I have another idea." Troy grinned at the kids. "If I help with barn chores, Cam and I could play cars while you ladies do hair. I won't be able to stick around long enough to make cookies, but can you save me some? I love cookies." He made a funny face and rubbed his stomach.

"Yay!" the kids shouted, and raced into the barn.

"But I… You… You're busy." Molly stared at him open-mouthed.

"Yeah, but I like kids and I have to hang around until the contractor gets here." He checked his phone and then turned it off. "Deal?" He gestured to the kids, who were already putting on their barn boots, and then held out his hand.

"I guess." Before Molly knew it, her hand disappeared into his, the brief contact making her palm tingle.

"Are you coming? We hafta get started," Cam hollered.

"On our way," Molly hollered back, all of a sudden lighthearted.

With the children nearby, Molly could avoid an uncomfortable moment alone with the man who occupied her thoughts way too much. For now, she could relax, have fun and forget that he was only back in her life because he was her boss.

# *CHAPTER FOUR*

TROY LOCKED HIS truck where he'd parked it in front of the bank on High Valley Avenue and crossed the town's wide main street decorated with pumpkins, hay bales, paper lanterns, black cats and smiling ghosts.

He must have temporarily lost his mind. That was the only reason he'd ducked out of work with hardly a second thought to spend an hour yesterday afternoon playing cars with a little kid. It had been fun, though, and he'd gotten a kick out of Cam, as well as Paisley and Skylar. And their auntie Molly who was so sweet and distracting any man would find her hard to resist.

At least that's what Troy had told himself as he'd tossed and turned most of the night alone in his big, almost empty house at the Bitterroot Ranch. For the first time in years, it had been thoughts of a woman instead of his job keeping him awake—something that couldn't continue since the woman was Molly.

*Coffee.* That's what he needed to jump-start his day. A café sign beckoned out of the early morning mist, and warm yellow light spilled onto the street along with the scent of fresh roasted coffee beans. He pushed open the door of the Bluebunch Café and a bell jingled overhead. The dark-haired woman behind the counter gestured in greeting as she spoke to another customer. It was only late October, not even winter, and already the weather was cool and crisp, so the café's warmth was welcome.

Troy rubbed his chilled hands together as he studied the chalkboard menu. He'd have to buy a few pairs of thick gloves and warmer clothes. Despite his years in California, he was Montana born and had always considered the state his true home. He'd cope with winter without complaining in exchange for the joy of being back in this land of big sky, fresh air and natural beauty everywhere he looked.

"What can I get for you?" The woman behind the counter turned to him with a friendly smile. "If I was to guess, I'd say you like an espresso but might occasionally be tempted by a foamy cappuccino." She tucked her hands into the pockets of a red apron with Bluebunch Café in white script across the bib. "You strike me as a muffin guy. Blueberry oat, maybe? Although I bet you wouldn't turn down chocolate." She laughed at his surprised expression. "I'm Kristi Russo. Café owner and barista with a sideline in matching coffee and muffins to my customer's personalities. You must be Troy Clayton."

"Yeah, I am, and an espresso with one of those blueberry oat muffins sounds good." In his local coffee place back in California, he'd never exchanged more than a few words with any of the baristas. None of them had ever presumed to guess his coffee and muffin preferences either. Even if they had, he couldn't imagine they'd be so scarily accurate.

"Coming right up. You'll soon get to know everyone. I knew who you were because the town's been buzzing about the Bitterroot's new owner." Kristi operated the gleaming silver espresso machine with ease. Then she popped a muffin from the glass display case onto a white plate. She seemed to be assessing him, and then she nodded. "Take any free table through there." She indicated the main part of the café. "If there isn't one available, go ahead and share."

"I… Okay." He took his tray, laden with his espresso cup, muffin plate, utensils and a pot of butter, by reflex. He'd planned to get a coffee to go but it wouldn't hurt to sit for a few minutes. He could catch up on email here as easily as at home.

"Good food and good coffee should be savored, not rushed." Kristi glanced over his shoulder. "Hey, Molly. I'll be with you in a minute. I just need to check on my sunflower bread."

*Molly?* Had Troy somehow conjured her up because in the past twenty-four hours she'd never been far from his thoughts? He turned and tightened his grip on the tray. She was real enough, and the hair on his arms rose. She was in jeans and a dark blue jacket, and her pretty blond hair was tucked up under a lighter blue knitted hat with only a few tendrils sticking out to frame her face.

"Hi." Her face was already pink from the cool morning, but as Troy returned her greeting, the pink deepened. "Small-town life. We can't escape each other."

Not that he wanted to. The realization shot through him, and jerked him into awareness before he'd taken even a sip of his espresso. Only a brief glimpse of Molly would brighten the gloomiest day. "You're in town early."

"I'm part of the volunteer crew getting things set up for this weekend's art fair, and there's a meeting at the craft center. The fair is showcasing some of my late brother Paul's paintings along with work by other local artists. The event's raising money for a disability charity. You might have seen the posters around town." As she spoke, Molly pointed to one on the café's wall.

Troy nodded and took a closer look at the poster. Paul, Molly's eldest brother, had died from complications of cystic fibrosis before Troy had worked at the ranch, but he remembered folks talking about him with respect and fondness. "I'll stop by." And make an anonymous donation to the charity in Paul's memory.

Kristi returned and glanced between them. "Your usual, Mol?" To Troy, she added, "Our Molly's an everyday black coffee fan. No nonsense, keep things simple, old school."

"That's me." Molly's laugh was light. "And a muffin of the day, please. I dream of Kristi's carrot muffins in Atlanta."

While Molly and Kristi exchanged teasing banter, Troy considered his espresso. What did it say about him? Maybe that he was busy, driven, valued efficiency and knew what he wanted? "I was about to find a table. You're welcome to join me, Molly, if you're staying."

"What did I say about savoring food and coffee? Adding good company makes it even better." Kristi's eyes twinkled. "A table for two just opened up by the front window. You'd better grab it before someone else does."

As others in the line that now snaked behind them to the café door murmured agreement, Molly's face went from pink to red. "Thanks, but I have to head straight over to the craft center. We're having a working breakfast."

"Another time then." Kristi's smile was knowing. "I expect you two have lots to catch up on."

"I...uh, sure." Her face still flaming, Molly grabbed her takeout coffee and muffin bag and made her way through the crowd to the outside door.

Kristi waved Troy toward the free table while simultaneously boxing up a dozen muffins for a white-haired man talking on his cell phone. "Along with you having worked at the Tall Grass, you and Molly are two country kids who made it in the big city. You must have lots in common."

"Of course." Troy made his expression neutral. Long ago, he'd learned to never let his face show what he was thinking, but something about Molly—and this close-knit town—made him perpetually second-guess himself.

Inviting her to share his table had been an impulse, something else he'd schooled himself never to do. Yet, as he made his way to that window table, which currently framed Molly's trim figure disappearing into a building across the street, unfamiliar regret prickled.

He wasn't used to neighbors taking an interest in his personal business, and if he'd sat here with Molly he might have gotten the town talking. But if yesterday with her and the kids had shown him anything, it was that the two of them *could* be friendly and collegial. Despite his ill-judged comment about being her boss.

Kristi was right about him and Molly having a lot in common, and maybe like him, Molly now felt somewhat out of place here. Although Troy was a country kid at heart, living in bigger places had changed him. It had likely changed Molly too. He'd never let what others might think or say bother him, and he wouldn't now. Maybe he and Molly could find a fresh start, or at least common ground to build on.

Troy sipped his coffee and ate the delicious muffin, ignoring his phone and the waiting messages and instead looking out the café window. As the sun burned away the mist, and the small town came to life, that sense of regret grew. Good coffee, good food and good companionship *were* important. Maybe, in keeping his life so closed and prioritizing work, he'd missed out on other things.

"Mind if I join you?" Mr. Kuntz hovered by Troy's table with a laden tray and a beaming smile.

"Go ahead." He could linger here a bit longer, and it would be useful to get Mr. Kuntz's input on different types of cattle feed.

However, as Mr. Kuntz set out his breakfast and chatted about the weather, Troy's regret increased yet again. The other man was a reminder of who Troy really wanted to sit here with.

*Molly.* And the unfinished business that still loomed large between them.

MOLLY SQUEEZED HER mom's hand as a boy and girl from the local elementary school cut the ribbon to proclaim the *Paul Carter Memorial Art Fair* open. Cheers and applause rang out from the crowd gathered outside the Medicine Wheel Craft Center. While this event was wonderful, it was also emotional, and her mom had been on the verge of tears all morning.

"Thanks, honey." Her mom sniffed and patted her eyes with a tissue. "I truly feel your brother is here with us." She glanced at Zach, Cole and Bryce, who stood on her other side. "Your dad is too, so despite missing them both, my memories make it a happy day."

Even good memories could be bittersweet, and Molly had a lump in her throat as she and her family made their way into Rosa's craft center with its adjoining gallery space. While most of Paul's paintings were displayed here, some had also been hung at the Bluebunch Café, High Valley's community center and the town hall. They'd visit those venues later, following the map in the town's "art trail" leaflet that Carrie, Bryce's fiancée, had designed. There was even a children's corner where some of Cam's drawings were on show. Her nephew loved art as much as Paul had, and it comforted her to think of that talent continuing into the next generation.

"Welcome." Rosa hugged Molly's mom and the two friends stood close together for a moment. "I gave Paul his first real drawing pad, do you remember? The kind true artists use."

"It was for his sixth birthday because back then he drew on every scrap of paper he could find," Joy said.

Rosa's eyes were soft with emotion. "I knew then he had a special gift, and I'm thrilled his work is now on display for everyone to see and enjoy."

As Rosa led them through the exhibition, Molly was in awe of Paul's talent. Only in his early twenties when he died, she'd always thought her brother hadn't had a chance to live, but she'd been wrong. He'd left a legacy in their hearts and through his art that was bigger and more profound than some who lived many more years.

As locals and out-of-town visitors thronged the gallery space, Molly stood in a quiet corner to study a large, gold-framed oil Paul had titled *Montana Summer*. Between the vibrant green fields stretching to the distant Rocky Mountains and a herd of the Carter family's red cattle with their distinctive brand, she drank in details large and small. In the foreground, the state's bluebunch wheatgrass framed a curious brown rabbit, while above, a meadowlark soared high against a vivid blue sky.

It was a stunning piece of landscape art in its own right, but it was even more meaningful because it was home. Molly knew the exact hill from where Paul had captured the scene, and his painting took her there with him.

A memory surfaced of a long-ago summer day when their folks had gone to town and left Paul to babysit her. They'd been on the front porch and, still as statues, watched a butterfly that had landed on one of their mom's rosebushes in the garden below. Paul had told her all about butterflies, and their journey from caterpillar to cocoon and beyond. Now from Molly's adult perspective, she thought he might have been talking about himself and living life with resilience despite challenges. Now she was the one who needed a tissue, and she dug in her crossbody bag for one.

"Here." A strong hand passed her a travel-size tissue pack.

"Thanks." Troy had always had a knack of being there when she needed comfort, and it seemed he still did. She swallowed the tears and dried her eyes. "I didn't know Paul well as a person because he was so much older than me, but seeing his work here…" She gestured around the busy gallery and craft center. "It hits me, you know? Maybe in his art Paul recorded his life and everything he loved for all of us. I know he wouldn't want us to be sad, but I can't help it."

"I bet he'd understand." Troy's quiet voice soothed her. "I expect he'd tell you to go ahead and cry if you need to. Lots of others are." He gestured to Molly's mom being consoled by her fiancé, Shane, and even the usually unsentimental Cole had his face buried in his wife Melissa's shoulder. "There's no shame in honest, heartfelt emotion."

"I know but…" Molly found another tissue as her tears flowed again. "Paul's death so young was tragic, but since I can't change what happened to him, I've tried to learn from it." Maybe that's why she'd set goals and gone after them with such single-minded determination. More than many people, she understood how life could be cut short, so she'd crammed as much as possible into hers so far. However, in keeping herself so focused on work and school, had she missed out on other, maybe even more important, parts of living?

Troy patted Molly's arm, his touch tentative

at first and then, as she didn't shrug it off or move away, his hand settled in the crook of her elbow like it once had. "Paul would be proud of you for working as a nurse with kids. It's a fine job, and you're making a big and important difference in lots of lives."

"Nowadays that's mostly through medical research rather than patient care." When Troy took his hand away, Molly felt a sense of loss as surprising as it was unsettling. "I like research, but I miss working closely with children and their families."

"Couldn't you do both?"

"Not at the moment. My new job is in a research institute, not a hospital ward." Molly fell into step with Troy as they moved through the gallery. "I'm working with one of the doctors I got to know through my master's project. She won grant money and put together a team for a project focused on cystic fibrosis in teenagers. It's a fantastic opportunity I'm excited to be a part of." For Molly, it was also personal. In her own small way, she could contribute to advancing knowledge so future families might not experience the heartache and loss that cystic fibrosis had brought to hers.

"Sounds impressive." Troy put out a hand so a group of teenagers absorbed in their phones wouldn't bump into her.

"To an outsider, maybe." Molly smiled her thanks. Troy had always looked out for her, and while she could take care of herself, she'd forgotten how good it felt to have him by her side. "Research is the kind of job where not a lot happens from day-to-day but then, if you're lucky, there's an exciting breakthrough that makes everything worthwhile." The hope of such a discovery was why she loved her job. Yet, did she really want to spend her whole life in a lab? There was a special and more immediate excitement in ward nursing when a sick child got better, and Molly shared in a worried parent's relief and gratitude.

"I get it. I want to make a difference in my work too. My business partner and I are working on a clean energy project where we're hoping for one of those 'exciting breakthroughs' of our own." Troy's voice held the passion Molly remembered, except, back then, he'd been talking about the life and future they wanted to make together.

"That also sounds impressive." Molly's fingers tingled with an urge to reach for his hand and clasp it in hers.

"It will be if we can pull it off, but more than a few people have said it's wishful thinking." Troy laughed. "I've learned to ignore the doubters, or at least not let them get to me."

"That's a good way to be." Molly wasn't there yet, but she'd grown in confidence since she'd left small-town Montana, and when it came to work, she wasn't afraid to stand up for herself and what she wanted. Now she had to figure out how to do that in her personal life—once she had one.

As they reached the children's art corner, Molly stopped in front of one of Cam's drawings. A horse, Daisy-May, according to the name he'd printed in green crayon, stuck her head over a barn stall in the middle of a group of stick figures Cam had labeled as his dad, soon-to-be stepmom Carrie, sister Paisley and Molly's mom.

"Do you like it?" Cam tugged Molly's hand. "Mrs. Rosa asked me and the other kids to tell visitors about our pictures. We're official tour guides." He showed her the "Junior Guide" badge pinned to his blue-and-white-checked flannel shirt.

"I love it." Molly studied the bright crayon drawing. It was simple, but Cam had captured the feeling of ranch life and family in a way some much older and technically skilled artists had never mastered.

"I'll draw a picture with you in it next." Cam looked at her trustingly. "Two pictures so you can take one with you, and I can keep one. I can make your hair the same color as Paisley's." He pointed to his sister's fluorescent-yellow tresses and looked between Molly and Troy. "Doesn't my aunt Molly have nice hair? She's really pretty, don't you think?"

"She sure is." Over Cam's head, Troy caught Molly's gaze. The attraction that was both familiar and new sparked between them once more.

Troy made a choked sound, and even Molly had to smile. Kids didn't have a filter, and it didn't mean anything important that Troy thought she was pretty.

"There you are, Molly! I've been looking for you everywhere. Isn't this wonderful?" Molly's mom appeared with Nina Shevchenko, one of the fair organizers, and several members of the Sunflower Sisterhood.

"She's been in Troy's capable hands almost the whole time. Not literally, of course." Nina laughed, and the others joined in with the joke while giving Molly and Troy interested, sideways glances.

"Troy's been kind in keeping me company." Molly sent Nina and the others a quelling look. She knew about small-town life. Two single people of a similar age could hardly spend more than a few minutes in each other's company before the gossip mill went into overdrive. "This fair's great. You've done a fantastic job. I've heard lots of people say they hope it becomes an annual show and sale for all local artists. Keep Paul's name, but make it into something bigger for both the town and the charity."

"Wouldn't that be amazing?" Joy's expression was tender. "Rosa said somebody made an anonymous five-thousand-dollar donation in Paul's memory. Can you imagine? I wish I knew who it was so I could thank them personally, but we're going to put a notice in the local newspaper and online. Hopefully they'll see it and know how grateful we and the charity are."

Molly glanced at Troy, who stood with his back to them, listening to Cam chatter about the different drawings. Troy hadn't known Paul personally, so he'd have had no reason to make such a big donation. It had to be someone else, but who? Perhaps a group of businesspeople had gotten together, but why stay anonymous?

"You and Troy look like you were enjoying yourselves. It seems you have a real connection," Nina said conspiratorially. "Werner and I both noticed it." She nodded at Mr. Kuntz, who'd joined them. "Your mother says you don't have anyone special in Atlanta. You never know, you might meet a special someone here."

"I'm going back to Atlanta in a few months." Molly liked Nina, but what was it about small-town life that made people who'd known you from infancy offer well-meaning advice like you were their own child? "Besides, I'm not looking to meet anyone right now. I'm too busy."

Nina laughed. "Love hits when you least expect and don't think you're ready or have time. That's the beauty of it, my dear."

"Look at Shane and me." Molly's mom spoke up, and a smile played at the corners of her mouth. "Never say never."

As the conversation moved on to the upcoming weddings, Molly took a glass of sparkling water from a passing server and made her escape.

Of course, she couldn't plan love, but she did have a life plan and it didn't include settling down in High Valley—or with Troy. And while today had been great, and maybe she and Troy could even be friends, this kind of small-town nosiness was one of the many reasons she loved the anonymity of Atlanta. There, nobody expected her to be paired up or made embarrassing personal comments.

But whether she liked it or not, Troy was back in her life, and there was still something between them. As she pretended to study a pencil sketch of a flock of chickens, she eyed him, now drawing with Cam and several other kids at a low table.

Something she had to deal with.

# *CHAPTER FIVE*

SEVERAL DAYS AFTER the art fair, Troy stepped outside onto the front porch of the Bitterroot Ranch house, *my house*, he reminded himself, and almost tripped over a red cooler sitting by the front door.

He bent to read the handwritten tag tied to the handle. *A few of my homemade Italian goodies to welcome you to High Valley. All good wishes, Angela Moretti.* In case Troy didn't know who she was, she'd also added: *Nina Shevchenko's friend, and Carrie Rizzo's aunt. You can leave the empty cooler at the Tall Grass Ranch next time you're passing.*

Last week Nina had delivered a blue cooler filled with food, and on Sunday afternoon various neighbors had dropped off chocolate chip cookies, an apple pie, three casseroles and a towering orange chiffon cake.

"More treats?" Cathy McCabe joined Troy at the door.

"Yep."

She gave him a teasing grin. Cathy's folks had been friends of his grandparents. She was older than him, in her forties now, but Troy remembered her from when he was a kid. The two extended families often met up for the Fourth of July weekend. She was what his folks called "good people," and when Troy heard she now lived in High Valley, he'd been happy to reconnect. He'd ended up hiring her to do general housekeeping for him at the Bitterroot. "In the freezer with the rest?"

"I guess so." Troy brought the cooler into the house and opened it. "I'm keeping a list so I can thank people, but I don't expect to be fed. I can cook, you know. My mom taught me."

Cathy exclaimed over the treats as they unpacked them. "I'm betting your mom didn't teach you to make Italian food like Angela Moretti. You haven't lived till you've tried her lasagna, risotto and gnocchi."

"No." Troy laughed. "You and your kids are welcome to join me in eating this stuff. Look at the size of this lasagna. It's for a family." A familiar hurt tugged at his heart. He wanted a family of his own, but even if he found the right woman, would he be able to trust in her—or love?

"My boys love Angela's lasagna so yes, please."

Cathy was a single mom with teenagers at home, and her expression was both honest and grateful. "You're really generous to us. Thank you."

"You don't need to thank me. You guys are like family." Troy checked to make sure he had the keys to his pickup. "I appreciate everything you're doing around here." In less than a week, the house had gone from dusty to sparkling clean. From the fall wreath on the front door to the flowering indoor plants that now lined his sunny office window, the place felt more like a home. "Take some cookies for the boys too."

"You're becoming the uncle my kids have never had." Cathy's brown eyes shone. "I'll send Wyatt over later to take a look at that snow-blower in the shed. You'll soon need it, and my son can fix anything mechanical. No need to buy new when something can be fixed."

That was the motto Troy had been raised with too. "Great. Call me if there's a problem. I'm heading to the Tall Grass so I should be in cell range most of the time." He didn't need to drop by the ranch this afternoon, but somehow he kept finding reasons to be there. Today, it was the arrival of Cole's rented bull.

"Sure. Tell Joy and Molly I say hi." Cathy grinned. "Molly's going to look gorgeous at the double wedding. I sew for the dress shop when Donna, the owner, gets busy, and I'm working on Molly's gown now. The guys will all be lining up to dance with her at the reception. If you want to have a chance, you'd better ask her early."

"I won't be at the reception. I mean, there's no reason for me to be invited," he added. He was Cole's temporary business partner, not a family member or a close friend.

"The actual wedding ceremonies are small, and I heard they're having a lunch afterward that's for family only, but the reception's a pot-luck and most everyone in town's going. Shane's hosting it at the Squirrel Tail Ranch—that's his spread. It's a resort so there's a lot of event space."

"But I'm new here and—"

"It'll be a great way for you to meet folks," Cathy broke in, and her eyes narrowed. She studied him from behind a stack of foil-wrapped food parcels. "If you don't go, people might get the idea you're too big for your boots."

Although Troy didn't want to let himself get any closer to Molly, he couldn't tell Cathy the truth. "As long as I won't be intruding, it sounds like fun." If most of the town was there, he might not even see Molly except at a distance.

"Great. You can bring something for the pot-luck. Show off your cooking skills. Women like men who are handy in the kitchen." Cathy's laugh was easy. "If you haven't guessed, you buying the Bitterroot has caused quite a stir. You sure won't lack for dance partners. Molly had better ask *you* early." Without seeming to take a breath, she continued, "I'll email you the potluck sign-up information. I'm on the organizing committee. Joy and Carrie wanted an old-time community fall supper, so we're making it happen for them."

Muttering something about needing to get to his meeting, Troy fled to his pickup. His thoughts whirled as he drove along the highway. He wanted to be part of the High Valley community, but he'd planned to get involved gradually. Maybe start by joining a running group or the woodworking club Werner had mentioned.

He'd also planned to avoid anything except a business relationship with the Carter family, at least while they were in business together. However, he'd only been back in town a week and so far he'd ended up in the middle of a Carter engagement party, he'd comforted Molly at an art fair where the Carter family was front and center, and now he was set to join the celebration for two Carter weddings. The line between business and personal wasn't just blurring, it had disappeared entirely.

Fifteen minutes later, and no closer to figuring out how he could get back to a business-only relationship, he turned into the long driveway that led to the Tall Grass Ranch, following what must be the livestock trailer with Cole's rented bull.

"Hey." Cole waved from the barnyard once Troy had parked by the fence.

Molly came out of the barn, bundled up against the cool October breeze in a pink fleece jacket, white knit hat, faded jeans and boots. From a distance, she looked eighteen again, and Troy's heart turned over. But he wasn't twenty and still wet behind the ears anymore. He was older, with enough life experience to be wary, no matter how pretty a woman's face. Yet, as Molly drew closer and he saw the woman she was now, not the girl she'd once been, it wasn't that old teenage attraction that had him churned up. Instead, it was a new and grown-up longing.

"Thanks for coming by." Cole approached Troy's truck and spoke to him through the half-open window. "You didn't need to be here when the bull arrived, but I appreciate it."

"No problem. Since I suggested you rent Cupid, I wanted to check him out."

"Cupid?" Molly joined her brother as Troy got out of his pickup.

"The owner's daughter named him." Troy laughed, and she and Cole joined in. "His mom's called Venus."

As Cole guided the driver to back the livestock trailer toward the barnyard gate to unload, the wind caught Molly's loose hair, and blond strands brushed against Troy's jacket. He tensed, and his pulse raced at the memory of how soft and silky her hair had been and how he'd liked to run his fingers through it.

"I talked to Cole and have started to tackle his paperwork." Molly tucked her flyaway hair under her jacket collar. "I've made an online schedule and contact list from the handwritten notes Cole had scattered across his desk." She rolled her eyes. "It's shareable so we can all access and update it as needed. Now Cole has to get into the habit of using it, so I set a reminder on his phone."

"That's great. I need to set myself one of those reminders." Despite having a virtual assistant, paperwork was still the bane of Troy's life. "Thanks for getting Cole on the right track."

Her expression turned impish. "I made him a deal."

"Yes?" He liked this new, more confident grown-up Molly.

"No more early barn chores for me until Christmas." Her smile was smug.

"Good for you." Heat radiated through his chest. With his employees, acquaintances and even people he considered friends, there was always an element of competition. However, with Molly things were comfortable and familiar. She wasn't trying to impress him, and it didn't seem like she wanted anything from him either.

"Cole says I drive a hard bargain." She bumped his arm, and he bumped hers back, lighthearted. "With four brothers, I learned from the best."

"It's a good skill to have." In business, as well as life. While Troy wasn't ruthless, he tried to make sure nobody took advantage of him. It worked both ways, though, and when it came to his team, Troy had confidence in them and hoped he'd earned their confidence in return.

While he and Molly had been talking, the livestock driver had gotten the trailer into position and now he and Cole unlocked the rear doors.

"Tell me more about this bull," she said. "Cole's excited about breeding him. It'll be tight, but there should be enough time this year before the truly cold weather sets in."

"We've talked about conditioning Cupid for breeding next spring too. He's a winner, and although it will take time, he'll get Cole where he wants to go in rodeo stock contracting."

As Troy told Molly about what made the bull special, she nodded and asked thoughtful questions, reminding him that unlike the women he usually met in California, she understood ranching and agricultural life. There was something reassuring and comforting about being able to be fully himself with her in a way he couldn't with friends and colleagues who hadn't grown up in this world.

Cole's voice interrupted them. "Come and see Cupid. You can stand on the other side of the fence."

"He's smart to use a bull staff." Troy indicated the pole with a fastening at one end that was clipped to Cupid's nose ring. It kept the animal at a safe distance as Cole led him into a separate paddock beyond the cow barn.

"Cole's calm and assertive so Cupid's already looking to him as the leader." Molly followed her brother's every move. "You don't mess with two thousand pounds of bull, but Cole knows how to work with them. You see how he doesn't hesitate? He might not have been the flashiest cowboy on the rodeo circuit, but Cole was one of the best. He's going to be one of the best stock contractors too."

Now in the paddock, the reddish-brown-and-white bull turned in a circle while Cole remained alert and aware without making eye contact.

Molly's loyalty to her brother was evident, and Troy respected her commitment to family. It mirrored his own. From what Troy had seen so far, Molly was as kind and natural as she'd been as a girl. Yet, she'd still broken his heart and he'd never reconciled how she'd ended things between them with the person he'd thought he knew and loved.

As Cole moved toward the paddock gate, never turning his back on Cupid, Molly offered the trailer driver a drink and snack from the small staff kitchen in the ranch's barn office. Like the rest of the Carter family, she was friendly and built relationships that were honest, genuine and lasting.

So why hadn't she been that way with him?

Troy met Cole as he slipped out through the gate and closed it behind him, leaving Cupid to explore his new surroundings. "Wow. Fantastic job."

"No problem." Cole grinned. "At least if you know what you're doing. Take it from me, a cowboy with the scars to prove it. Never trust even the mildest mannered bull because he can always surprise you."

Like Molly had surprised Troy, and why he had the emotional scars to prove it. That was why he'd been guarded ever since and only dated casually, not willing to risk getting his heart broken a second time. So no matter how honest and genuine Molly seemed, was it possible to ever trust her again?

"Happy Halloween, kids." At Healing Paws, the town's animal physical therapy clinic associated with its veterinarian's office, Molly put chocolate bars into four trick-or-treat bags.

As the pirate, ghost, princess and lion shouted their thanks and left for the next stop on High Valley's Halloween "No Tricks, Just Treats" tour, she went behind the reception counter to refill the pumpkin-shaped bowl. She'd worked at the vet clinic during the summers she was home from college. Now, whenever she was back in town, she filled in at Healing Paws if they needed extra staff. Her presence here today, however, was for fun, not work.

Carla, the receptionist, smiled at Molly from her seat at the computer. "If you see a bumble bee, cat and caterpillar, that'll be my three. Give me a shout, okay? My hubby texted they should be in soon."

"Sure." Molly poured treats into the bowl, ready for more children to appear. She still loved decorating her place and dressing up to greet trick-or-treaters. This year, with a bag, balloons and sign Cam made for her, she'd fashioned a jellybean costume to wear over a black T-shirt and leggings. With her hair in two ponytails and colorful makeup, it was simple but effective.

More important, it reminded Molly of her

dad. She couldn't remember a time when he hadn't called her "Jellybean," the childhood nickname that had stuck when, as a premature baby, he said she was hardly bigger than a jellybean. He'd loved Halloween as much as she did, and even though they didn't get many trick-or-treaters out on the ranch, they'd always decorated the house together.

She swallowed a lump of emotion as the bell over entry door jingled. "Happy Halloween, I hope you like..." She came back around the desk with the treat bowl but stuttered to a stop as Troy appeared in front of her with a small brown dog on a leash.

"We keep running into each other." A smile tugged at the corner of Troy's mouth. "Meet Acorn. The vet sent us over to make an appointment."

"I didn't know you had a dog. I mean...there's no reason I should have known. It's your business." The more Molly said, the more flustered she got.

"Acorn's a recent addition. She's a senior dog the rescue was having trouble finding a home for. Her owner died a few months ago. When I saw the ad, I applied to adopt her." Troy's smile broadened as he took in Molly from head to toe, and her face heated. "Cute costume."

"Thanks." She took an instinctive step back,

and her balloons bobbed between them. "I…
uh…chocolate bar?" She thrust out the candy
bowl. "We also have dog treats if Acorn would
like one. Kristi at the Bluebunch made them."

"When it comes to chocolate, you don't
have to ask me twice." He took a bar and then
grabbed a dog treat from the container Molly
indicated and knelt to Acorn's level. "Would
you like a cookie, sweetheart?"

Acorn thumped her tail, and by her adoring
expression, she was already head over heels in
love with her rescuer.

Just when Molly thought she'd hardened her
heart to Troy, he did something like adopting
sweet Acorn that made him even more appealing. Sharing a rented condo and working shifts,
she couldn't adopt a dog, and she wouldn't let
herself long for something she couldn't have.
While it wouldn't be the same, she could volunteer at an animal shelter in Atlanta. That would
keep her busy outside of work, and if she was
busy, she wouldn't have time to think.

After Acorn had crunched the treat and wagged
her tail again, Troy scooped the little dog into his
arms. "Here, girl, come say hi to Molly. Acorn's
timid from being so long in the shelter, but she
likes having her ears rubbed." He demonstrated
as Acorn rested her head against his broad chest.

Molly moved closer and reached over her balloons to pat the dog's soft ears.

Acorn rewarded her with a gentle nose nudge.

"I think she's saying 'more, please.'" Troy chuckled. "I only picked her up last night, so we're still getting to know each other. The vet says she's healthy, and some canine physical therapy will get her more active."

"Yes, you wanted to make an appointment." Troy hadn't come here to see *her*. She knew that. He was just being friendly like he would be with any acquaintance. "All the therapists are great but Cole's wife, Melissa, works here and she specializes in older dogs. If she has an opening, she'd be great for Acorn."

The bell over the door rang again, and more costumed children came in with parents taking pictures on their phones.

"Happy Halloween." She turned to the kids and handed out candy. "Amazing costumes."

A toddler dressed as a green dinosaur let out a wail as a Great Dane bigger than he was came out of a treatment room with its owner.

Molly stood between the child and dog. "Zeus won't hurt you. I know him, and he's a softie. Are you scared because he's so big?"

The boy nodded, clung to his mom's leg and cried harder.

Molly untied an orange balloon from the end

of the Halloween arch she'd made earlier. "There you go." The little boy took the balloon and a sob turned into a hiccup. "I know a song about a dog and a balloon. Would you like to hear it?"

The child gave her a solemn nod and sniffed.

Molly launched into the upbeat tune and then danced around the clinic's waiting area as she sang. "Come on." She waved at the boy, and he and his mom, followed by Troy, joined in.

As Molly's gaze caught Troy's, he shrugged, and his blue eyes twinkled before they sang the catchy chorus together. He had a good voice, but it was the expression on his face and in his eyes that make her legs tremble and heat surge through her body.

Acorn let out an excited bark, and the Great Dane sat on his haunches and watched them like the gentle giant he was.

Molly finished the song with a flourish, and the boy clapped and laughed. "All better now?"

Still clutching the balloon, he gave her a shy smile.

"You're fine, aren't you, William?" The mom ruffled his curly, dark hair, and the affectionate gesture made Molly's heart squeeze. "William hasn't been around dogs, any animals really, because his sister has allergies. Thanks for helping him feel comfortable. You're great with kids."

"Anyone would have done the same." Since

the other children and parents had left, Molly gave William a few extra treats. "Have fun." She turned to William's mom. "Before he sees a dog again, the two of you could think about how to handle it. Planning always makes me feel better." It was also a way for her to feel like she had some control in an uncontrollable world.

"Great idea." The mom nodded. "My husband and I moved to High Valley last month, and everybody's been so kind and welcoming. I'm Brooke Kaplan."

Molly introduced herself, exchanged numbers with Brooke and invited her and William to visit the ranch. But the whole time, an awareness of Troy coursed through her.

She hadn't planned it, but the connection between them was stronger than ever.

After Brooke and William left, followed by Zeus and his owner, Troy and Acorn made their way to the clinic door.

"Bye." Molly's mouth got dry.

"I guess I'll see you at the ranch." Troy's deep voice reverberated above Molly's head and forced her to look at him. His eyes were so blue and framed by eyelashes she used to tease him were too long to be real.

"Yeah."

"Like Brooke said, you were great with William." Troy's warm breath brushed her cheek as they both reached for the door handle at the same time. "I remember my mom singing that song to me."

"My mom sang it to us too." Once, Molly had been certain she'd sing it to her own kids. However, to be a mom, she had to meet the right man and be in the right place in her life to settle down and have kids. "It was nice of you to join in. I never knew you liked to sing." He'd be a great dad to some lucky child. The thought intruded and she forced it away.

"As a hand, I used to sing to the cows." Troy's eyes teased her. "My dad said it kept them calm, but don't tell anybody." He put a finger to his lips. "Also promise me you won't tell anyone I was singing and dancing around." He winced and tugged at his jacket collar.

"I won't but I can't speak for Carla." She darted a glance at the receptionist who'd been clapping along and was now clearly eavesdropping on their conversation. "Or Brooke. She and William were pretty impressed with you."

Although Brooke was around Molly's age, like Carla she'd given Troy the kind of approving look usually reserved for a mom checking out their daughter's date. She'd mentioned having a daughter so maybe that was why, but it had reminded Molly that if she'd stayed here, she'd likely have been married or at least engaged by now. Most of her close friends in Atlanta were single, but here she was surrounded by couples and not only in her family. The majority of her high school friends had gotten paired up long ago. "William looked like you were his new hero."

"He's a cute kid." He hesitated as if he was going to say something more but instead looked at Carla and then opened the clinic door. "See you."

As he and Acorn disappeared into the street thronged with costumed kids and families enjoying both the event and sunny October afternoon, Molly hugged the treat bowl. That ER doctor she'd gone out with a few times would never have sung and danced with a scared little kid, maybe not even one of his own. For him, appearances were everything. Unlike Troy, who wasn't afraid to show his silly side.

And who was a good man to his core, something she'd sensed but hadn't been mature enough at eighteen to fully appreciate. From dogs to people, he'd be there for those who needed him without expecting any kind of return.

That was the kind of man she needed. Memories, loss and then regret mixed together inside her. But Troy was here in High Valley, and she wasn't, at least not long-term. Like they'd always been, their lives were on different paths, and then as now, she couldn't...*wouldn't* let herself be distracted.

# *CHAPTER SIX*

ONE OF THE things Troy prided himself on was never losing control either in business or his personal life. But there was something about Molly that made him forget himself and lose his usual inhibitions. That had to be the reason he'd sung and danced at Healing Paws like a goofy kid. Almost a week later, he still cringed at the memory.

However, he seemed to be the only one who was embarrassed or thought he'd done anything out of the ordinary. When he'd taken Acorn back to the clinic for her session with Melissa, Carla had greeted him warmly and invited Troy to join her and her family for a Sunday dinner. And when he'd bumped into Brooke and William at the grocery store, the little boy had hugged him right in the middle of the produce aisle.

As Troy rode out of his barn on Winnie, a Morgan horse the previous owners of the Bitterroot had sold with the ranch, he considered how much his life had changed since moving here. For a start, he couldn't remember when he'd last stopped work at midday on a Friday to do anything else, let alone go riding. However, on this first Friday in November, the sun was high in the clear blue sky, and with harvested fields stretching around him to the horizon, the weather was perfect to take a look at his new property. There was no better way than on horseback to get to truly know land, and just then, there was a part of Troy that felt like he was king of the world.

In California, he'd been crowded between the ocean, mountains and people, but here he could breathe in a way he'd almost forgotten. He waved to his foreman and two ranch hands working in the barnyard before taking a rutted path down a low rise that led alongside the fields closest to the house. He could already picture next summer's crop here with grain waving in a warm breeze. He planned to buy more cattle and build up the Bitterroot's herd. *So many plans, so little time.* He chuckled. It was a good problem to have, and out here he had both new energy and a fresh sense of optimism.

Half an hour later, he and Winnie rode along the fence line by pastureland that bordered the Carters' horse barn. He hadn't planned it, but thanks to an old path across the fields, Troy had ended up on Carter land. Since he was here any-way, he might as well check on Cupid. And if he happened to accidentally run into Molly, so much the better. His skin tingled and he caught his breath. Where had that thought come from? While it was both surprising and new, it some-how felt right. Although he didn't want to ex-amine his feelings too closely, Molly was one of the reasons his life had changed for the better.

Dismounting in the barnyard, he introduced Winnie to one of the nearby hands. "I won't be long so no need to put her in a stall. She's a friendly girl and will be fine in the pasture with the others." He gestured to where several of the Carters' horses had gathered near the fence.

"Sure." The man nodded, and he and Troy began to untack her, both of them speaking in a reassuring tone.

Troy had always talked to horses. Now with Winnie, it was a way for them to get to know each other and build a trusting bond. He gave her a final pat and then went into the barn, blinking as his eyes adjusted from bright sun-shine to the dimmer interior. Cole was usually here at this time of day, so he'd find him before going to see Cupid.

"Hey, girl." He greeted Cindy, Joy Carter's seal-brown mare, who was on stall rest due to a muscle injury. "I know being stuck in here is boring but it's only for a few more days."

Cindy nickered, and Troy reached across the stall door to rub her forehead. Pigeons cooed in the barn loft, and muted sunlight patterned the floor of the central aisle. As Troy stepped away from Cindy's stall, he whirled around at what sounded like a sob.

"I can't talk to anyone except you." Although Molly's voice was muffled, Troy would have known it anywhere. "I like Shane, but I miss Dad. You remember him, don't you?" There was a gulping noise like Molly was choking back tears. "Of course you do. He raised you from a foal. Everything is changing. Not for you, Daisy-May, but me. Mom's moving, and Zach and Beth will be living here and I… Home won't be the same."

Troy hesitated. He could leave the barn right now, and Molly would never know he'd heard her crying and sharing private thoughts with her horse. Except, he wasn't that kind of guy, and he'd have wanted to comfort *anyone* who was hurting or in trouble. Even though she'd hurt *him*, he still hated to think of Molly being upset and alone.

Cindy stomped her front feet and whinnied.

"It's okay." Troy spoke to her soothingly. "I'll go see what's wrong."

The crying stopped as if someone had turned off a water faucet. Troy walked along the aisle, but the other stalls were empty as was the tack room. "Hello?" His voice echoed, and wings fluttered as the pigeons flew overhead. "Molly? Cole?"

A horse nickered. Troy stopped in front of a towering stack of straw bales, which were new since the last time he'd visited. "Anyone here?" He poked his head around an end bale, and Daisy-May let out a loud whinny.

"Hi." From the horse's other side, he glimpsed Molly's tearstained face. "If you're looking for Cole, he had to go into town, but he should be back soon." She fiddled with one of Daisy-May's rear hooves.

"I wanted to check on Cupid but thought I'd say hi to Cole first. If you need—"

"I'm fine. I was riding on the creek path and after last night's rain, it was muddy."

She sniffed and returned to untacking the horse. "You can wait for Cole in the office."

"I could but..." Troy drew in a deep breath. Once, he'd felt so connected to Molly, like she was the other half of himself. And while he'd convinced himself he was over her, maybe he never truly would be. Seeing her now, all he wanted was to help and make things better in whatever way he could. "You're upset and I don't want to leave you alone."

"You heard that?" Her face, which had been a mottled red, paled.

"I wasn't eavesdropping, but when I came into the barn, well…I couldn't help overhearing. Maybe I should have left but I couldn't do that either." Troy drew closer to her. "Of course, with your mom marrying Shane things will change, but she'll still be nearby."

"I know but…" Molly gulped and rested her head against Daisy-May's neck, and Troy's heart squeezed at the memory of how she'd once laid her head against *his* neck. "I want Mom to be happy and although she's marrying Shane, she'll never forget my dad. I'm not a kid so Shane won't be my stepfather in that way. But even though I moved away and changed, home has always been here and the same, you know? Beth and Zach are talking about redecorating, and I thought I was okay with everything, but I guess I'm not."

Troy understood what she meant. He'd lost his own childhood home on the cusp of adolescence. "Your brothers all have their own places and families, but the Tall Grass Ranch and your mom being here, that's your anchor."

She nodded. "I miss my dad so much. Shane would never think of trying to replace my dad, but this kind of change is hard. I guess I hadn't truly realized that even here, nothing can stay the same." She dug in the pocket of her jeans for a tissue. "I'm being foolish. Forget I said anything."

It was too late for Troy to forget because for the first time since they'd both returned to High Valley, he'd seen the real Molly. "You're not being foolish. I bet if you talked to your brothers, you'd find they're having some of the same feelings."

"I doubt it. Zach's excited about the baby, Cole's focused on his stock contracting business and Bryce is about to have his own new start with Carrie." More tears welled in her beautiful blue eyes. "I'm the only one who…" She gulped. "I have my own life, but it's not here. The next time I come back to High Valley, everything will be different."

"It will, but some differences can be good." Troy paused. She'd been vulnerable with him, so now he needed to take a risk and let himself be open with her. "When my folks lost our ranch, it took a long time for me to accept what had happened. I was angry and hurt and sure I'd never settle anywhere else, especially in a city. But I did." He'd had to. "My mom and dad kept a lot of our family traditions the same and that helped. But most of all, I came to realize that what makes a house a home is family, no matter where you are. You'll still have your family, only in different places."

She rubbed her eyes. "Zach says he won't change Dad's basement workshop, and they're keeping all our height measurements on the wall by the kitchen door. Beth's even talking about framing them. It's right they make the ranch house their own, and for now I'll still have my bedroom here but…" She shrugged and more tears fell. "I guess after losing Paul and my dad, I focus more on any changes here being bad rather than good."

"Come here, Mol." Troy closed the space between them and held out his arms.

She stepped into them, and he hugged her— as a friend who wanted to offer comfort, he reminded himself as awareness of her warmth and closeness surged through him. He touched her cheek to wipe away a tear and then held her even closer.

Troy's knees went weak as he breathed in her recognizable fragrance, that delicate jasmine overlaid with a hint of vanilla. Holding Molly was like coming home to someplace familiar but also new. And as feelings Troy had tried to forget flamed into life, he never wanted to let her go.

MOLLY LET HERSELF relax into Troy's embrace. Although she prided herself on being independent, there was no shame in leaning on someone when you needed to. Especially when that someone was Troy, who'd always held her in the right way, not too tight but with a gentle firmness. Like he was taking her burdens and making them lighter simply by being there.

With her face buried in his shoulder, she savored his scent. The crisp cotton of his Western shirt beneath his unbuttoned jacket, and the warmth of his skin below were better than any aftershave. It was the familiar "I'm here for you no matter what" aroma that had once represented comfort, love and a sweet tenderness she'd never found with anyone else.

Molly didn't know how long they stood there together, only that hugging Troy was even better than she remembered. When Daisy-May nudged her shoulder, as if to remind Molly she'd left the horse half untacked, she had to force herself to take a step back.

"Thanks." She rubbed her face and tried to quell her panicked thoughts. She never let anyone see her inner turmoil, so why, out of all people, had she let down her guard with Troy? "I'm not usually so emotional."

"Forget about it." As if he sensed her embarrassment, he stared up into the barn loft instead of at her. "I'm glad I happened to be around."

She turned to Daisy-May and secured the stirrups and then Troy unbuckled the girth, the two of them working together in silence like they used to.

Troy had never been a big talker, but after his care and concern, the next step was up to Molly. "I owe you an explanation." He'd broken down her protective walls, and she couldn't live with herself any longer if she didn't tell him at least part of the truth.

"About what?" His voice had a hint of a quiver as he put the girth on top of Daisy-May's saddle.

Maybe the hug had affected him as much as it had her, but she couldn't let herself think about the torrent of emotion it had unleashed—one that had shaken her to her core. They kept bumping into each other and for her, it was often when she was at her most vulnerable. Once and for all, she had to deal with the past and the pain she'd caused. Maybe that way they could both move on. Troy with his business, the ranch and making a life here. And her with her future in Atlanta. Not here and not with Troy.

"About why I broke up with you." She gripped the saddle by the pommel, and he took it by the back as they lifted it up and off Daisy-May.

"You were going to college. It was a summer

romance." He took the saddle and put it on a nearby rack keeping his back to her.

"That's true, but..." Molly studied his stiff shoulders. "I also thought I was too young to be so serious about you—about anyone." And because her feelings for Troy had been so big and intense, she hadn't known how to handle them. She'd been afraid. The only option she'd seen then was breaking up with him, but she hadn't counted on the magnitude and intensity of those feelings either. "I didn't only *want* to go to college, I *needed* to." She took a steadying breath as Troy turned to face her. Had his eyes always been so blue?

"I knew how important college was for you. Did you really think I'd have tried to stop you from going? I thought what we had together was important too, and we could have lasted no matter what." Now those eyes held both disbelief and hurt. "We were both young, but that doesn't mean what we felt for each other wasn't real."

How could she make him understand something she'd never truly understood herself? Maybe those feelings had been too real. At eighteen, she had been confused, overwhelmed and still grieving her dad's death, and the only thing she had known with any certainty was that she had to leave the ranch. "I knew you wouldn't have stopped me from going to college, but I was scared of being like my mom. My mom *wanted* to go to college when she was my age, but she didn't. She married my dad instead, so she's only taking college classes now. I always wanted to go to college and become a nurse, but I also *needed* to follow my dreams. If I hadn't, I'd have regretted it. I might have ended up resenting you and us." She stared at her feet as her thoughts turned inward.

"But I planned on college too. We talked about how I'd already taken a few courses at night and was saving to go full-time." Troy leaned against the barn wall and crossed his arms in front of his chest. "I'd never have held you back. We could have both gotten our degrees and supported and encouraged each other." His mouth settled into a stubborn line that Molly remembered. "I asked, but you wouldn't even try to make a long-distance relationship work."

Because she'd thought it would be better to break things off before she got in even deeper. Yet, the hurt had lingered for years. "My mom and my brothers sacrificed a lot to give me a college education. I didn't want to disappoint them."

Even to her own ears, Molly sounded unconvincing, but it was the best she could do. Troy was astute and always went right to the heart of the matter. It was undoubtedly one of the qualities that had helped him succeed in business, but it was also a reminder she needed to be on guard with him.

"So, you disappointed me instead." Troy's voice was flat before he took Daisy-May's bit and wiped it with a clean cloth.

"I'm sorry." Her chest hurt, and the world seemed to spin around her.

"I'm sorry too." Troy exhaled. "But it's ancient history." He gave her a pained smile, and his eyes were dull. "We were kids. Despite what I thought back then, we probably wouldn't have lasted together anyway."

In any relationship, but especially a long-distance one, communication was key. Molly's stomach flipped. She'd done what she thought she had to and had saved both of them more hurt later on. "No hard feelings?"

"Of course not." He focused on the bit and avoided her gaze.

"Cole will be back soon." She had to change the subject. It wouldn't do any good to prolong this conversation. If she did, she risked saying something she couldn't take back. "From what I've seen, Cupid's settling in great. As bulls go, he's a sweetheart."

"Good to hear." Troy shrugged as if Cole and Cupid were the last things on his mind.

"I guess I'll see you at the weddings, if not before." Molly took the bit from him and gathered the rest of the tack. She'd let Daisy-May into the pasture once Troy was on his way.

"Sure." But as he turned and went down the barn aisle without looking back, his boots left a dull echo that stabbed her heart. Because of how he'd comforted her, Molly's emotions churned even more than before.

Except this time, they weren't about her mom's remarriage and the changes it would bring. They were about Troy and, despite the years and history between them, how he still made her feel.

# CHAPTER SEVEN

"HEY, MOM." Putting his phone on speaker, Troy lifted the steak from the pan to a plate already loaded with a baked potato and green beans. The meal was basic but filling, perfect for one person. "What's up?"

"Nothing. I wanted to hear your voice." His mom's warm laugh bridged the distance between San Francisco and Montana. "Your dad's at the golf club, and I just came back from my tai chi class. We're going out to dinner and a movie later. It's been a busy week at work for both of us, so we've hardly seen each other."

Although neither of his folks had to work, they wanted to and said part-time hours kept them active. His mom was an office administrator, and his dad loved serving customers at a neighborhood hardware store. What did it say, though, that his folks, at almost sixty, had a more active social life than Troy?

"That sounds fun." He sat at one end of the

rustic kitchen table the previous owners had sold with the house and put the phone beside it. Troy could picture his mom curled up on the living room sofa near the table with a display of framed family photos. No matter where they lived, those photos were a constant. A symbol of roots, family unity and cherished bonds.

"What about you? Any news? Even after all these years, I still miss Montana." His mom's voice had the wistful quality it always got whenever she talked about her home state.

Troy stared out the kitchen window into the darkness interspersed by shadowy outlines of the leafless trees that encircled the rear of the house. "Everything's okay. The usual. The ranch foreman and hands are doing great." The Bitterroot ran as efficiently as he suspected it always had, and Troy sometimes felt superfluous. "Pete and I are ramping up for a new product launch. It's looking good to be on schedule and under budget."

But his business partner, Pete, was carrying more of the load while Troy found reasons to visit the Tall Grass Ranch. Although he'd tried to keep from thinking of Molly and how perfect it had felt to hug her in the barn, he couldn't stop himself. For a moment, he'd forgotten how things had ended between them, caught up in the power of a hug meant to comfort her but, for him, had become so much more. In the past few days, though, he'd only glimpsed her a couple of times around town. Once coming out of the Bluebunch Café with several other women, and then when she and her mom were heading into the craft center as Troy parked his truck nearby.

"As for Montana, we might have snow when you're here for Thanksgiving." Would his parents and sister, Sara, make the ranch house feel more like home? "You and Dad will like seeing snow."

"As long as we don't have to shovel it." There was a pause on his mom's end of the phone. "What's wrong, honey? Aren't you happy at the ranch?"

"It's great. Everybody in High Valley has been really welcoming." There was no reason for Troy to be so restless and unsettled.

"What about the Carter family? Is everything... okay there?" Troy's mom was the only person who knew about his heartache over Molly. He'd assured her that investing in Cole's stock contracting venture was only business, but now he wondered if he'd deceived himself and then her.

"It's fine. Molly's back in town because her mom's getting married again, but anything between us is water under the bridge." *Liar.* Troy's skin still tingled at the memory of holding Molly close and the way her head had nestled into his shoulder. "Joy's having a double wedding just before Thanksgiving. Her son Bryce—Molly's brother—is getting married too."

"That's so romantic." His mom's voice softened.

"I was about to have dinner so can I call you tomorrow?" The last thing he needed was for his mom to start talking about weddings.

"Don't mind me. We can chat while you eat." His mom laughed again. "When we visit, I'll bring a card and a small wedding gift to leave with you to give Joy. What about a basket of my homemade jams, jellies and pickles?"

"I'm sure she'd like that." What else could Troy say? His mom was kind and thoughtful— she and Molly's mom were a lot alike in that way.

"That summer you worked at the Tall Grass, Joy guessed how I worried about you. She'd email me every few weeks to say everything was okay. As a mother herself, she understood the pain of the empty nest."

Troy rolled his eyes, even though his mom wasn't there to see it. "I was twenty. You didn't need to worry." He cut a piece of steak, but his appetite had disappeared.

"No matter how old your child is, you worry about them and you miss them. We raised you to spread your wings, and your dad and I are so proud of everything you've achieved. But that summer was the first time you'd lived away from home. You'll know what I mean once you have children yourself." She didn't huff, but she might as well have.

"I'm not ready to become a parent yet." It had been fun spending time with Molly and her nieces and nephew, and with little William at Healing Paws. His heart constricted. He'd love to be a dad but right now it was an *if*, not *when* he had kids.

"Have you met anyone in High Valley?" His mom's tone was too casual.

"I've met lots of people here." There was hardly a day that someone didn't drop by, usually with food, and whenever he went into town, he stopped and chatted with folks.

"That isn't what I meant, and you know it." His mom's mock chiding made Troy chuckle.

"Subtle, Mom. When I meet a special woman, I'll let you know." A siren wailed in the background on his mom's end of the phone. After only a short time in High Valley, he'd adjusted to country life and didn't miss city sounds. "I have a work call soon and—"

"You're working in the evening?" His mom made a tsking sound. "You work far too much. You're only young once and—"

"It's fine, Mom. Nobody's telling me I have

to work. It's my choice." But was that because he didn't have much else in his life? "Can you message me your recipe for snickerdoodles? I signed up to bring a dessert to the Carter wedding potluck and your recipe for those cookies is the best ever." It wasn't a lie, but he needed to divert his mom from his single status. "I'm also making that pumpkin chowder you and Dad like."

"Of course, but..." A pause and Troy could almost guess what his mom was thinking. "You're going to the weddings? Are you sure that's wise, honey?"

"I'm not going to the ceremony, but there's a community reception afterward. Everyone in town's invited. It would look strange if I didn't go."

"I suppose, and with a crowd, it's not like you'll have much to do with the family, will you?"

His heart pounded. He was a grown man, but he still valued and respected his parents and their opinions. "If you need to say something to me, go ahead." His meal forgotten, he rubbed at his temples where a headache had started.

"I'm glad you're being sensible about Molly. You never forget your first love nor should you, but you've both moved on. The two of you are different people now. You might be able to be friends, but you have to think of the future, not the past."

"You know me, Mom. I'm all about the future." He gave a hollow laugh. "Talk to you soon. Say hi to Dad for me."

As they said their goodbyes, Troy's stomach knotted. His mom was right. He and Molly *were* different people now, and she no longer even lived in High Valley. But each time he saw her, it was like he went back to who he'd been— where that future he thought of was with her. Even if they were able to somehow be friends, would he always yearn for more?

MOLLY WAS USED to city traffic, which was the reason she'd left the ranch half an hour earlier than necessary for the short drive into High Valley. When she wasn't in medical scrubs, she was used to city clothes too. After parking her SUV near the Bluebunch, she again glanced at her tailored jeans, chunky gray sweater, black heeled boots and black puffer jacket. Did she look too dressy for a Sunflower Sisterhood meeting to make wedding favors? Even if she did, it was too late to change.

She left her vehicle and locked it with the key fob, though it was unlikely anyone would try breaking in here.

Minutes later, she entered the café and greeted

the women seated in a big circle behind tables arranged in the center of the room. "Hi, everyone. I thought I'd be early but you're all here!"

Kristi, the café owner, welcomed Molly with a smile while others waved or called out friendly hellos. "You *are* early. Everyone else is even earlier. We like chatting, that's all."

Molly's mom patted the empty chair at her side. "Sit by me, honey."

As Molly sat, there was a ripple of whispering around them. The other women seemed to be conspiring for a moment. Before Molly could ask what was going on, everyone shouted, "Surprise," and she and her mom stared at each other, wide-eyed.

"What's... I thought we were making the honey jar wedding favors." Her mom laughed and put a hand to her face as Nina and Angela unrolled Bridal Shower and Bride-to-Be banners, and Rosa appeared from the café's kitchen with a yellow and white balloon arch decorated with artificial sunflowers.

"I didn't know about this shower, I swear." Molly shook her head and laughed with the rest.

"We didn't tell you because Joy would have gotten it out of you." Rosa set up the balloons behind Joy's chair.

"It's all good." Kristi set out plates of party

snacks and the other women carried more decorations out of the back.

"But you already had an engagement party for me at the community center." Molly's mom looked near tears. "It's too much. I don't know what to say."

"That party was for everyone. This shower is only for the Sunflower Sisterhood. And you don't have to say anything except shout surprise when Carrie, Paisley and Skylar get here. Double wedding, double bridal shower." At Molly's other side, Melissa tied more balloons to the café walls. "I asked Carrie to pick up the girls from gymnastics to delay her. Bryce just texted me they should be here any minute. Right on time." Melissa gave Joy a mock glare.

Taking a sparkly princess-style crown from Nina, Molly set it on her mom's head. "I didn't think anything of it when you called and said you were staying in town, and you'd see me at this meeting. If I'd known about the shower, I'd have come up with a reason to get you to come home instead."

"Don't worry," Melissa reassured her. "Joy has a sixth sense when anybody's keeping a secret. That's why we couldn't risk telling you. Living in the same house, she'd have had it out of you in no time."

A chill crept up Molly's spine. The only big secret she'd ever kept from her mom was that summer romance with Troy. Had her mom known all along?

"So that's why everyone but me is dressed up." Her mom glanced around the group. "Even you, Molly. You must have suspected something was up."

"I didn't, truly. I'd have found a way to get you to come home and convince you to dress up, I swear." In her city clothes, although still casual for her, she didn't look out of place. However, clothes or not, for the first time since coming back to High Valley, she felt like she belonged in a way she'd never done in Atlanta.

"Carrie's truck just went by," Angela said. She was keeping watch by the café door. "Now she's parking down the street. Everybody ready?"

An excited murmur went around the group, and Molly squeezed her mom's hand. Although she'd been to wedding showers in Atlanta for friends from school and the hospital, this event was personal and extra special.

"I'm glad you're here." Her mom squeezed Molly's hand back, and tears shimmered in the depths of her blue eyes.

"Me too." Molly's heart was full. She'd come home lots of times during her years away, but until now she'd never felt the tug of home so strongly. It must be prewedding emotion, but as she glanced around the circle of faces—family and friends old and new—fresh longing rose inside her.

As Beth and Melissa chatted, their expressions animated as they talked about Beth's pregnancy, Molly's heart tugged in a different way. Like Carrie, who'd soon become a stepmother to Paisley and Cam, all three of her sisters-in-law were mothers *and* independent career women right here in High Valley.

Before she could get too caught up in her own thoughts, the bell above the door jangled again. Everyone, including Molly, shouted, "Surprise!" as Carrie, Skylar and Paisley came into the café.

Kristi flipped the sign over to read Closed, though she didn't lock the door, saying something about a delivery. As the party got started and plates of food began to circulate, Nina nudged Molly's arm.

"Want one of Kristi's mini quiches?" She held out a plate.

"Thanks." Molly took one of the delicious savory pastries, as good or even better than anything she'd had in Atlanta.

"Be sure to save room for Kristi's huckleberry cheesecake," Nina said. "It's well on its way to putting High Valley on the culinary map."

"Oh?" Molly asked politely.

"Mmm-hmm. When Kristi won the cooking

competition in High Valley's Spring Food Festival, the Bluebunch was featured in a state tourism campaign. An East Coast food journalist saw it and came here on vacation. She wrote a magazine article about the café and that cheesecake and included lots of pictures. As soon as it came out, the phone started ringing with people wanting to order food and café hats, mugs and aprons online. Carrie got her set up with the technology side of things, so Kristi hired me for several extra hours a week and now Angela as well to fulfill orders. Last Monday alone we sent out fifty packages. We even shipped three dozen Montana blueberry muffins to Alaska."

"I'll have to place a regular order once I'm back in Atlanta."

As Molly passed the plate of mini quiches around the circle, she discovered that since this was a second wedding for Joy, and Carrie was moving into the home Bryce had shared with his late wife, none of them needed a lot of household items. As a result, the Sunflower Sisterhood had decided to make the shower a charity fundraiser with the theme of Shower High Valley with Compassion. However, the women had still gone in together to buy two group gifts.

"Wow!" Carrie exclaimed over a coffee maker and selection of gourmet coffee. "Thanks, everyone. You know I need coffee to get started on those early mornings. Actually, every morning." She stuck a gift bow on Paisley's head while Molly's mom did the same with Skylar, and both girls laughed. "Now Bryce's old coffee maker can go in the barn, and we'll use this new fancy one in the house."

"You know me well." Joy had unwrapped a wicker basket holding a teapot, "Mr. and Mrs." mugs, and a range of tea accessories and specialty teas.

While Molly admired the gifts with the others, her thoughts swirled. High Valley was still the small town she'd grown up in, and as interconnected as it had always been, but it was more outward looking now. Or maybe the town had always been that way, but Molly was seeing it—and the people who lived here—through new eyes.

"Hey, guys. You can leave the chairs in my new workroom behind the kitchen." Kristi's voice rose above the conversation as the café door opened to let in several men.

One of them, Nina explained to Molly as she pointed him out, was Kristi's fiancé, Alex Greenwood, the chef at Ruby's Place, a restaurant across town.

"Help yourself to food from the platters on the kitchen counters," Kristi added. "I made a batch of mini pizzas for you guys. There's also BBQ chicken bites and pretzel dogs." She kissed Alex's cheek, and he smiled as the women greeted him and the others.

"What about the table? You want it in the workroom too?" Werner leaned on the open door. "Sorry to disturb you, ladies. We won't be a minute." His smile broadened as Nina joined him and held the door. "I'll take the other end, Troy. That's right. Hold it steady and lift sideways."

Molly couldn't help it as her gaze connected with Troy's.

He nodded in greeting, and she waved back.

Molly's mom put her tea gift basket by her purse at Molly's side. "Kristi's offering cooking classes for team building events. There's one for the town council tomorrow, but there was a mix-up and the rented chairs and table were delivered to the hardware store instead of here. Werner got a group of fellows together to move them over. It's nice how Troy's becoming part of the community."

"Yes." But Molly barely heard her mom's words. Troy was only moving a table, but she couldn't take her eyes off him. No other guy ever wore a pair of faded jeans so well. And when his winter jacket fell open to expose a blue T-shirt that hugged his toned chest, her mouth went dry.

As she took a slice of huckleberry cheesecake from Beth, she had to make herself focus on the luscious dessert rather than Troy's voice coming from Kristi's kitchen.

She could get used to life here, but admitting it to herself would turn everything about who she'd always thought she was upside down. And while that would be hard enough, how could she ever admit to anyone that for the girl in her high school graduating class voted most likely to succeed, true success might be entirely different from what she'd always thought and said?

# CHAPTER EIGHT

"GO DO YOUR THING, CUPID," Troy said, as Cole opened the livestock trailer and let the bull into the pasture with the cows.

Beside him, Molly grinned, and she quirked an eyebrow. "His 'thing'? I grew up on a ranch. There's not much about cow breeding season I don't know."

Troy's face heated but he didn't reply.

Cole shut the pasture gate behind Cupid and joined them by the fence. "Molly used to pitch in with us for calving season. Good practice for delivering human babies, right, sis? Same idea."

Molly gave her brother's shoulder a playful swat. "In theory, yes, but don't talk about calf birthing around Beth. She's nervous about labor and delivery."

"I won't." Cole made a zipping motion across his mouth. "Zach's sure a bundle of nerves. He's got a stack of books about pregnancy and birth in the barn office, and different route maps on his phone to get Beth to the hospital depending on the time of day and weather. I've never seen him so worked up."

"Sometimes the dads are more anxious than the moms," Molly said. "I've seen all kinds."

As Molly rested her elbows on the fence, and the wind caught her ponytail, Troy's heartbeat sped up. In jeans, a barn jacket, cowboy boots and a white cowboy hat, she looked as much a part of this vast landscape as the tall pasture grass, distant mountains and grazing animals. Out here, it was easy for him to picture Molly always being at his side, and the two of them working their own ranch together. Having a couple of kids one day as well.

Troy shook himself and turned back to Cole. He needed to focus on work, not dreams that could never come true. "If you're all set, I'll get going." Back to the Bitterroot, his home office and whatever crises had come up while he'd been out of cell phone coverage.

"Sure. Do you mind giving Molly a ride back? Bryce asked me to take some soil samples for him."

"I expect Troy's busy. I don't mind waiting for you. I could even help with the samples," Molly replied before Troy could say anything.

"I'll be a few hours. I also need to check the fence line. Don't you have to help Mom with the last of the wedding baking?" Cole looked at his sister with a bemused expression.

"Yes, but—"

"What's the issue?" Cole's gaze went to Troy, and his eyes narrowed. Despite his easygoing, laidback manner, Cole was sharp, especially when it came to people he cared about. "Is there something going on with you two I don't know about?"

"There's nothing going on," Troy interjected. "And it's no problem for me to take Molly back to the Tall Grass." He kept his voice and expression neutral, found his keys and gestured to his truck parked beyond the livestock trailer. The drive would only last fifteen minutes or so. He could make small talk that long.

"Okay." Molly's voice was small, and she hugged herself. "Let's go."

Ten minutes later, Troy drove his pickup along a rutted, dirt track that edged the hilly pastureland. They'd already talked about the weather. Sunny and unseasonably warm for Montana in November. How Acorn was settling in. Fine, and the dog was at the Bitterroot with Cathy. The chance of the hometown hockey team making it to the league finals. Excellent, they both agreed.

Now, hunched in the passenger seat, Molly stared out the window. Clearly, she'd rather be anywhere else but trapped in the truck's cab with him. However, if she wasn't going to address the awkwardness between them, Troy had to.

"When we talked in the barn about why you broke up with me, and we spoke about your mom remarrying, and your dad…how you're feeling…" The truck jolted into a rut, and he floored the accelerator until they'd cleared the next rise of land. "I want to make sure you know that conversation is only between us."

"Thanks." Her voice hitched.

"It's okay, truly." He couldn't see inside her head, but it made sense that even without everything else, her mom's wedding would be emotional. "I know I said before we couldn't be friends, but now…" He took a deep breath. "Why don't we give it a try? What have we got to lose?"

Maybe everything. And possibly his heart most of all. Troy had to ignore his doubts. He and Molly couldn't go on this way, edging around each other like polite strangers or the alternative, a closeness too reminiscent of the intimacy they'd once shared. He hadn't missed the curious looks they'd attracted at the art show, and back there with Cupid and the cows even Cole had been suspicious.

"You're right." Molly tugged on her jacket. "If

Cole gets the idea there's something between us, he won't let it rest. He'll talk to Zach and Bryce and my mom, and they'll all make something out of nothing. Along with being the only girl, I'm so much younger than my brothers. They've always been protective." She chewed her lower lip. "When we talked we sort of cleared the air and dealt with the past, so okay, friends."

Although a statement, her voice rose at the end making it more of a question.

"Friends," Troy echoed as he turned into the gravel lane leading to the Tall Grass Ranch.

"We both want Cole's stock contracting business to be a success," Molly added. "After Melissa and Skylar and the rest of the family, it's the most important thing in his life." She looked out the truck window again as if, like Troy, she didn't know how to navigate this new "friendship" between them. What to say, what to do and, most of all, how to pretend their past had indeed been dealt with.

"Cole's lucky to have you. All of you." Like Troy was lucky to have his parents and sister. "Family first and—oh no."

"What?" Molly turned to look where he pointed and gasped. "What are Bryce's pigs doing on Mom's lawn? Mom and Shane want to have wedding pictures taken there."

As soon as Troy stopped and parked the truck

in front of the ranch house, Molly jumped out of the vehicle and ran toward the four red-and-white pigs that rooted in the lawn amid scattered fall decorations.

He followed her, shutting both truck doors. "Hang on." The biggest pig must weigh around seven hundred pounds, and although Molly was strong, she was slight. Herefords were docile and usually quiet, but who knew how they'd act when cornered.

"They either broke through the fence or someone left the gate open." Molly stopped at the edge of the lawn strewn with half-eaten pumpkins and squash, several flattened floral wreaths, an upside-down scarecrow, three broken porch chairs and various ripped cushions. "Look at the mess they've made. Stop that…go away…you bad boy." She waved her arms at a piglet, albeit at least a two-hundred pounder, digging in a patch of lawn beside an overturned white garden trellis. "Mom's still in town. We're the only ones here except for the dogs." She indicated Joy's collie, Jess, and her beagle mix, Gus, who barked from inside a front window.

Molly's face was red, her chest heaved, and she looked like she was about to burst into tears. In the entire time he'd known her, Troy had never seen her so worked up. "I'm here, I'll help. It'll be okay."

"How? Even once the pigs are penned, we'll need a landscaper and carpenter." She gestured to several broken porch rails, the wrecked trellis and mud-churned lawn. "Today's Friday. The wedding's next Saturday just over a week away."

"First things first." Troy touched Molly's arm. "Take a deep breath and get a bucket of feed from the barn. While you're doing that, call Bryce. We can make a food trail and lead the pigs to a fenced area. In the meantime, I have some grain in my truck. I'll make a start and try to divert them."

"Thanks." Molly put a hand to her face. "I don't know what's wrong with me. I'm usually good in a crisis. As a nurse I have to be."

"There's a big difference between a medical crisis and pigs running rampant where you're about to have wedding pictures. What these guys have done is personal." He patted her arm one last time before taking his hand away. He wanted to comfort and hold her close like he once would have, but he didn't have that right.

"My dad built that trellis and I... It's special to Mom and all of us." Her voice wobbled as she darted to the barn. She took off her cowboy hat as she ran, and her blond hair tumbled around her shoulders.

Troy's mouth went dry, but he turned away and grabbed the almost-empty feed container from his truck bed. *Focus*. He had to get the pigs penned, and then he'd figure out the rest.

Pigs or no pigs, Joy Carter would have the wedding photo setting she wanted. As Troy scattered grain in a trail, he pulled his phone out of his jacket pocket and scrolled to Werner's number.

Folks in High Valley pulled together. When Werner had called Troy to help move that furniture to Kristi's café, Troy had been happy to lend a hand. Now he'd ask Werner to get the word out that Joy needed the town to pitch in to rescue an important part of her wedding.

Troy glanced at the piglet who'd abandoned digging the lawn to snuffle the grain Troy had sprinkled. "That's it, boy. Bring the others with you." He grinned as the mama pig followed her piglet and, as a group, they snuffled and ambled away from the lawn.

He left a message on Werner's voicemail and emptied the dregs of grain from the feed container along the path the pigs had decided to follow.

Joy had always been kind to him, and now Troy would return that kindness in whatever way he could.

"I filled a feed bucket and got hold of Bryce. He's nearby so he'll be here in a few minutes." Molly handed Troy the bucket, and as her hand brushed his, he drew in a breath as longing rushed through him.

"Great." Troy clutched the feed bucket handle, and his fingers tingled.

Molly put her hands on her knees and gasped for breath. "You distracted them." A slow smile spread across her face. "Good job."

"For now anyway. I appealed to their natural herd instinct." Unlike Molly, Troy hadn't been running, but he was still short of breath. He dug a scoop into the feed bucket and scattered more grain.

"Here, piggies. See what we've got for you? Yum, yum." She cajoled the animals, and there was a flutter in Troy's chest.

"Nice, pigs. Come on, baby." Troy held out more treats and made a soft, cooing noise at the smallest piglet.

"You should sing to them."

"Sing?" He raised his eyebrows.

"If it worked for those cows you milked back in the day, maybe it will work for these pigs. But choose something upbeat. We need to keep them moving."

"I guess." Troy looked around but they were alone. "Okay, here goes." He launched into "Dancing Queen" by ABBA. It was the first catchy song he could think of, likely because his mom had it on what she called her "happy" playlist.

"Yeah. Good one. My mom's a huge ABBA fan." Molly joined in, her soprano blending with his deeper voice.

The mama pig's curly tail wagged and then the whole group picked up the pace, hoovering up scattered grain as they followed where Troy and Molly led.

"Teamwork." As Molly glanced at him, her smile became softer, more intimate and for an instant, she linked her fingers with his.

That smile and brief touch, her windblown hair and the sweetness of her voice all pulled Troy to her in a way that was both familiar and new. A way that if he was any kind of friend he couldn't—wouldn't—act on.

THE NEXT MORNING, the Tall Grass Ranch bustled with activity. "Ready?" Molly lifted one end of the broken garden trellis.

"Yep." Her mom took the other end and they headed toward a sawhorse Zach had set up in front of the house.

"What are you two doing?" Shane took the trellis from Joy and called a ranch hand to help Molly. "You're the bride, Joy. You should be re-laxing and getting ready for our big day. Put your feet up or go to the spa in town." He glanced at

Molly. "Can't you get your mom to stop work-ing?"

She grinned at her soon-to-be-stepfather. "Nope. She likes to keep busy. We're alike that way." But here at home, for the first time in years, Molly's life wasn't taken up by school or a job and she was unexpectedly aimless. She also had too much free time to think about Troy, and the job in Atlanta waiting for her in January.

"Looking at this mess, how can I relax?" Wear-ing a barn jacket that had belonged to Molly's dad and with her hair covered by a blue bandanna, Joy gestured to the wrecked lawn and battered porch. "It's worse than when the tornado went through ten years ago. It only took off the shed roof and went in a straight line through the pas-ture. Whereas those pigs…" She huffed out a breath and shook her head.

"It is what it is, isn't that what you usually say?" As Cole and Bryce assessed the damaged trellis, Molly wrapped an arm around her mom's hunched shoulders. "Who'd have thought those Herefords would have dug under a supposedly pig-proof fence? Or that their snouts would be strong enough to lift the fence posts clear out of the ground? It's part of ranch life, I guess. We're always learning something new." The pigs were only being true to their nature, and she had to admire their determination and ingenuity, if not the chaos they'd caused.

"It is." Her mom gave a short laugh. "But among other things, my porch chair cushions are beyond saving. I only bought them this spring. I didn't intend them to be used for pig bedding."

"With everyone pitching in, we're saving the most important things." Molly gestured to the volunteer work crew who'd given up their Saturday to tidy the lawn and repair the porch and trellis. "Like Dad's trellis." Her voice cracked.

"We are, and I'm not usually so on edge." Her mom fiddled with a button on her jacket.

"You're allowed. It's wedding nerves." Molly clasped one of her mom's cold hands. She'd been so focused on her own feelings about the wedding she hadn't considered her mom might be struggling. "If you're having seconds thoughts about getting married, you—"

"It's not that. Of course I want to marry Shane," her mom broke in. "But I'm too old to be so nervous."

"You're not old and anyone would be nervous, but you and Shane are going to have a wonderful life together." The more Molly got to know the older man, the more she liked him. Maybe in time, he could be a friend and someone she could turn to for the kind of wise advice her father would have given. "Look at how he stepped up yesterday and again today? Some people wouldn't understand how important it is for you to have photos here, but Shane does and along with everyone else, he's making that happen."

"I know." Her mom's voice wobbled. "We could have had pictures taken at Squirrel Tail. Shane's ranch is already set up for weddings, but here he is, getting his hands dirty with the rest of us because it's important to me."

"There you go." Since becoming an adult, Molly hadn't spent enough time with her mom for them to become friends, as well as mother and daughter, but in the past few weeks their relationship had shifted, and she was grateful.

"Will this cushion work for you?" Rosa stopped beside them, along with Nina, Angela and the rest of the Sunflower Sisterhood. Except for Rosa, who held out a sunflower-patterned throw pillow, the others carried garment bags and their faces held suppressed excitement.

"It's beautiful but what did you do?" Joy looked at her friends.

Rosa hugged Joy. "I had enough fabric and foam in my workroom, so last night we got together and made you replacement porch cushions. They're a gift from all of us."

"You must have worked all night. You… Thank you." Joy swiped away a tear.

"It was a pleasure." Angela's voice was gruff. "You're always there for us and anyone in town who needs anything, so these cushions are the least we could do. Here." She handed Joy a pink gift bag tied with white ribbon. "This one is an extra from me. I had material left over from a baby quilt I made for the church's holiday bazaar. It seemed fitting."

As Molly looked around the group of women, her heart squeezed. They all had busy lives, but they hadn't hesitated to drop everything to support a friend in need. While Molly had friends in Atlanta, were they *true* friends like the Sunflower Sisterhood was to her mom? Or were they only friends for a reason and season in her life, linked to each other by work or school and little else?

"Oh, my goodness." Her mom's laughter drew Molly back to the conversation. "It's perfect." Joy held a rectangular pillow patterned with pink pigs aloft for everyone to see.

As Molly joined with the laughter and joking, she knew she'd remember today for the rest of her life. Although ranching was hard, there was a sense of community here she'd never found anywhere else. And, as the saying went, little things could indeed make the difference between hope and despair.

Leaving her mom to exclaim over the cushions, Molly went to a folding table Kristi had set up by the fence. "Can I do anything?"

"Yes, you're a lifesaver." Kristi paused in setting out a tray of oatmeal cookies. "If you can look after drinks and snacks, I'll head back to town. With the weddings and then Thanksgiving, it's extra busy at the Bluebunch. I love my job and my life, but right now I need an extra pair of hands."

"Sure. Tell me what you need."

"Just keep folks fed." Kristi collected her purse and several empty baking trays. "There's more food in the green cooler, and juice and water in the white one. Zach ran an extension cord from here to the house for the coffee maker. Rosa said she'd bring everything back to town for me."

"Wait." Molly gestured to the table filled with several kinds of sandwiches, cookies, muffins and a streusel-topped Bundt cake. "What about a price list and making change?"

"A price list?" Kristi's mouth fell open, and then she patted Molly's arm. "You've been away too long. Your mom needs us, so we're lending a hand. I can't sew, and I'm a hazard to myself and others using power tools, but I can show I care with food."

"Yes, of course." Molly's face heated. She'd spoken without thinking. Had she tried so hard to make herself into someone else, sophisticated city Molly instead of a country girl from an isolated Montana ranch, that she'd forgotten who and what she truly was?

Kristi's expression softened. "It's okay to love city life, but you're home now, at least for a while. And you don't have to choose city or country, but…" She stopped.

"You can't take the country out of the girl, right?" Molly had heard that expression too often, and each time it had made her either defensive or embarrassed. Now, though, it was different. She was proud of coming from a place like High Valley.

"No, that wasn't what I was going to say." Kristi studied her with a serious expression. "All I meant is when you go back to the city, you can take some of High Valley and us with you." She spread her arms wide, taking in the surrounding landscape and the friends and neighbors busy with various tasks.

As Kristi dug out her keys and walked toward the Bluebunch delivery van parked outside the fence, Molly stared after her. She'd always thought her two lives were separate and Montana was the one she wanted to leave behind, but now, she wasn't so certain.

"Can I get a coffee and slice of cake, please? Kristi's pumpkin Bundt cake is my new favorite."

Molly turned at Troy's voice. "Sure." Her hand trembled as she picked up the coffeepot and filled his mug with one of the delicious local roasts Kristi served in the café.

"Are you okay?" When Molly raised her head, Troy looked at her with a concerned expression.

"I'm fine." She cut a generous slice of cake and put it on a paper plate for him.

"It's different being back in Montana, isn't it?" Troy's tone was kind.

Out of everyone, he was perhaps the most likely to understand how Molly truly felt. "It's good but I feel torn, you know?"

He nodded. "I'm a small-town, country boy who made good in the city but sometimes..." He took a sip of coffee and looked beyond Molly. "It's like I don't really belong anywhere."

"Me too." A weight lifted from her chest as she acknowledged a truth she'd never shared with anyone. "What do you do when you feel that way?"

"What can any of us do?" Troy laughed before sobering. "Be yourself, find folks who 'get' you and make it work. Like Beth." He gestured to Molly's sister-in-law who sat in a lawn chair and handed Zach and Bryce the tools they needed to fix the trellis. "She must miss things about Chicago."

"She does, but she says she now misses Montana when she visits Illinois." Molly had been so wrapped up in her own life, she hadn't thought about what it was like for Beth to move from Chicago to High Valley to marry Zach. However, she'd never seemed to regret that choice and went between both worlds with ease.

"It'll work out, Molly." He gave her a teasing grin. "But I have to say, it's hard to escape the place you grew up. Or the sound." He jerked his chin toward the speakers Cole had set up on the porch, which blasted country music. "The only advice I can give is for you to be you, the whole you. Why can't you be as at home here in cowboy boots and jeans as you are in Atlanta in medical scrubs?"

Yet, as Troy returned to helping Zach and Bryce with the trellis, and Molly served coffee to Nina and Werner, all she wished was that it could be that simple.

# *CHAPTER NINE*

CROUCHED IN THE choir loft at the church near downtown High Valley, Troy double-checked the internet connection and gave a thumbs-up to Mitch, the camera operator. "It's working now." While Troy hadn't planned on attending the Carter double wedding, the team Carrie had hired to livestream the ceremony had all gone down with food poisoning. In the ensuing panic, Troy and anyone else with technical expertise had been drafted to help.

Mitch, a college freshman who was home for the Thanksgiving break, darted an anxious glance at Carrie's dad behind Troy. "We're ready to start the wedding livestreaming, Mr. Rizzo. Your family in Italy will feel almost like they're here."

"Good." Frank Rizzo, who Troy had met a quarter of an hour earlier, clapped Mitch's shoulder before turning to Troy. "You'll stay here to make sure there aren't any more problems?" He gave Mitch a sideways glance as if he doubted the teenager's capabilities.

"Sure, but Mitch is experienced. We've also got the high school film production teacher and his students on the main floor recording from there, along with a camera technician and backup equipment." Troy made his tone reassuring. "Try to relax. Although it's not exactly what Carrie and Bryce planned, we'll manage."

Mr. Rizzo patted his face with a white handkerchief. "I'll be more relaxed once this whole shebang is over. What kind of place doesn't have consistent internet?"

"That's rural Montana for you, but see?" Troy indicated the computer he'd set up at one end of a pew. "Looks like they're all here now. Carrie wanted them to have their cameras on and not be muted so they can join in." On the screen, people waved and clapped.

Mr. Rizzo waved back.

The organist, who'd introduced herself earlier as Kim, began to play "Ave Maria," one of Troy's mom's favorite songs.

"Um, sir, it's time." Mitch gestured to the grooms, Bryce and Shane, at the front of the church with the other Carter brothers and Shane's son.

"Oh, right." Mr. Rizzo thanked Mitch, and then spoke in an undertone to Troy. "You keep an eye on him, you hear?" He rolled his eyes in Mitch's direction. "I don't want anything to spoil my daughter's wedding day."

"It won't." Out of Frank's view, Troy crossed his fingers. "Now go walk Carrie down the aisle."

With a final dubious look at Mitch, Frank disappeared down the stairs to rejoin the rest of the wedding party.

"Here goes." Mitch spoke to Rob, the high school teacher, through his headset, and Troy did a final check of the internet connection, including the backup network he'd set up just in case.

Kim shuffled her music and began playing another classical piece, this time joined by a male soloist, Carrie's cousin from Kalispell, who sang an Italian aria.

Keeping one eye on the computer, Troy watched from above as the brides, Joy and Carrie, and their attendants moved down the aisle to the front. He drew in a harsh breath when the overhead lights caught Molly's blond hair as she preceded her mom.

Troy barely noticed the brides, the other bridesmaids or Skylar and Paisley, the adorable flower girls. Instead, his gaze followed Molly. She wore a silver-gray dress, and while most of her hair was loose, the back part was caught up

in a delicate floral headpiece. As she reached
the front of the church, she took Paisley's hand,
and her smile made Troy's mouth go dry. From
here, they could have been mother and daughter, and the sweet scene made him imagine how
Molly might care for her own child one day.

"Troy. We're losing signal." Mitch's frantic
whisper pulled Troy back to what he was supposed to be doing, and he turned to the computer to switch over to the backup network.

As the ceremony went on, there was more
music, several readings, oohs and aahs from the
Italian family on the livestream and those in the
church and a burst of applause as both newly
married couples kissed. Then Joy with Shane,
and Carrie with Bryce came back up the aisle,
beaming. Carrie's cousin, as comfortable with
country as opera, sang a Rascal Flatts hit, this
time accompanied by Kim on guitar, and two
of Joy's nephews on banjo and ukulele.

Troy tapped one foot in time to the music and
laughed along with the congregation as Bryce
gave Carrie a twirl at the end of the aisle.

When Frank escorted Carrie's mom from
their front pew, he glanced up at the choir loft
and gave Troy and Mitch an approving nod,
and Troy exhaled with relief. It had been last-
minute, but they'd pulled it off. In Italy, Carrie's
family clapped and cheered, and Mitch darted

downstairs to film a message from Carrie and Bryce to their virtual guests.

"Troy?" At Molly's voice, he whirled around.

"Hey." At a distance, she'd taken his breath away, but up close she was a vision. Her face was flushed, and her blue eyes sparkled. "Aren't you supposed to be down there doing maid of honor stuff?" He tried to joke as her nearness made him lightheaded.

"Mom won't miss me for a few minutes. I wanted to thank you for pitching in. I…all of us…we really appreciate it."

Her lips parted and as she smiled and moved closer, Troy inhaled her sweet jasmine fragrance. "Not a problem." His breathing quickened, and his heart pounded.

"Well, thank you…for everything. With the pigs and now today, you've been a real friend." She wet her lower lip with her tongue, and Troy noticed, not for the first time, how appealing her mouth looked. "I should go." She glanced at the musicians who chatted as they gathered up their music. "There's photos and then a lunch for family and close friends, but see you at the town reception at Squirrel Tail later?"

"Of course." He fiddled with a computer cable. Molly had been pretty as a teenager and maturity had simply added to her beauty. It wasn't only her looks, though. She was gorgeous inside and out. "It's a long day for you."

"Yes, it had to be a morning wedding because of the time difference between here and Italy." Her gaze dropped to her bouquet of pink roses mixed with some kind of white flower and greenery. Did she also feel the unspoken attraction that hummed between them and was she as uncertain as Troy about what to do about it?

"Right." Although Molly had called him a "real friend," his feelings for her were more than friendship. And, if he was honest with himself, he'd never gotten over her the first time and maybe he never would.

When she looked at him again, her expression took away whatever breath Troy still had left. Tenderness, and maybe something even deeper, flickered in her eyes and across her face, and they both stepped forward to close the remaining distance between them.

"Mol? We're waiting for you to take pictures on the church steps." Cole's voice echoed up the stairs, and Molly jumped away from Troy as if someone had poured a bucket of ice-cold water over her. "See you."

"Yeah." As she darted away, followed more slowly by the soloist and banjo and ukulele players, Troy's chest was heavy, and his stomach knotted. He packed up the rest of the computer equipment, and his thoughts turned inward, ruminating on the past. He'd loved Molly with all his heart and a foolish part of him still did.

"You finished up here?" Kim, who was around Troy's mom's age, gave him a curious look as she put on her coat.

"Almost. I'll turn off the lights when I leave." He made a show of winding up the last electrical cord.

"Thanks." Kim hesitated. "I've known Molly her whole life. I'm not saying there *is* something between the two of you, but if you'd like there to be, why not take a risk and tell her?"

"It's not that simple." Troy put the cord in his backpack and added a laptop.

"Or maybe you're making it too complicated?" Kim's laugh was light, her smile warm. "Beneath that city gloss, Molly is still a country girl. Look at the weddings today. They mixed city, country and even Italy just fine. When it comes down to it, people are people and much the same no matter where they live."

They were, and maybe Troy *was* overthinking everything. He took risks all the time in business, and that was part of the reason for his success. Was it a mistake to be so guarded in his personal life?

As Kim left, he considered what she'd said. He couldn't ignore his feelings for Molly any longer, and maybe he shouldn't. He was beginning to realize that he'd idealized Molly back then, but she was as human as any other woman. Some light flirtation might be exactly what he needed to put his feelings for her behind him once and for all. Now, he only had to convince his heart to follow his head and not want anything more.

MOLLY HAD WANTED to kiss Troy right there in the church choir loft, in full view of the musicians and anyone else who might have seen them. In the wood-beamed barn at Squirrel Tail that Shane had converted into a reception venue, Molly put a hand to her face as embarrassment rolled over her again. So far, she'd managed to avoid Troy at the party, and with most of the town around, it should be easy to continue to keep her distance.

Carrying a plate of food from the buffet, Molly glanced around trying to find a spot to sit. Since this reception was informal, there wasn't assigned seating, and she'd lost sight of her brothers in the crowd. She moved toward a round table with several empty chairs. If she texted Cole, they could find each other and—

"Hey, Molly." Troy patted the chair beside his. "I'm on my own. Want to join me?"

She looked around again but anybody she

knew was already with a group. "Okay." She smiled at a couple engrossed in conversation on the other side of the table. She recognized the woman as one of Carrie's cousins. As Molly sat next to Troy, two gray-haired couples took the remaining empty seats and introduced themselves as ranching friends of Shane's from Wyoming.

"It's a fantastic spread." Troy indicated his plate piled high with food.

"Yes." It was like every Montana "fall supper" Molly could remember, and a true community gathering with good food, friends and cheer. "Although there's a caterer for the meat and other big dishes, it's a typical High Valley potluck like Mom and Carrie wanted."

It was also the kind of event Molly hadn't realized she'd missed, but now, looking at her own plate where one of Angela's mini barbecue chicken calzones nestled beside Nina's traditional Ukrainian cabbage rolls, along with other treats she remembered from childhood, her mouth watered.

Troy grinned as he dug into his meal. "After the ceremony, I went home and chopped wood. Werner told me I'd need to work up an appetite for tonight."

"Smart." Molly pushed away the image of Troy lifting an axe and bringing it down on a block of wood. Since it had been a warm day, he might have taken off his jacket and in short sleeves, his forearms would... *No.* She took a bite of the savory calzone and chewed with determination. Carrie's cousin and her boyfriend were still absorbed in each other, and the couples from Wyoming talked about corn and barley prices, so she and Troy were on their own. "Nobody goes home hungry after *any* High Valley party."

Troy laughed and as they ate their meals, Molly relaxed. He was good company and as easy to talk to as he'd been long ago. Until tonight, they'd talked mostly about ranch business, but as their conversation ranged from movies to books and travel, she found they had more in common than she'd expected.

"You ate what?" She stared at him wide-eyed as he recounted a business trip to Hong Kong.

"Duck's tongue and goose feet. They're both delicacies." He showed her a picture on his phone. "Pete's, my friend and business partner, family is from China. Thanks to him, I didn't embarrass myself or our hosts."

"I'd like to travel." She admired a picture of Troy and Pete on the deck of a ferry with the impressive Hong Kong skyline behind them. "I've only been outside the US once, and that was to Canada." But once Molly started her new job, along with saving for a place of her own, she wanted to plan some vacations.

"Where do you want to go?"

"I've been thinking about Costa Rica. All the wildlife. The rainforest. I'd also like to visit England. The Carter family came from there way back. There's all that history and old buildings and fish and chips."

By how he listened to her and asked attentive questions, Troy seemed truly interested in what she had to say. Unlike some guys she'd dated, he was focused on her rather than looking around for someone else or trying to take over the conversation. *Hang on.* She wasn't dating him. They were only chatting because they'd ended up sitting together.

As she mentioned other destinations, she realized she was babbling, but how Troy looked at her threw her off center. Although surrounded by other people, there was an intimacy between them that made her nerve endings quiver. And although he looked great in ranch clothes, in his navy suit, crisp white shirt and perfectly knotted striped tie, he oozed a different but similarly appealing masculinity.

"London's a fantastic city." As Troy talked about visiting a customer there, his words washed over Molly. *Big Ben. Westminster Abbey. Buckingham Palace. The Tower of London.* All places she'd read about or seen in movies and longed to experience in real life. "Sorry, what did you say?" Caught up in a daydream about walking by the River Thames with Troy, she realized he'd stopped talking and was looking at her with his eyebrows raised, having evidently asked a question.

"I said it looks like there will be a lot of leftovers." He nodded toward the buffet table.

"There always are, everything gets donated to the local food bank." It was part of the ethos of "giving back" that Molly had grown up with and one she now tried to live in her own life.

"That food bank helped my folks once. It was the Christmas they lost the ranch and before we moved to Bozeman. They didn't want to go to the one closer to home where people knew them, so they came here. I'm glad it's still going. I'll have to drop by and thank them." A faint flush crept across Troy's cheeks as if he was embarrassed to have shared something so personal.

"The team would appreciate that." Molly paused with her last piece of cabbage roll partway to her mouth. "Lots of people need a helping hand at one point or another. The food bank's discreet and…" Her face heated and she stumbled over her words. Troy was such a success now she'd almost forgotten how his family had struggled.

Troy focused on the remains of his meal as if

Rosa's delicious bannock bread held the meaning of life.

Molly decided to redirect their focus away from the awkward moment. "So, what are you doing for Thanksgiving?"

"My parents and sister are coming here." Troy's anxious expression eased as if he was grateful for the change of topic. "I told my mom I'd make Thanksgiving dinner, but my stove conked out yesterday. Since I can't get a replacement delivered until after the holiday, we may end up microwaving something." His laugh was forced. "I found a few questionable recipes online for microwaved holiday meals, but maybe we should go to Billings and have Thanksgiving at a hotel there instead."

"What's this about Thanksgiving at a hotel?" Cole stopped behind Molly's chair.

"Troy's parents and sister are joining him for the holiday, but his stove's not working so he's—"

"You can't go to a hotel." Cole's eyes widened, and he shook his head. "Join me and Melissa at our place. We're hosting everyone this year since Mom and Shane will be on their honeymoon."

Molly's heart squeezed. She'd already been preparing herself for her first Thanksgiving apart from her mom. But spending it with Troy on top of that? She couldn't. "I'm sure the—"

"Thanks for the invitation, but we couldn't." Troy spoke at the same time as Molly. "Thanksgiving's for family and—"

"The more the merrier. When I was riding rodeo, I spent too many Thanksgivings and other holidays away from home eating overcooked turkey in some soulless hotel or diner. Melissa won't mind me inviting you and your family." He patted Molly's shoulder. "Like Mom says, Thanksgiving's about bringing people together and sharing food and friendship. It wouldn't be the holiday without a few extra, would it?"

As she nodded, Molly's stomach lurched and she put her cutlery back on her plate, her appetite gone. She'd kept her previous relationship with Troy secret from her family, so she had only herself to blame that Cole and the others had welcomed him like a long-lost relative. Another awkward moment.

"If you're sure it's okay, we'd love to join you. I'll let my folks know." Troy's voice was strained, suggesting he was as uncomfortable with forced holiday proximity as Molly.

She gave Cole and Troy a bright smile. It was only a day, but between now and Thursday, she'd do her own online research. Starting with tips about spending Thanksgiving with your ex.

As Troy turned to speak to one of the Wyoming ranchers, Molly shivered as coldness swirled from her stomach up her windpipe.

Troy *was* her ex, and though she'd spent years trying to convince herself he was only a teenage crush, she could admit now that he had been much more. They shared common interests and values, and if he lived in Atlanta, he was the kind of guy she could get serious about.

But he didn't, so she couldn't let herself think about anything long term—no matter how much she might want to.

# CHAPTER TEN

ON THE MONDAY morning of Thanksgiving week, Troy sat behind the desk in his home office, held his phone to one ear and stared out the window at the harvested fields etched in silver frost. "It's not a good time for me to come to Texas. Why don't you come here instead?"

"Why would I come to Montana?" On the other end of the phone, Pete's voice was astonished. "I thought we agreed that when we needed to meet in person, you'd either travel to me in Austin or we'd meet in San Francisco."

"We did but…" Troy paused and rubbed his free hand across his forehead where the start of a headache throbbed. He hadn't lived here long and didn't want to leave the ranch, even for a few days. Or leave Cole on his own with the stock contracting business. Sure, he'd be within easy contact by phone, text and email, but it wasn't the same as being here and available for anything that might come up. And not that he could say so to Pete, but if were honest with himself, he also didn't want to miss any opportunities to spend time with Molly. "Think about it, will you? You can see my ranch. I could even get you on horseback."

Pete laughed so hard he snorted. "Ranch, okay, as long as it's not too rustic, but riding a horse? I live in Texas. If I wanted to, I could ride horses at home. But I'm a city guy, remember? Being too far from the bright lights could be fun for a few days in summer but not that far north between October and April." He made shivering noises.

"Sure, but…" Troy looked at the fields again. He'd met Pete in college and although the guy was his best friend, Troy had never talked to him about where and how he'd grown up. "It's important to me."

"What's going on? Truly?" Pete's voice softened, and children's laughter echoed in the background. Pete and Tina had married soon after they'd both graduated from college and now had two young kids. While Troy liked spending time with them, their family togetherness also made him feel lonely.

"Nothing's going on. I want to show you my new place, that's all." A pickup truck drove along the highway that bordered his ranch, and Troy craned his neck to take a closer look. Was that the Tall Grass Ranch logo on the door?

He hadn't seen Molly since the wedding reception at Squirrel Tail, and although she'd tactfully changed the subject, he still cringed at how he'd opened his big mouth and let her see his vulnerability. He'd never spoken with anyone about those lean years when his folks had struggled.

"Okay." Pete gave in. "I'll do it, but only because you're family to me. But I'm not getting anywhere near a horse except for looking through a window at one, or if it's safely on the other side of a stall door or fence from me."

"Deal. Thanks, buddy." Troy let out a breath he hadn't realized he was holding. Outside, an engine rumbled and then stopped and what sounded like a truck door slammed. "I have to go."

"Hang on, it's a woman, isn't it? That's really why you want me to come to the back of beyond." Pete's voice sharpened with interest and curiosity.

"Of course not." The front doorbell rang and, still holding the phone, Troy left his office to go to the top of the stairs.

"But—"

"Let me know when you've booked flights." Troy looked out the stairwell window. That truck, now parked in front of his house, did belong to the Tall Grass Ranch, but from here he couldn't see who was at the door.

"You've got it bad, buddy." Pete laughed as Troy disconnected, went to the bottom of the stairs and checked his hair in the mirror by the front door.

Maybe he did have it bad. Since the wedding, he hadn't been able to stop thinking about Molly, but it was too new and confusing for him to talk to Pete or anyone else about.

He opened the door and made himself give a neutral smile. "Hey, Molly." She'd looked elegant in that dress at the wedding and now, in jeans and a cozy blue jacket the same color as her eyes, she looked cute. Either way, she was gorgeous and turned him inside out and upside down.

"Hi." She held a soft-sided cooler bag, and her smile was tentative. "We're on our way to town." From the truck, Cole waved at him. A dog's head bobbed excitedly in the back window. "We, um…here." She thrust the bag at him. Her cheeks turned a pretty shade of pink. "With your stove not working, and Cathy away visiting her sister, I…we wanted to make things easier for you."

"Thank you." The tension in Troy's shoulders eased, and he put his free hand to his chest. "That's really kind and thoughtful."

Molly waved away his appreciation. "I should have thought to save some food from the reception for you but—"

"It's fine." The food bank needed it a lot more than he did. "I…uh…I guess I'll see you at Thanksgiving at Cole and Melissa's."

"Yes." She fiddled with the tassels of her blue-and-white scarf.

Cole beeped the truck's horn, and his beagle, Blue, stuck his head out the half-open rear window and barked.

"I should go." Molly half turned.

"Wait." Troy took a deep breath. "I saw posters in town about a holiday tree lighting ceremony the Friday after Thanksgiving. I wondered if you'd like to go with me. As a friend, of course."

"I… As a friend. Sure."

She smiled, then nodded in the direction of the truck and jogged down the porch steps to rejoin her brother.

As the Tall Grass truck disappeared at the end of his lane, Troy closed his front door and went to pat Acorn. Either because of her age or history, the dog never came to greet visitors, instead preferring to stay in what was now "her" chair by the living room window.

*Some light flirtation.* There had been too many people around for Troy to flirt with Molly at the wedding. However, and although his invitation to the holiday tree lighting had been a spur of the moment impulse, maybe it was what he needed. Even if she was still a country girl at heart, anything between them didn't have a future with him here and her in Atlanta. Once Molly was past history, Troy could move on and stop comparing every woman he met with her.

He scratched Acorn's ears, and after stowing the food in the kitchen, as he went back upstairs to his office, the dog followed. Thanksgiving with Molly and her family would be fine. The tree lighting ceremony would be as well. They were the kinds of things friends did together.

But as Acorn hopped onto Troy's lap, blocked his view of his laptop screen and nudged his hand so he'd scratch her ears again, Troy couldn't shake a persistent sense of unease.

What if his plan didn't work? And what if flirtation made him fall further into whatever "this" was with Molly? Something that made him think about a future with her rather than their past.

"Happy Thanksgiving." Molly handed Melissa the tin of pecan pie brownies she'd made, took off her coat and smoothed her cozy, cream-colored sweater dress. Paired with brown Western boots, it was casual enough for a Carter family gathering but a step up from the jeans and T-shirts she usually wore around the ranch.

Melissa thanked her as she led the way to the back of the cozy, two-story frame house. The place, a few miles from the main ranch house, had been built by Molly's great-grandparents. In their day, what was now the family room had been a summer kitchen.

"It's my first time hosting a holiday celebration for a crowd. I'm nervous, especially because we only moved in here two weeks ago." Melissa's laugh was quick and high-pitched. "I'm still getting used to the kitchen."

"Don't worry." Cole joined them as they reached the comfortable den, and he wrapped an arm around his wife's shoulders. "We're all family here. Well, almost." He indicated Troy and a couple who must be his parents, who sat on the sofa at the far end of the room near Carrie's folks and her aunt Angela. "The Claytons are so happy to have been saved from microwaved turkey burgers, they're sure not going to complain if anything goes wrong. Come on, Mol. I'll introduce you."

"That's okay, I'll—" Molly looked around, but having driven herself, rather than coming with Zach, Beth and Ellie, she was the last to arrive and everyone else had already gathered in groups. She made herself smile as if the Claytons meant nothing more to her than any of the other guests her family invited each year.

Cole made the introductions, and Molly smiled harder, hyperaware of Troy, who'd nailed Thanksgiving casual with style in black jeans, a pale blue button-down shirt, navy blue pullover sweater and boots.

"Please call us Val and Jeff." Mrs. Clayton, whose light brown hair fell around her shoulders, gave Molly a warm smile. Her smile and her eyes were like her son's.

Molly swallowed and turned to Jeff, a balding man with a silver beard, who shook her hand and said, "Good to meet you. Troy's talked a lot about you."

"Jeff." Val shook her head and gave her husband a mock glare. "Here's our daughter, Sara." She turned to a young woman with long, dark red hair who, except for her striking blue eyes, didn't look like Troy or either of their parents. "Sara's a college senior in Oregon, but I expect Troy already told you that."

Molly nodded and kept her smile in place as she greeted Sara. Troy hadn't told her anything about his sister or his parents, at least not recently. She wondered what he'd told his folks about her, then or now.

"Since everyone's here, let's eat." Cole clapped his hands and began directing people into the dining room much like Molly had seen him herd cows. As she started toward her usual spot at the kids' table, Cole added, "No, Mol, you don't need to stay here with the kids. They'll be fine with Ellie looking out for them." He gave their niece a fond pat on one shoulder.

She followed his lead and found herself seated—of course—next to Troy, with his family across the table from them.

"The place still looks the same," Zach said as he held out a chair for Beth. "But I guess we only moved out a few weeks ago."

"How are you settling into the main ranch house?" Bryce waited for his new bride, Carrie, to take her seat. They'd postponed their honeymoon to spend Thanksgiving with Paisley and Cam but were heading to Jamaica for a week in December in a gap between Carrie's rodeo competitions.

"Apart from the boxes still piled everywhere?" Zach chuckled as he took his own seat beside Beth. "We've left a lot of stuff still packed up because we're going to do some painting to make the house our own. Starting with the baby's room, of course."

To Molly, he said, "And you'll always have your room to come home to. Don't worry about that, sis."

"We'll keep a space for you here too, Mol."

Cole sat at the head of the table decorated with turkey art made by the kids, mini orange pumpkins and red, yellow and brown paper leaves. In only a few months, her brother had taken to domestic life like the proverbial duck to water.

"Our guest room is yours whenever you want it," Bryce added.

Molly nodded and tried not to grimace. She didn't have a place of her own right now, but she would again soon. And although her brothers meant well, she wouldn't spend every vacation in Montana. Besides, when she did visit, she could stay with her mom and Shane.

As Melissa carried a golden-brown turkey in on a platter from the kitchen and set it in front of Cole, her brother bowed his head to say grace, and the familiar words her dad used to say rolled over Molly. Thanksgiving was about family, and although her dad was gone, and her mom was now married to Shane, traditions continued and were added. Nothing stayed the same, least of all Molly herself. She needed to embrace change instead of resisting it.

"Has anybody heard from Mom?" Cole started to carve the turkey, and Melissa passed around serving dishes with mashed potatoes, roasted vegetables, corn bread and, new this year, Carrie's mom's Italian charcuterie board and Angela's homemade Asiago bread.

"Not apart from a text saying they'd arrived safely in Sedona." A small smile played around Zach's lips. "You'd better not be messaging her either. Let Mom have a honeymoon without thinking or worrying about us."

Since Zach and Beth's baby was due so soon, Molly's mom had wanted to stay in the United States for a honeymoon trip, but she and Shane planned to go to Europe in the spring. After so many years of sticking close to home, her life was changing in big ways and travel was likely only the start.

"All of us except for Molly are settled," Cole said. "And unlike me, Mol's never caused Mom any grief, so what does she have to worry about?"

"Mothers always worry, no matter how old their kids are." Val gave Troy and then Sara a loving smile. "So, Molly, tell us about your job. Troy says you're a nurse."

As Molly answered Val's questions about the hospital and her master's research, she was conscious of Troy next to her, his chair so close that his knee bumped her leg when he passed a bowl of green beans to his dad.

"Sorry." Troy moved his leg away, but then bumped Molly's knee again when Sara asked for the corn bread.

Molly's whole body tingled and, as Troy's folks and Sara chatted with Beth and Zach about the baby, she tried to focus on her food instead of his nearness. The table was crowded with so many people around it. Under the circumstances, he'd have bumped anyone. And Cole had placed them beside each other, so it wasn't as if Troy had sought her out. As she lifted her eyes from her plate, they exchanged a brief glance, and his slow smile made the hair on her arms rise.

"It was nice of Cole and Melissa to invite my family to join yours for Thanksgiving." Troy spoke in an undertone, although since Cole was telling a funny rodeo story with Skylar perched on his lap making horse sounds, nobody else was paying attention to him.

"It's good to have you here. I…we…my family's always welcoming," Molly stammered. They weren't touching, but it was as if the two of them were connected at an emotional level that superseded any physical contact. Flustered, she set her cutlery down on her plate and rested her hands on her lap.

He leaned closer. "I have a lot to be thankful for, but I've always been grateful for that time we shared. We were young, but what we had together was important."

"It was." No matter where Molly went, she'd always carry the memory of Troy in her heart.

One of Troy's hands clasped hers beneath the

table. She froze. This touch wasn't an accidental knee bump. It was purposeful, and as his fingers curled around hers, she let her hand relax in his.

Molly's stomach fluttered and then, with a quick squeeze, it was over, Troy let go and he turned away to speak to his sister.

He'd only held her hand for a brief moment, but it was intimate, intense and opened Molly's heart to his in a way she'd never experienced with anyone else.

It also meant she, and her heart, were in big trouble.

# CHAPTER ELEVEN

LATER THAT NIGHT, Troy flipped on his kitchen light and made his way to the cupboard next to the sink. Since the antacids weren't in the medicine cabinet in the upstairs bathroom or the powder room, the only other place they might be was here.

He pressed a hand to his rolling stomach and opened the cupboard door. On a Montana ranch, there wasn't a 24/7 pharmacy or grocery store on the corner so he should have remembered to stock up.

"Troy?" Footsteps padded from the living room, and he turned to see his mom in a pink housecoat, fluffy pink slippers and a sleepy Acorn nestled in her arms. "I thought you'd gone to bed. I hope you're not up working."

"No." He'd tried to work, but after fifteen minutes of sitting and staring at the computer without seeing the document he'd opened he'd given up and headed to bed. "I can't sleep." He grabbed the bottle of antacids, found a glass and filled it with water from the sink faucet. "Too much rich food or maybe I'm coming down with something." He didn't feel sick, though, only unsettled. Joining Molly's family for a special holiday like Thanksgiving could have been awkward. Instead, it had felt right and comfortable, like he belonged. And when, on impulse, he'd taken her hand, the two of them had fit together in a way he'd never felt with anyone else. "Where are Dad and Sara?"

"Your sister's talking to a friend, and your dad's watching football." Still cuddling Acorn, his mom pulled out a stool and sat behind the kitchen island. "It's a clear night. I opened the living room curtains and looked out at the fields. With the lights off, and in the moonlight, I remembered the Thanksgivings we had on our ranch. You were little and Sara hadn't been born yet. Your dad's folks and mine were still alive, and all the aunts, uncles and cousins would travel to be with us." Her voice was tinged with sadness. "Still, life goes on."

Troy swallowed one of the tablets and sat across from her. "If our old ranch ever comes up for sale, I'll buy it for you."

She shook her head. "That's sweet but no. That ranch is the past, and I don't want to revisit it. You have a wonderful place here, and it's your future. If you ever need help, your dad's itching to get back in a cattle pen or behind the wheel of a tractor."

"I'd be happy to have you both come out and work with me." He loved having his folks and Sara here, but there was still an emptiness in his house—or maybe his heart—that not even his closest family could fill.

"Molly's a beautiful young woman. She's smart and clearly devoted to her family, but…" His mom shifted on the stool and fiddled with Acorn's collar. "Be careful, that's all."

"What are you talking about? Molly's a friend, nothing more." He tried to make the words casual, but his mom knew him too well to be fooled.

"Do you usually hold hands with your friends at the dinner table?" His mom's eyes twinkled.

"I… No…but…" Troy headed up a multimillion-dollar business, but his mom could still make him feel like a kid caught raiding the cookie jar. "You saw?"

"Not at the time but Skylar told me. She asked if you were going to be her new uncle." His mom chuckled. "Not much gets by kids, and she was on Cole's lap. I guess she had a good view."

Troy dropped his head into his hands. "Do you know who else Skylar told?" He might have some questions to answer the next time he was around Molly's family.

"My guess is Paisley because those two girls are best friends, but I also told Skylar that whatever was going on between you and Molly was private and not anyone's business." His mom's expression softened. "Like I said when Cole talked about Joy, mothers worry about their kids even when they're grown up. Molly hurt you, and I don't want you to get hurt again."

"I won't get hurt because I *am* grown up." He shrugged. "It was a bit of flirting, that's all." Flirting that had been a lot more intense than he'd expected and, for a moment, he'd forgotten they had an audience.

"You've never been one to flirt unless you were serious about a girl." His mom studied him, and Troy's face heated. "And from what I've seen Molly's the only girl, or woman, you've ever been truly serious about."

"I've dated other women. Like Kelly."

"Kelly was wonderful, but you broke things off with her and now she's married to someone else. I know because I bumped into her mom at the yoga studio a few weeks ago. So, what's going on?"

"I don't know." And that was the truth. Troy had cared about Kelly, but he hadn't loved her in the way he knew he should. The way he'd once loved Molly. "I'm not in a rush to settle down."

"If you met the right woman you would be, and Molly…can you trust her?"

That was the issue. Troy prided himself on being a good judge of people, but with Molly he'd been wrong. And with Kelly and the few other women he'd dated, he'd always held part of himself back.

"I *want* to trust Molly. She knew me before… everything." He raised his arm in a sweeping gesture that took in the ranch house and surrounding land. "These days, I never know if people like me for me, or what they think I can do or buy for them." It was the first time he'd voiced the fear that ate him up inside. "Apart from you guys and Pete, I keep to myself."

"Oh, honey." His mom got up, set Acorn on the floor and came around the kitchen island to wrap Troy in a hug. "Your dad and I are so proud of your success, but none of the money or what it buys matters if you aren't happy."

"I *am* happy." As Troy returned his mom's hug, the backs of his eyes burned. "I have you and dad and Sara. Pete and his family. This ranch. Interesting work that more than pays the bills. Compared to lots of folks, I'm lucky."

"You are but…" His mom squeezed his shoulders before she stepped back. "You remember after we lost our ranch? Your dad worked the night shift at that factory. I was doing days at the grocery store, and you worked part-time at the gas station while you were still in high school, and you babysat Sara. The four of us were crammed into our small apartment that always smelled of greasy food from the restaurant below."

Troy nodded. How could he forget? It had been one of the hardest times of his life.

"Looking back, I often wonder how we survived it, but we did. And that Thanksgiving, I remember sitting at our kitchen table and feeling thankful. I didn't have much, but I had a loving husband and two wonderful children. We all had our health, and I had hope and faith that things would get better. They did, eventually, and thanks to you, as far as material things go, I've been blessed beyond my wildest imaginings." She hesitated and a frown creased her forehead. "All I'm saying is I could lose everything tomorrow and as long as I still had your dad, you and Sara, I'd be thankful. That's what I want for you. A loving partner and a family who'll be there for you no matter what."

Troy wanted that too, but he didn't know how to get it. And even if he did, could he trust it would be the kind of forever relationship his folks had?

"The right woman won't care about what you can buy for her." It was like she could read his thoughts. His mom gave him another hug. "She'll love you for who you are. 'For richer, for poorer,' like in the wedding vows."

Troy admired her optimism, but he couldn't be so certain. Life hadn't made him cynical but it, and the rough-and-tumble of the business world, had made him wary.

"I want the best for you, honey, and if that's Molly, well, the two of you were so young before. Now, you've both done a lot of growing up. Any child of Joy Carter's is bound to have a sensible head on their shoulders. And you're right. Molly did know you before, so she's not likely to be dazzled by riches."

"No." Troy had to chuckle. Molly was the least pretentious woman he knew.

"I won't interfere, but I'm always here for you. Your dad is too." His mom moved toward the fridge, and Acorn followed. "As for your tummy upset, ginger tea will fix you up better than any of those store-bought pills. I brought fresh ginger with me." She opened the fridge door and rummaged in the crisper drawer. "I expect you drink too much coffee. Along with all that screen time, it's no wonder your digestion and sleep are upside down."

"Mom." Troy huffed in frustration.

"Or I could make you warm milk?" She sent him a teasing glance. "Remember when you were little? A cup of warm milk sent you right off to sleep."

"I'm fine but okay, ginger tea." He rolled his eyes like he'd done as a teenager. He'd admitted enough embarrassing stuff to his mom tonight. He wasn't about to acknowledge she was right about his coffee drinking and what his doctor called "bad sleep hygiene."

Still, shutting off screens several hours before bed and homespun remedies like ginger tea and warm milk wouldn't cure what truly ailed him.

Once again, Molly had gotten under his skin. And rather than running away from what was happening between them, the only cure, if he could call it that, was facing those feelings head-on.

On Friday night the week after Thanksgiving, Molly tucked her fuzzy blue scarf into the neck of a parka she'd last worn in high school and pulled the hat that matched the scarf and gloves farther down over her ears. Waking up this morning to a light dusting of snow on the fields and a thin skim of ice on a half-filled water bucket she'd left outside the barn made her feel like a kid again, excited with the changing seasons.

Or was her excitement more about going with Troy to tonight's town tree lighting? She stole a glance at his profile as he stood by her side in Meadowlark Park. He'd picked her up at the Tall Grass half an hour ago, and although neither of them had said much on the way into town or while strolling past bustling and brightly decorated stores as Christmas music played, the silence between them was comfortable.

Despite that hand-holding at Thanksgiving, which she was pretty sure no one had spotted since none of her family had mentioned it, they were here as friends. Nothing more. Yet, no matter how many times she reminded herself of that, it still felt like a date.

"Are you warm enough?" Troy took Molly's arm to shield her from several kids who darted through the crowd with glow sticks that lit up the night like winter fireflies. In jeans, and bundled up in a parka, hat and gloves, he looked like most of the other men here, but there was something about him. No matter what he wore, he made Molly's stomach flip.

"I'm fine." If anything, she might be too hot, but that was because of him. Even though the kids were gone, Troy still held her arm and despite her parka and sweater beneath it, her skin tingled with awareness.

"Would you like a hot chocolate?" With his free hand, Troy indicated the nearby stand trimmed with red and white holiday lights.

"Sure, but I can—" She reached for her purse, but he stopped her.

"My treat." He grinned. "I invited you so you're my guest. It's the least I can do after your family hosted mine for Thanksgiving."

"Did your folks and Sara get home okay?" Molly liked Troy's family, but she hadn't missed his mom's assessing looks.

"Yeah, and my new stove was finally delivered this morning. Out here, I'm learning I have to order stuff early and stock up on food and other supplies in case of emergency." He shrugged and shook his head. "I'm going to San Francisco for Christmas so it will be a while before I get to try the stove out to cook a big meal."

"Oh." Of course he'd want to spend Christmas with his family. She was surprised at how much she'd gotten used to having Troy nearby. As he ordered and paid for their drinks, he took his arm from hers, and Molly hugged herself, unexpectedly bereft.

"Hey, Molly." Hannah, an old friend from high school, came over. "I heard you're back in town for a while. You should come to one of our group dinners. The guys watch the kids so we women can have a night out and enjoy ourselves." She darted a curious glance at Troy while also helping a dark-haired toddler with his mittens.

"Thanks, I'll keep it in mind. So far, I've been busy with family things." Molly smiled at the little boy, who happily told her that his name was Noah. He looked to be about two, and judging from the bulge under the front of her coat, Hannah was pregnant again.

"It's the third Thursday evening of the month at Ruby's Place, the Western-themed restaurant off High Valley Avenue. Most of the old crowd turns up. We meet at six." Hannah grinned at her husband, Mike, who'd been a few years ahead of Molly in school.

"Sounds good." Molly took the paper cup of cocoa from Troy and introduced him to Hannah and her family. She smiled at Noah again and pushed away a surprising tug of longing.

"Noah, no. That's Ben's, not yours." Hannah removed a glow stick from her son's mittened hand, which he'd apparently taken from another boy.

"But I want to be a superhero." Noah's small face screwed up, and he started to wail.

"Sorry. We'll have to catch up another time." She gave Molly an apologetic glance.

"Hey, buddy." Troy crouched to Noah's level and said something to him. The boy stopped crying, nodded and then grinned.

As they said their goodbyes, Molly told herself she should enjoy this time of being on her own. She had her path, and she was happy with it. Yet, in Atlanta, far away from her nieces and nephew and working in a research institute, she missed the joy of children in her life.

"What next?" Troy looped his arm through Molly's again as they moved away from Hannah and her family and rejoined the crowd.

"The tree lighting will start soon." She sipped the sweet cocoa, enjoying the feel of Troy's arm in hers. She hadn't heard what he'd said to Noah, but it had charmed the little boy and diverted his attention, which was the point. She suppressed the way-too-appealing thought of Troy with kids of his own, and the less-welcome one of whatever woman he'd become a parent with. "The town's also collecting money and gifts for a toy drive over by the pavilion." With the weddings and Thanksgiving, Molly hadn't had time to shop, so she'd given a check to one of the organizers when she'd been in town getting groceries.

"Already taken care of. I dropped some things off this afternoon."

"He sure did." Nina appeared on Troy's other side, accompanied by Werner. "The bed of his pickup truck was full to overflowing. You were much too generous, and we sure appreciate it.

Some lucky kids on Christmas morning will as well."

"It was nothing." Even in the growing darkness, Molly spotted the faint flush on Troy's cheeks.

"If that's nothing, I can't imagine what 'something' is," Werner said. "Don't be so modest. Between that and your check for the food bank, you gave us over—"

"Great to see you both but we need to get going," Troy interrupted. "We have to get a good spot to see the holiday lights go on, don't we, Molly?"

"Yes, but…" As Troy steered her away from Nina and Werner, she shook her head at him. "What did you do?"

"Nothing important, but it was also supposed to be private." Troy tossed his empty cocoa cup in a nearby recycling container and then did the same with Molly's.

"Haven't you learned nothing much in High Valley is private?" Yet, although people here liked to talk about their neighbors, they were kind and caring to anyone in need. "If you keep on this way, the town will name something after you. You're too young for a statue and besides, you're still alive…" She stopped at Troy's expression, which showed not only embarrassment but verged on annoyance. "Sorry, I was teasing."

"I know, but it bugs me when people make a big deal about me giving to charity. I got lucky in my life so I want to give back. I shouldn't be celebrated for that."

As a ranch hand, Troy had had no reason to be arrogant or pretentious, so Molly hadn't thought his kindness and humble nature were anything special. Now, she knew differently. "I shouldn't have joked. You were always private, and I respect that." She respected him too and, if she wasn't careful, it would be easy for her to fall in love with him again.

"*We* were private." His face was troubled.

As it turned out, that privacy had been for the best because when Molly had left for college, nobody, Troy most of all, had known the heartbreak she'd taken with her.

"What about here?" He stopped near a tall tree. "We have a good view but it's not as crowded."

"Fine with me." Along both sides of High Valley's main street and here in the park, trees and lampposts were strung with holiday lights and decorations. In a few minutes, the town's mayor would say a few words and then Santa would flip a switch to light up the town at this dark time of year. "I came to this event with my parents and brothers when I was small. My

JEN GILROY                    183

dad carried me on his shoulders so I could see
everything. Then after Paul passed, we stopped
coming. Paul loved holiday lights so being here
hurt. Mom and Dad didn't even decorate much
at home for a few years."

Troy squeezed her gloved hand. "It must have
been so hard for all of you."

"It was and still is in a lot of ways. There are
gaps in my family that will never be filled, but
we make new memories, right?" She made herself give Troy a bright smile.

"We do but—"

Static crackled and cut off whatever Troy had
intended to say. Then the mayor's voice came
over a loudspeaker as she welcomed everyone
and made a few announcements. Then it was
time for the main event. "Now it's my pleasure
to invite Santa to turn on the holiday lights for
us." She gestured to the jolly man in a red suit
and white beard that Molly had spotted strolling
along High Valley's main street earlier giving
out candy and having photos taken with kids.

"Ho, ho, ho." Santa hopped onto a temporary
wooden platform beside the mayor.

"That's... No, it can't be." Molly glanced
around. She'd seen Melissa and Skylar over by
the pavilion, but come to think of it Cole hadn't
been with them.

"What? Who?" Troy looked around as well.

Molly lowered her voice. "I think that's Cole up there. Rosa's husband usually plays Santa, he's the deputy mayor, but that's not him. And look at how Santa is walking over to the light switch. That's Cole's cowboy gait for sure." She put a hand to her mouth, covering a laugh as Santa bantered with the mayor.

"Wow. Cole's disguised his voice but it's him all right." Troy and Molly chuckled together.

"Shush. We don't want to spoil anything for the kids."

Santa flipped the switch and the park was illuminated with multicolored lights. Then, as Luke Bryan's rendition of "Run Run Rudolph" blasted from the sound system, everyone began to dance. Melissa even jumped up to join Santa while Rosa's husband, who'd stayed behind the other town councillors, extended a hand to the mayor.

"I'm not much of a dancer but shall we?" Troy gave Molly his hand.

"Sure, everyone else is." From couples to families spanning multiple generations, High Valley was in a party mood. Yet, as Molly's hand slipped into Troy's like it belonged there, and he drew her close to him, her laughter stopped. And as they swayed together, her heart caught in her throat.

"Look." Troy gestured with his chin toward the sky.

Molly glanced up. "It's snowing." Fluffy flakes drifted lazily around them, landing on their faces and parkas. The colored lights and smiles in the crowd swirled together as the song changed to Thomas Rhett's "Christmas in the Country."

"Magical, isn't it?" Troy's voice was husky in her ear, and then Molly's head was on his shoulder as she nodded. She loved this song, although when she'd had to work last Christmas and hadn't been able to come home, it had made her cry.

Without her noticing, they'd danced away from the crowd into what in summer was a small ornamental garden shielded by a high and bushy cedar hedge.

"Troy, I…" The music and crowd noise faded until it was only the two of them.

"May I kiss you?" The softness in his eyes and gentle smile almost undid her, unlocking feelings she'd thought were gone forever.

"This is probably a mistake but…yes," she whispered in response to his question as his lips drew closer.

"You and me were never a mistake."

Then he kissed her, or she kissed him because she didn't know which of them moved first.

"Okay?" He drew back and studied her face.

She nodded, unable to speak. For the first time in years, she was complete and felt like she was where and with the person she was meant to be. Her legs shook, and she held him tight so she wouldn't fall over.

"I tried, Molly. I really did, but I still have feelings for you. I can't help it."

"I can't either. I still have feelings for you too." The intensity of that kiss didn't lie. And after years of being cautious in her dating relationships and never meeting the right guy, maybe now she needed to take a chance.

"Good." He gave her a half smile and then another kiss mixed with a snowflake landed on the end of her nose. "We're adults. We can enjoy each other's company for the next few weeks and see what happens."

"Yes." Molly didn't have any long-term expectations. She was still going back to Atlanta, although right now it might have been Mars for how remote it seemed, but she couldn't plan her whole life. And being an adult meant she knew how to keep herself and her heart safe.

She tilted her head for one more kiss and didn't let herself think about the future or the past. All that mattered was now.

# CHAPTER TWELVE

TROY GLANCED AT Molly in the passenger seat of his truck where her blond hair shone in the muted light from the dash. Outside, snow still fell and now covered the two-lane highway that led back to the Tall Grass Ranch.

"The road's getting slippery. Otherwise, I'd hold your hand." Kissing her had been the best and now she seemed too far away. He hadn't planned to kiss her, but when the right moment had presented itself, why not? It was only a kiss. Still, that one kiss had turned into a few more, and when they'd stepped away from each other and returned to the main area of the park, he couldn't pretend that something momentous and maybe even life-changing hadn't happened.

"I'd rather you keep both hands on the wheel than we end up in the ditch." At the warmth and teasing in Molly's voice, Troy's spirits lightened. He'd been afraid she regretted those kisses, but she'd only gotten quiet like she used to.

He chuckled. "Does High Valley still have a towing service?" Forget about the road conditions, he might be on a slipperier slope with Molly than in the truck.

"Yes, Mike's older brother runs it now, but he and his crew will likely be busy in town. Lots of tourists were at the tree lighting, and some of them won't have winter tires on yet. You'd have better luck calling someone with a tractor." Gazing out the truck window, her eyebrows drew together, and she fidgeted in her seat. "The weather's getting bad. Will you be okay to drive home after dropping me off? I'm sure Zach and Beth would make up a spare bed for you or, if not, there's always space in the bunkhouse."

"That's a good idea. I could ask one of the hands to look after Acorn." Troy peered out the window as well. Even with the truck's high beams, he could hardly see more than a few feet in front of them. "The last time I checked, a storm was forecast but it wasn't supposed to hit until three or four hours after midnight. I'd forgotten how fast winter can blow in out here."

"Me too." When he stole another glance at her, Molly bit her lip. "We had a dusting of snow last night, but this storm's the real deal. What can I do?"

"Look for any landmarks." Maybe they should have stayed in town, but the snow and wind hadn't been bad then. And he'd been so caught up in Molly, Troy hadn't paid attention to anyone, or anything, else or thought to check for an updated weather report. "Do you still have cell service?"

She pulled her phone out of her bag. "A weak signal. I'll text my brothers in our group chat. We—"

The truck veered across the road, and Troy gripped the wheel and steered into the skid. "Hang on." After a few endless seconds, he righted the vehicle.

"Ice?"

He nodded, slowed the vehicle even more and put on the hazard lights. He and Molly were both Montana born. No other words were needed. Ice was dangerous enough on its own, but mixed with heavy snow and high winds, the weather conditions were like driving blind.

Molly pointed her phone's flashlight toward the swirling snow. "We should be close to the ranch by now, but my text didn't go through. Wait, is that a light?"

"Where?"

"There's Bryce's driveway on the right. He's got the porch lights on."

Troy drew in a breath and turned the truck to where he thought the driveway should be.

"Whoa." Molly's voice rang out as the vehicle lurched forward and there was a prolonged crunching and cracking noise before they slid to a stop in a snowdrift.

"Are you okay?" Adrenaline surged through Troy as he hit the emergency brake and then reached for her.

"I'm fine. What about you?"

"Fine." Except for feeling like a fool. He squeezed her gloved hand. "I'm so sorry. I'd never do anything to put you in danger and—"

"In this weather, it could have happened to anyone." Although her words were reassuring, was that laughter in Molly's voice? "You missed the ditch, but I think you hit the mailbox and the shelter Bryce built for Paisley and Cam to wait for the school bus."

*Way to go, Clayton.* This situation was embarrassing enough without him having destroyed Carter property. Troy released the brake, shifted gears and pumped the accelerator to try to reverse the truck, but they were stuck. He leaned his head on the steering wheel and accidentally hit the horn.

"Troy, it's…" Molly's voice shook.

Was she laughing or crying? He raised his head. She was laughing, but was it because she was in shock? "Molly, I swear this was an accident. I'll talk to Bryce and pay for the damage I've caused and—"

"I know. It's okay." She gulped. "Only in Montana. The two of us should have known better."

Answering laughter rose up in Troy's chest. "You're sure you're okay?"

"Absolutely."

"We'll have a funny story to tell one day." He took her hand again and tenderness washed over him. He wanted it to be a story they told to their family and friends, children and then grandchildren. Laughing at themselves, but laughing together as they were now. No matter what happened, Molly put Troy at ease and made everything better. What would it be like to go through his life with her by his side? "Molly, I—"

Someone banged on the outside of the truck, and a beam of light shone through Molly's window. She yanked her hand away.

"It's Bryce," she said shakily.

Although Troy appreciated the help, he wished it hadn't been one of Molly's brothers. "Can you get your door open?"

"I think so." Molly pushed on her door until it opened partway and then swung her legs out of the truck's cab.

"I've got you, Mol." In a parka and snow pants and with his face almost obscured by a hat and scarf, Bryce half carried his sister to what must be the laneway before returning to the truck.

As Troy shut off the vehicle and slid across

the bench seat to exit the truck in his turn, another beam of light almost blinded him. "I'm sorry. Before I knew it, we were sliding and—"

"Molly told me." Bryce lowered the flashlight, and Troy blinked. "All that matters is the two of you are safe." He gave Troy a hand to help him over a snowdrift and shut the truck door. A small smile played around his mouth. "We needed a new mailbox anyway. As for the school bus shelter?" The smile broadened, and Troy breathed easier. "I should warn you my daughter will try to negotiate for a fancier replacement than that wooden shed I knocked together."

"No problem." Troy followed the path cast by Bryce's flashlight as they rejoined Molly and waded through snow to the house. "Whatever you all want, I'll cover it."

"Good. You're off the road so we can get the tractor and pull your truck out in the morning." Bryce sobered. "As for the rest of it…" He paused as they reached his front porch. "What do you say we keep whatever's going on with you two between ourselves?"

"There's nothing going on." Molly stopped, and her gaze caught Troy's.

Bryce chuckled as he looked between them. "I wasn't born yesterday. It's your business, but I hope you know what you're doing." Then he opened his front door, and Carrie greeted them with blankets, hot cocoa and insisted they stay the night—Molly in the guest room and Troy on a pullout sofa in the family room.

An hour later, after he'd called one of his ranch hands to see to Acorn and once the house was quiet, Troy stretched out on the sofa, warm and cozy as snow still fell heavily outside. Yet, Bryce's warning echoed in his head. He didn't know what he was doing and maybe Molly didn't either, but it sure felt good.

Perhaps, and for now, that was enough.

AT CARRIE'S FARMHOUSE the next day, where Joy and Shane were living while their own house was being built, Joy stored her empty suitcase in the bedroom closet.

"I think that's everything unpacked. I appreciate you coming to help, honey." She glanced at Molly, who sat on the dressing table bench by the window. "I'm sure it won't take long for me to feel at home here, but right now, it's all new and strange."

Joy had lived at the Tall Grass Ranch for more than forty years. In the past few weeks, everything in her life had changed, from a different view beyond her bedroom window to a kitchen she was still finding her way around to getting used to being married to Shane.

"You're happy, right?" Molly set out toiletries on top of the dressing table with her back to Joy.

"Yes." So happy Joy was almost afraid to say so out loud, afraid she'd jinx this unexpected later-in-life love that had blessed her beyond her greatest imaginings. "I'm getting used to Shane's habits as he is to mine. Our honeymoon was wonderful, but I must say I'm glad to be home." Not that Carrie's farm was home yet, but as soon as the plane's wheels had touched down in Montana, Joy had been home in the way that counted the most.

"That's great, Mom." Molly put Joy's jewelry roll in one of the dressing table's drawers, the only piece of furniture Joy had kept from her old bedroom because it had been her mother's.

"So, what's going on here? Tell me all the news." Joy patted the cushioned window seat that overlooked a snow-covered pasture.

"Nothing much. You've probably already heard most of it from Rosa." Molly padded across the carpeted floor in her sock feet, joined Joy on the window seat and sat cross-legged.

"I sure heard about Cole stepping in to play Santa at the tree lighting. Rosa said her husband thought it was time for someone new to take over, but who would have thought it would be Cole? Certainly not me." Which showed Joy that no matter how old they were, her kids could still surprise her. "How are you doing, Jelly-bean?" Something was different about Molly and although Joy didn't have proof, from what Rosa had said, she suspected it had something to do with Troy.

"I'm fine." Her daughter's smile was innocent, but a faint pink tinted her cheeks.

"I bumped into Troy at the Bluebunch earlier. I thanked him for looking out for you the night of the storm." Joy gazed out the window at the snowy fields and the ridge of low hills behind Carrie's house. She wouldn't ask a direct question, but it didn't do any harm to lead the conversation in a way that might get her daughter to open up.

"Mom, you didn't have to. I'm a grown woman. Troy and I looked out for each other." Molly fiddled with a curtain tie, and the pink in her face deepened.

"That's what he said, although he seemed keen to emphasize it was him, not you, who'd hit Bryce and Carrie's mailbox and bus shelter." Joy suppressed a smile. Troy had been so embarrassed it was both awkward and sweet and that, more than anything, told her he had feelings for Molly. "I won't interfere but from what I've seen, you and Troy might have something more than a working relationship. He's a good man and—"

"Oh, Mom." Molly dropped her head into her hands. "I don't know what to do. I never told you, but Troy and I were involved before, the summer after I finished high school. We broke up before I left for college but now... I guess you never forget your first love." Her laugh had a hollow sound.

Joy's heart pinched. "You don't, but..." Her words trailed off as she studied Molly's bent head. Joy had married her own first love, Dennis, so who was she to advise? However, now she loved Shane too, so she knew you could have more than one love in a lifetime. "Back then, I suspected you and Troy had feelings for each other. But because of how things were between you and me, I didn't want to say anything. It was hard." How hard, Joy had never told anyone, not even Rosa. "And when you came home for Thanksgiving and Christmas, it seemed like you were avoiding me."

"I wasn't, not really, but those things were hard for me too."

"It's okay, I understand." Finally, she and Molly were talking honestly with each other, and Joy didn't want to mess anything up. "I knew you needed to become your own person, and separating from me was part of growing up." However, in the intervening years, Joy had wondered if she'd ever get her daughter back and have the closeness they'd once shared.

"I thought if I told you about Troy, you'd be upset. You wanted me to go to college and do all the things you never had a chance to. I also wanted to go to college for myself. So, with Troy, it was only a summer thing. I never forgot him, though, and when I came back here in October, seeing him again stirred up all sorts of feelings." Molly finally raised her head and tears pooled in her eyes.

"Oh, honey." Joy hugged her daughter, and Molly snuggled close like she'd done as a little girl. "All I want for you, all I ever wanted, was for you to be happy. I'll be okay with whatever that happiness means to you. It's wonderful having you home and—"

"You'd like me to stay." Molly's voice was flat.

"Of course, but I know it's not that simple. From the time you were in grade school, you wanted to live in a city. Your dad and I had a lot of time to accept you'd be leaving the ranch. We never tried to stop you either and now you're thriving. You did so well in college and grad school and you have a great career waiting for you. You've only gotten started on that journey." Joy hesitated. "When you tell me about going to shows and parties with friends, I'm glad. You deserve to have fun and get all dressed up to go to fancy events in style." There had been times when Joy had imagined that kind of life and now, with Shane, she'd have it. Still, she'd loved her years on the ranch with Dennis and their family. "I see why you're torn. I like Troy, but when you go back to Atlanta one or both of you could be hurt."

"We're realistic so nobody will get hurt. Whatever's between us isn't serious." Molly stuck her chin out.

So they did have a relationship now, one that was new and fragile. Joy stopped herself from saying something that might push Molly away again. "Even so, there's Troy's investment in Cole's business to consider. I have to look out for all my children. If Troy were to pull out of that deal, Cole would be devastated. He's finally happy and settled and his stock contracting venture has only just begun to turn a profit." Joy patted Molly's back before her daughter straightened and brushed away the tears.

"I'd never do anything to put Cole's business at risk. Besides, Troy's smart. He knows he's made a good investment, and the money he loaned Cole is separate from anything to do with us. Not that there is an *us*, not really. You don't have anything to worry about." Molly's smile was forced.

"I hope you're right, but I'm always here if

you need to talk or…anything." Joy stuttered to a stop and clasped her hands together. There wasn't a map for this stage of the parenting journey, but the one thing Joy knew, had learned with Zach, Cole and Bryce, was that she had to respect her adult kids' boundaries. Although she still wanted to protect them like when they were small, she couldn't. So, somehow she had to find the right balance, which was different for each of them.

"Thanks, Mom." Molly stood and smoothed her pretty hair. "I'd appreciate it if this conversation could stay between us. I don't want my brothers to get involved. Well, Bryce already suspects, but it's private."

"Of course." Joy stood and followed Molly to the bedroom door as her daughter's cell phone chirped.

"Oh, that's Troy. I need to call him. I'll meet you in the kitchen in a few minutes. We can unpack your last boxes, at least the ones you moved here and aren't storing until the new house is ready. I'm glad you brought Grandma's dishes. They'll look great in that glass-fronted cupboard." Molly took her phone out of the back pocket of her jeans and went to the open area at the end of the upstairs hall where Joy planned to set up her sewing machine and craft table.

As she went down the stairs to the kitchen,

Molly's soft voice reached her, the words inaudible, but their warmth and affection unmistakable.

Despite her daughter's reassurances, Joy *did* have something to worry about. But like with all her kids, she had to trust Molly to figure things out for herself—and only give a nudge when, or if, it was needed.

Joy had her own new life to focus on. The back door swung open, and Shane came in stamping fluffy snow off his boots. He hung his parka on a hook in the mudroom, then stepped into the kitchen with a grin. He opened his arms to her, and Joy went into them.

And as she wrapped her arms around her husband, she willed herself to focus on the happiness she had rather than worry about a future that might never happen.

# CHAPTER THIRTEEN

"SHE'S GORGEOUS." From across the paddock fence at the horse rescue, Molly patted Cara, the fourteen-year-old bay mare Troy had brought her to visit. "You've seen her vet records?"

"Yes, and everything health-wise looks good. The staff here hasn't seen any behavioral problems with her either." Troy stood across the fence from Molly, next to Cara. He gave Molly a lopsided grin. "It's my fourth visit here. Cara started off as a show horse and then became a companion animal. When her owner had medical and financial issues and couldn't keep her any longer, Cara came to live here. The staff promised they'd find her a loving home."

"She seems like a sweetheart. Friendly and easy to catch and lead. Have you tried grooming her yet?" From what Molly had seen, Cara would make a wonderful family horse. She listened well, appeared eager to please and as a Morgan she'd be versatile, as good with beginners as with more experienced riders. If Molly was setting up her own barn, Cara would be a perfect choice.

"No grooming yet. Since she's already tacked up, why don't you come into the paddock and see how she handles?" Troy's expression was boyish and here, twenty miles north of High Valley, he was more like the ranch hand Molly remembered.

"Okay." Molly had stayed on the other side of the fence to keep her distance from Troy, not Cara. Her lips still tingled at the memory of those life-changing, earth-shattering kisses the night of the tree lighting ceremony. While she wanted to kiss him again, her mom's gentle warning brought some of Molly's own doubts to the fore. Yet, when Troy had texted and asked her to come and see Cara, it had been impossible to resist spending more time with him.

She climbed the paddock fence and hopped to the ground on the other side like she'd done as a kid. She rode sometimes at a horse barn in Atlanta. There, she'd have used the gate, but the place had antique chandeliers hanging from skylights and custom leather seats in the tack room. The only time most of its clientele scaled fences was atop eye-wateringly expensive horses on a show jumping course. "Hey,

Cara. You're so pretty. Are you going to show me what you can do?"

The horse studied her and then, as if deciding Molly was someone she could trust, nudged her hand. "She's between fifteen and sixteen hands?" Molly dug in her pocket for one of the treats she'd stashed there earlier. She assessed Cara from all angles, giving the mare a chance to get to know and feel comfortable with her.

"You still have a good eye. According to her vet records, she's fifteen two." Troy's expression was approving. "Do you want to ride her? She was fine with me on my last visit, but I'd like to see how she responds to a woman."

"Sure." Before Molly returned to Montana, it had been at least six months since she'd made it out to that equestrian center in Atlanta. But even on the rare times she'd ridden there, it hadn't been the same. She might have adjusted to an English instead of a Western saddle, but it wasn't home so she hadn't felt comfortable.

She donned the riding helmet Troy handed her, and then he gave her a boost onto Cara's back. She settled and rubbed the horse's sleek neck.

"You okay up there?" Troy shaded his eyes against the bright sunshine that reflected off the white snow. Fine lines that hadn't been there before gave his face both maturity and character.

It was a face Molly could still let herself love and, as she eased Cara into a walk, she drew in a shaky breath. "I'm great." With Cara's reins between her hands, a saddle beneath her seat and Troy walking alongside, happiness surged through Molly. Despite the frosty weather, she was warm and cozy and, if she hadn't been on horseback, she might have jumped for sheer joy. No matter her conflicted feelings for Troy, she loved Montana and she'd missed both the place and times like this one.

"You sure look great." Troy's voice was husky.

"So do you." His hair, which had grown a bit longer, stuck out from under his cowboy hat. And in his worn jeans and winter barn jacket, against the backdrop of this big and rugged landscape, he looked like he belonged here.

Maybe she did too. As she settled into the saddle, they smiled at each other, and Troy raised one of his hands to hers. For a moment, as their gloved palms connected, a different kind of warmth, electric rather than cozy, surged through Molly and left her breathless. When he took his hand away, she fumbled with Cara's reins. "Want to see her trot?"

"I'd like to see both of you trot." While Troy's eyes and expression teased her, the faint flush on his cheeks wasn't only from the cold weather, suggesting he was as attracted to her as Molly was to him.

Molly laughed and, as Cara turned her head as if to ask what was funny, she encouraged the horse from a walk to a trot. Cara made the transition seamlessly, and Molly patted the horse's neck before waving at Troy who now stood by the fence to watch.

Molly didn't only feel happy. She also felt content, as if life had brought her almost full circle back to Montana and this man, where she'd always been meant to be.

"WHAT DO YOU think of this dark red one?" In the middle of a display of sofas at a furniture store in the nearest big town to High Valley, Troy turned to Molly. He'd taken a rare day off work and didn't want his time with her to end. After visiting the horse rescue, he'd asked her to check out living room furniture with him.

"I like it. Since it's modular it will be more versatile." With her hands on her hips, Molly considered the one they'd both looked at first and had then come back to.

Troy dragged his attention away from the rosy curve of Molly's lips and back to the sofa. "What do you mean?"

He'd never been big on shopping, preferring to either buy online or get in and out of a store as fast as possible. Being here with Molly, though, was different, and he saw the sense of taking the time to pick out something that would suit both his house and his life. It was also fun to watch her consider the different pieces of furniture, wave away the sales guy and instead guide Troy through what was to him a bewildering maze of styles, upholstery choices, arm height and trim.

"Modular means it comes in different pieces, and you can arrange them in different ways or even add parts later. You could use this sofa all together in your living room or have a smaller piece in another room. This one doesn't have a pullout bed, but it's a lot like the sofa you slept on at Bryce and Carrie's the night of the snowstorm, remember?"

How could Troy forget? He couldn't stop thinking about that night. Kissing Molly, enjoying each other's company like they used to and then laughing together when he'd missed Bryce's driveway and driven into a snowbank. Some women would have mocked him, but Molly had seen the funny side and her good humor had lessened Troy's embarrassment. Then, as now, he wanted to throw caution to the wind and ask her to stay here so they could be with each other forever.

"This smaller piece would fit in what used to be the parlor. Acorn and I like to watch movies in there." Since Cathy had repainted the room for him, it was snug and inviting. Troy could imagine Molly curled up next to him on this sofa with a bowl of popcorn and mugs of cocoa.

"Nice. This piece has been pretreated with an upholstery protector so if you spill anything, the stain will come out." Molly grinned as she pointed to a label attached to one of the sofa's arms.

"How do you know all this stuff?" Troy understood complex computer coding, but this world was alien.

"I worked in a hardware store part-time in college. It also had a furniture and appliance department, and I sometimes had to cover that area."

"You must have been their top salesperson." Troy sat on one end of the sofa and patted the space next to him. "Come on. Try it out with me."

Molly hesitated and then sat where he'd indicated. "Working in the hardware part of the store reminded me of the ranch. After my brothers left home, I worked with my dad. He taught me how to shingle a roof, build a chicken coop and do rudimentary plumbing. If your toilet ever backs up, I'm your woman. I've saved lots of money over the years doing repairs myself."

"I used to work alongside my dad as well. Those were good times." Nowadays, Troy missed working with his hands and although he'd hired Cathy to paint several rooms, part of him wanted to grab a brush and join her. "Coincidentally, my dad has a part-time job in a hardware store in San Francisco. He loves it."

"He told me about that job." As Molly shifted on the sofa, her thigh brushed against Troy's and even that brief touch made his breath catch. "Your folks and Sara are great."

"Like you are with your family we've always been close." Although Troy loved High Valley, he missed having his folks nearby.

Molly's smile faded and she stood, putting more space between them. "So, are you going to buy this sofa?" She inclined her head toward the middle-aged sales guy who hovered at a distance. "If you want, I'll negotiate to try to get you free delivery and maybe even one of these small end tables." She rubbed the scratch on a table displayed by the sofa. "A bit of sandpaper and stain would fix up this beauty in no time, but they can't sell it as is, at least not for full price."

"I could use you on my team. I mean my work sales team, not at the ranch, although you'd be terrific there." His tongue tripped over the words. The more he said, the worse it sounded.

"It's okay. I know what you meant." Molly's eyes twinkled. "Not having money has taught me to be financially savvy. I guess it's become a way of life."

"Even when you have money, it's still good to pay attention to what things cost." Troy had worked hard for his success, and he'd never spend recklessly or risk losing the security money gave him. "I like the sofa so go for it."

As Molly spoke to the sales guy, who introduced himself as Mark, Troy watched with both amusement and awe. Like most people, he wanted to get a good deal, but since the sofa was already on sale, it wouldn't have occurred to him to bargain. Along with free delivery and the damaged table, Molly also got him a coupon for a discount on any future purchase over two hundred dollars—which he'd use because Troy's house was still half empty.

Troy thanked Mark as he rang up the purchase.

"Don't thank me. Thank your wife." Mark smiled before glancing at Molly, who'd wandered over to the recliner section and was now chatting with a white-haired woman.

"She's not my wife. Just a friend." Troy rushed to clarify.

"Too bad, buddy, she's a keeper." Mark shook his head. "A woman like her is one in a million. I should know. I've been married to one of my own for almost twenty-five years."

As he put his credit card and the store coupon in his wallet, Troy's good mood evaporated. "I'll be back here for sure. I moved onto a ranch near High Valley in October."

"Nice area. My mom grew up around there."

"Definitely a nice area. Thanks again!" Troy waved at Molly, hoping she'd understand the urgency of his gesture. In small-town and rural Montana, the usual "six degrees of separation" was more like one or two. Mark's mother was undoubtedly related to someone who knew Troy or Molly, and news the two of them had been furniture shopping would make it back to town before they did. And with each retelling, the story would be embellished until they hadn't only bought a sofa but an entire primary bedroom suite because they were planning a Christmas wedding.

"All set?" Molly rejoined them. "Mrs. Klein over there is looking for an ottoman to match her recliner. Since you were busy, I made a few suggestions." She grinned at Mark. "She's from High Valley and knows your mom and mine."

Mark grinned back while also giving Troy a sideways glance. "A keeper, remember?"

"Yeah." As Troy shepherded Molly out of the store, he was torn between laughter and embarrassment.

"What did he mean about a keeper?" Molly's expression was curious.

"He was talking about the sofa. That it would last me a long time." Troy improvised before laughter won out. "Folks in High Valley will likely find out we've been shopping for furniture together."

"I guess I've lived away too long." As they reached Troy's truck, the embarrassment Troy had felt was mirrored on Molly's face. "Roots still run deep here. We may have some explaining to do, but I'll set anyone straight who asks." Her smile was rueful.

Which was what Troy would do too so why did he have a brief pang of regret? "As long as we're on a roll, why don't we give people something to really talk about?" They both knew it was a bit of fun, so the excitement coursing through Troy was only because he liked a good joke.

"Meaning?" Her eyes twinkled, and when Troy opened the passenger door for her, Molly hopped in. "Troy?"

Her jeans seemed to make her legs longer, and she looked good up there in his truck. "Oh, right." He went around and climbed into his own seat and started the vehicle. "I could either take you right back to the Tall Grass, or since Zach mentioned the youth hockey team he coaches is playing an early game, we could stop by the arena. Get something to eat at the concession stand and cheer on the team." His breath quickened as he waited for her to answer. It wouldn't be fancy, but unlike the tree lighting and going to look at a horse and then furniture, it was definitely a date.

He knew it and, by the way she tilted her head and smoothed her hair, Molly did as well.

"Sure, that sounds fun. Zach will be happy to have us there supporting him and the kids." Her voice was light but as Troy let the truck idle, she reached out and covered his free hand with one of hers. "I know we can't get serious, but I want to spend time with you. Let's make whatever moments we have together count."

Troy nodded and a lump rose in his throat. Those moments were going by too fast. What would he do when none of them were left?

# CHAPTER FOURTEEN

"Go, Grizzly Bears!" At Molly's side in High Valley's ice arena, Troy jumped to his feet and cheered as one of the players on Zach's team scored a goal. "Great shot! Way to go, Wyatt!"

"I didn't know you were such a big hockey fan." Molly finished her burger, which tasted just like she remembered.

"I wanted to play when I was a kid, but with all the equipment, registration fees and travel to away games, youth hockey's expensive. I had one season where I learned the basics of the game and worked on skating, but after that my folks couldn't afford to keep me in the program. I played soccer instead and ran track in high school." He shrugged as if it didn't matter, but in his expression Molly saw the disappointed boy he'd once been. "Wyatt is Cathy's older son. I've hired him to do odd jobs around the ranch when Cathy's working at the house. He's a good kid. I talked to Zach about him and well… I wanted to do what I could so Wyatt could play with the other guys his age." Troy's face reddened. "Let's keep that between us, okay?"

"Sure." Molly's heart squeezed.

Troy gathered up their empty food containers. "Chance, Cathy's younger boy, is more into music and academics than sports. He's a math whiz and made it into the state round of a middle school competition in Billings in March. Wyatt's going to hang out with me when his mom and Chance are away for those two days."

Without Troy saying a word, Molly knew that along with Wyatt's hockey equipment, he had something to do with covering Cathy and Chance's travel costs. "You're a good man, Troy Clayton, and those boys and their mom are lucky to have you in their lives."

"It's me who's the lucky one. The three of them are my family here." He put a paper bag with their garbage and recyclables under his seat. "Speaking of family, I mentioned Pete to you before, right? He's my business partner and closest friend, and he's going to be here for a couple days this week. We'll be working nonstop, but you might see us around town." The pink on Troy's face intensified. "If he was going to be here longer, I'd invite you over to meet him. And Cole, of course."

"Of course." If they were a real couple, Troy

would want her to meet his friends, but since they weren't, and even if he and Pete had time, it would be a business instead of personal get-together.

"Pete lives in Texas, so you'd think he'd know about ranching and cowboys, but he doesn't. He grew up in Florida and since moving to Austin, unless he's flying somewhere else, I don't think he ever ventures much beyond the city limits." Troy gave Molly a teasing grin. "He's a city guy like you're a city girl."

"I'm…" Molly stopped as Troy jumped to his feet again when the Grizzly Bears scored another goal. "That's it, guys!" Despite a pang of sympathy for the opposing team's goalie, who sprawled in the crease with his head in his hands, Molly clapped and cheered with the rest of the hometown crowd, most of whom she recognized at least by sight.

She'd almost told Troy she wasn't sure if she was truly a city girl, but she wasn't entirely a ranch and country girl either. So, what did that make her? Confused and torn between two places that in different ways were both her home.

The buzzer rang to signal the end of the game, and they began to gather their things. Molly folded the blanket they'd brought from Troy's truck to keep warm. It was so cold in the arena she hadn't even unzipped her parka and had only removed her gloves to eat. That was small-town hockey and once, when she hadn't known any different, she'd assumed all arenas were like the one here.

"Hey, Molly. You didn't say you'd be at tonight's game." Cole stopped by their seats. Bryce appeared behind him with Paisley, Cam and Skylar in tow. "If we'd known, you and Troy could have sat with us."

"Coming here was sort of…spur of the moment."

"Carrie's away for a rodeo, and Melissa had a work dinner, so we brought the whole crew." Bryce glanced between Troy and Molly, and a small smile tugged at his mouth. "Mom and Shane were supposed to be here, but they stayed with Beth. She wasn't feeling so good, and Ellie had a sleepover at a friend's. Zach didn't want to leave Beth alone when he had to coach." Bryce waved at Zach, who was still behind the home team's bench talking to his assistant coach and several players.

"I told Beth to call me if she ever needs anything. For a mom-to-be, no question or concern is too small." Molly wrapped her scarf around her neck. "That goes for the rest of you too."

"It's fantastic to have a nurse in the family." Cole fell into step with Molly as they made their way as a group to the arena exit. "I'm having this twinge in my right knee. I wondered if—"

"You've had that 'twinge' since your last rodeo accident, and your excellent physical therapist is already taking care of it." Molly gave him a playful swat. "Unless it's an emergency, I don't treat family members, I only answer questions."

"Don't the new accessible seats look good?" Since Zach wasn't with them, Bryce assumed the role of family peacemaker and diverted the conversation. He pointed to a reserved row on the arena's main level. "The Sunflower Sisterhood worked hard to raise money for them, and Mom says they've only gotten started. The next time you're home, I bet you'll see even more changes here, Mol."

"By this spring, my business will have really taken off," Cole added. "I've got a bunch of new rodeo contacts lined up, Cupid did his job and everything's looking good."

"Skylar and me are gonna compete in more horse shows after Christmas," Paisley said. "We want to win lots of ribbons."

Cam slipped one of his hands into Molly's. "You'll miss seeing us in the spring school play. I'm a villager. My teacher says that's someone who lives in a place even smaller than High Valley. Paisley and Skylar are stars in the sky, and they get to sing a song."

"That sounds great." Molly squeezed Cam's hand. "I'm sorry to miss it, but I'll see all of you in the Sunday school Christmas Eve pageant."

"We'll send Molly lots of pictures from the play and Carrie will video tape it," Bryce said with a quick look at Troy, who'd so far stayed silent.

Molly wasn't leaving until after the new year, but her family was already anticipating when she'd be gone. "And we can have video calls all the time." Except they weren't like being in the same place as people you loved. She manufactured a smile before Cam went ahead with his sister and Skylar. "Maybe you guys can visit me in Atlanta."

"Maybe." Bryce's smile was wistful. "It's a long trip, though, and with Carrie's rodeo schedule and the kids and the ranch, it's not easy to get away. Our honeymoon will be our biggest trip for quite a while."

They exited the arena into the parking lot, Molly said goodbye to her family, shivered and pulled her hat farther down over her ears. One thing she didn't miss about Montana was the winters.

"Are you cold?"

Molly nodded and tried to keep her teeth from chattering.

As they rounded the corner of the arena building, Troy held her close, his big body sheltering her from the worst of the blustery wind. "It was fun to see your family. Did you hear Paisley and Skylar telling me knock-knock jokes? Those girls are hilarious."

Molly hadn't because she'd been talking to her brothers and then Cam, but Troy was good with children, and they responded to his interest and attention. "Until I went to college, it used to bug me I couldn't go anywhere around here without bumping into someone I'm related to. Now I realize how lucky I am." She stopped by Troy's truck and looked at the clear, starlit sky.

"Are you making a wish?" Troy opened the truck door for her.

"I should. There's sure enough stars up there to wish on." Her pulse raced, and she had a new appreciation for this wonderful world and everything in it.

"Do you remember when we wished on a star?" His voice was low, and his warm breath brushed her cheeks.

Tongue-tied, she nodded and then clambered into the truck. As he closed her door and came around the vehicle to his side, memories flooded through her. That July night by the creek behind the ranch, they'd each wished on the brightest star they could find and then kissed and said they'd love each other forever.

"What did you wish for?" Troy started the truck to warm up the vehicle.

"I don't remember." She did, but she wouldn't tell him then or now.

"Well, I hope your wish came true." This part of the parking lot was mostly empty, and with the darkness outside, the truck's cab was like cocoon. "Mine didn't, at least not yet, but I can still hope."

At the warmth and yearning in his eyes, and gentle smile that had always turned her insides to mush, Molly's breath caught. Had he wished for what she had?

"Aww, Mol." He leaned close and his lips brushed hers in a kiss that was slow, sweet and soft. A reminder of their past and, if she still believed in wishes, maybe even a promise for the future.

She'd told her mom there was nothing to worry about, but as Molly returned Troy's kiss, she knew she'd been wrong. Spending time with Troy, and these achingly gentle but oh-so-meaningful kisses, didn't only risk Molly's heart but also her soul.

With each passing day, she was more torn between wanting to stay here and give her relationship with Troy a real chance or going back to Atlanta like she'd planned. And no amount of wishing on stars would give her the answer she needed.

"So that's downtown High Valley." On Wednesday, Troy stepped out of the Bluebunch Café with Pete and gestured to the town's wide main street.

"It's picturesque. I'd like to bring my family back in the summer, but I still don't understand how you can live here." Bundled up in a scarf, hat and too big parka he'd borrowed from Troy, only Pete's eyes and a narrow strip of his face showed.

"It's home." Those two simple words meant so much. No matter where Troy went in the world, this corner of Montana would always call him back.

"Where's that craft place you mentioned?" Pete looked toward the distant mountain range and then back to the windswept street. "I'd like to buy a few presents for Tina and the kids. Get a start on my holiday shopping."

"The Medicine Wheel Craft Center is just across the street, but when have you ever started holiday shopping before December 23?" Troy led them to Rosa's store.

"Since I married Tina, and she showed me the

benefits of thinking—and shopping—ahead."
On the other side of the street, Pete turned in a slow circle. "Wow. This town sure goes all out for the holidays." He gestured to what had to be a seven-foot-high candy cane hanging from one of the Victorian-style lampposts that lined both sides of High Valley Avenue.

"The town council likes to aim high. Halloween, Thanksgiving and Christmas are all a big deal here. It's a fun way of bringing people together. Tourists enjoy it as well. Or so I've heard," he added since Pete stared at him with raised eyebrows.

"I don't know what it is, bro, but something about you is different. You're more…" He paused as Troy opened the craft center door and they went inside into the warmth. "Chill maybe." Pete took of his gloves and rubbed his hands together. "Whatever it is, it suits you."

"Thanks, I think." Troy tried to joke but except for his family, Pete knew him better than anyone. While Troy didn't think he was different, maybe High Valley had changed him. "What do you want to look at first? I remember Tina likes pottery so there's a big display—"

"Troy?" Molly's voice stopped him.

"Hey. I'm… This is…" In dark jeans, trendy boots and a fuzzy white sweater patterned with cheerful reindeer, Molly was both cute and beautiful, and for a moment he was lost for words.

"You must be Troy's business partner. I'm Molly Carter. Troy invested in my brother's stock contracting operation." She held out a hand to Pete with a friendly smile.

"Yeah, I'm Pete Wong. Nice to meet you. Troy mentioned your brother. We're both diversifying our individual portfolios by investing in smaller businesses." After smiling back at Molly, Pete glanced at Troy and along with a knowing look, his dark brown eyes twinkled.

Troy knew that twinkle. It was the "there's something going on here you haven't told me about, but I'll find out later" expression. However, unlike in business, this time it was personal.

"Welcome to the Medicine Wheel Craft Center." Rosa appeared at Molly's side and introduced herself. "How can we help?"

*We?* Troy looked from Molly to Rosa.

Molly grinned. "I'm helping Rosa today because she's got some big holiday orders to finish, and her usual part-timer is sick." She turned the full beam of her gorgeous smile on Pete. "Troy said something about pottery. If you're interested, we have a range of items from mugs to larger serving bowls, all made locally."

As Pete followed Molly to the display, Rosa

224 A RANCHER'S RETURN

touched Troy's arm. "If Molly hadn't gone into nursing, she could have made a fortune in sales." She clamped her lips together briefly as if holding back a laugh. "I wanted to pay her for her time today, but she said she was happy to volunteer. She always was a kind girl. Can I show you anything? I've got some new silver and moonstone jewelry in. Molly admired a bear paw necklace earlier. Come, I'll show it to you."

"But…" Troy stuttered. He had to get control of himself. As Rosa led him over to the jewelry near the cash register, he tried to explain himself. "I'm not looking for a gift for Molly, but maybe for my sister or my mom for Christmas."

"Of course." Rosa opened the glass display case.

At the other side of the craft center, Molly had moved on from pottery to telling Pete about dream catchers and children's beading kits.

"Here's the necklace Molly likes." Rosa lowered her voice. "The blue matches her eyes, don't you think?"

It did, but Troy wasn't about to admit that to Rosa. A small blue stone sat in the center of a miniature silver bear paw, and while Rosa told him about the artist who'd made it, Troy's thoughts wandered. He'd never given jewelry to a woman he wasn't related to. But Molly wasn't just any woman. She was his friend, and this pendant would be a memory of going to the hockey game to see the Grizzly Bears play.

"I'll take it." He glanced over his shoulder to make sure Molly was out of earshot. "Could you wrap it for me as well?"

"Of course." Rosa leaned across the counter and her voice dropped to a whisper. "If you want it to be a surprise, I can set it aside for you to pick up later."

"That's great. I'd also like those green beaded earrings for my sister, and the white-and-blue bracelet for my mom." He pointed.

"I made those pieces myself. If the bracelet doesn't fit, tell your mom to bring it in the next time she's here and I'll alter it." Rosa tucked the earrings and bracelet beneath the counter with Molly's necklace. "It's like old times having Molly in town. She was a lovely girl and she's grown up to be a fine woman. I often wonder if she'd decide to settle here…if she met the right person."

"She seems happy in Atlanta." Troy spoke around what felt like a marble at the back of his throat.

"There are different kinds of happiness. What makes you happy at one point in your life might change. No, I can take your payment later." Rosa waved away Troy's credit card. "You came back here. Molly could do the same."

"I doubt it." He shook his head.

"But the two of you are good together."

Troy liked and respected Rosa. He might have told someone else it was none of their business, but Rosa was different. Along with Joy, she was like a town mom. "You shouldn't listen to gossip." He gave her a rueful smile.

"I don't." Rosa's voice was tart. "But I can't help seeing what's in front of me. You should do the same."

Pete trotted up to them, saving him from having to answer Rosa. Molly followed with one of the craft center's wicker shopping baskets piled high.

"Thanks to Molly, I've done most of my holiday shopping. They can also ship a box to me, so I don't have to carry a bunch of things on the plane." Pete beamed. "I even got a baby blanket for my cousin, and she's not due until February. Molly's amazing."

"She sure is." Troy made himself join in the easy banter. Molly *was* amazing, and the more time he spent with her, the more he knew that she was everything he wanted in a woman now and forever. However, he couldn't let himself fall in love with her again, and not only because she was leaving High Valley soon.

She'd broken his trust, and his heart, once. Now, despite all his good intentions, he was giving her a chance to do it again.

# CHAPTER FIFTEEN

"SINCE ZACH CAN'T be here, I appreciate you coming with me to this checkup." As they entered the lobby of the county hospital, Beth's face above her burgundy maternity parka was pale.

"I'm happy to be here." Waiting in front of the bank of elevators, Molly gave her sister-in-law's arm an encouraging squeeze. "It's nice to be in a hospital again."

"Nice isn't the word I'd use." Beth's voice was small. "I'd rather see my ob-gyn in her regular office. Being here reminds me of visiting Ellie's mom before she passed. She was so sick and I… Let's say hospitals aren't my favorite place."

"I understand and I'm sorry. I didn't think." Molly's voice softened in sympathy. She'd never want to hurt or upset Beth. They moved into an elevator, and Molly pressed one of the floor buttons. "All I meant is I miss nursing, and since I've spent a lot of time working in hospitals this one feels familiar." It had been built after she left for college, replacing an older hospital in town. Although smaller, it was as modern as those in Atlanta and, judging from the range of clinics listed on the main floor noticeboard, was a medical hub for the area. "Try to relax. You haven't had any unusual or concerning symptoms, have you?"

"To me, everything about pregnancy is unusual and concerning," Beth said as they left the elevator and walked toward the maternity assessment clinic where her doctor worked two days a week. "Maybe if I'd gotten pregnant for the first time in my twenties, it would be different but I'm in my late thirties. Whenever anyone describes me as at an 'advanced maternal age' I worry."

"I get that, but you're doing all the right things and you've had a normal pregnancy so far." Molly paused to give Beth a quick hug. "I also hear you have a great doctor, so you and the baby are in good hands. And Zach—"

"Is more worried than me. I'm the one trying to calm him down. He's upset about not being able to come with me today, but maybe it's for the best. Last time, he started talking about stages of calving and asked if it would be the same for me."

Molly laughed. "That's a ranch husband for you."

"I know and I wouldn't change him. He loves me and wants to help but sometimes…" Beth rolled her eyes and laughed too.

Beth checked in with the receptionist and was ushered into the exam area right away. Molly took a seat in the spacious and welcoming waiting room. The off-white walls and soft lighting were soothing, and combined with comfortable furniture in blues and greens, a basket of toys and a large fish tank, it appealed to her as both a nurse and a patient, if she were ever to…

She stopped herself. Although she wanted children, and thanks to testing knew she didn't carry the cystic fibrosis gene, she wouldn't be having them at this hospital. Besides, she was traditional and wanted to have a husband first.

A family came in—a heavily pregnant woman, a man and a toddler who ran around the room in circles with his arms outstretched like an airplane.

"Hang on, Thomas." The man chased after the boy and gave Molly an apologetic look. "He's full of energy."

"It's fine." Molly grinned and made airplane noises for the little guy.

"Hey, you look familiar." The man scooped Thomas up and studied Molly more closely.

"So do you." Her mind scrolled through various possibilities. "High Valley High School, maybe?" She introduced herself and gave her graduation year.

"That's it. I'm Cal Young. My wife was Kendra Jacobsen." He jerked his chin toward the pregnant woman at the desk. "We were five years ahead of you. Closer in age to your brother Bryce. That's why you look familiar. I came out to the Tall Grass a few times when Bryce tutored me in chemistry."

"Small world."

"That's Montana." Cal and Molly spoke together as Kendra joined them.

"What are you up to these days?" Cal sat beside Molly with Thomas on his lap while Kendra took a chair with a footrest across from them.

"I'm here with my sister-in-law, my brother Zach's wife." Best to get that detail in as soon as possible in case Cal and Kendra assumed *she* was pregnant. Even an innocent mention to someone else that they'd seen her here could take on a life of its own. "I'm home for an extended vacation. I'm a nurse in Atlanta."

"Small world, I'm a nurse here!" Cal said. "We both work at this hospital, in fact." He gave Kendra a fond look.

"I'm a physician assistant." Kendra beamed back at her husband. "We knew each other in high school but only started dating when we moved back here after college. Now neither of us can imagine living or working anywhere else."

As Molly passed the toy basket to Cal and Thomas, her heart twisted. It must be comforting to be so certain of yourself and your place in life.

Cal nodded agreement as he took out red, yellow and green blocks for Thomas to play with. "I worked in Los Angeles for a year and although I learned a lot, it was impersonal, you know? Here, I really get to know patients and their families. It's also a great place to raise kids."

"It sure is." Kendra rested a hand on her pregnant belly. "Between my family and Cal's, we have lots of willing babysitters."

"Too many, sometimes," Cal joked. "Still, it means we can have date nights."

"If you're interested, the hospital's hiring. I could put in a good word for you." Kendra studied Molly and, under her probing gaze, Molly's cheeks warmed. "Apart from the whole family and community thing, for me the best part about working here is that I feel needed. We're rural, and while I once thought that was a disadvantage, I like knowing I'm helping people who really need my skills."

"I'm not looking for another job right now, but thanks." Even as her stomach churned, Molly kept her voice light.

"Well, if you ever change your mind, give me a call. Here's my number." Kendra held out her phone and they exchanged details. "Before this place was built, you likely remember folks having to leave the area if they needed specialist treatment. My dad's fine now, but he had cancer two years ago. It meant the world to him, my mom and our family that he could be cared for here in a place that's familiar. If he'd had to go to Billings in the winter, he and Mom would have had to live there. Here, they both had family and friends for support." Kendra snagged her son as he darted toward the fish tank. "If you want to look at the fish, you need to ask Mommy or Daddy to go with you so we can lift you up."

"Molly?" The receptionist came from behind the desk. "Beth wants you to come in for a minute."

Molly got to her feet. "Great to see you guys. Good luck with everything." She grinned at Thomas.

"I'm going to be a big brother," he said. "I get to listen to the baby's heartbeat in Mommy's tummy."

"You'll be a super big brother." Molly knelt to Thomas's level. "When I was your age, I had four big brothers. They helped my mom and dad look after me." As far back as Molly could remember, Paul, Zach, Cole and Bryce had been there for her. Protectors, teachers, role models and her very own cheering section when she'd played sports or took part in activities at school or church. Zach, Cole and Bryce still looked out for her, even when she no longer needed them to.

"I like you." Thomas flung his arms around Molly and gave her an exuberant hug. "Can you come to my house?"

"Thanks for the invitation. Maybe another time, okay? I have to go see someone." Molly stood.

"Are you going to be a big sister?" As Cal picked up Thomas, the boy spoke over his dad's shoulder.

"No, an aunt. It's kind of like a big sister." Except, Molly would only see Beth and Zach's baby infrequently. Just like her other nieces and nephew. She'd be the faraway aunt who sent gifts for birthdays and Christmas but who, when she visited, would be almost a stranger.

As she waved goodbye to Thomas and followed the receptionist, Molly couldn't hold back a sigh. She couldn't be in two places at once, so she had to make the best of it.

"Hey, Beth. What's up?" Her sister-in-law lay on an exam table with an ultrasound technician on one side.

"I thought you'd like to see the baby. Zach and

I don't want to know whether it's a boy or girl, so if you spot anything don't tell me, okay?" She gestured to the screen.

"Wow." Molly leaned closer. Although she'd accompanied lots of pregnant women to sonograms, Beth was family, and that baby on the screen was her... Molly's throat tightened, and she reached for Beth's hand.

The sonographer, a middle-aged woman whose name badge said Lynn, smiled. "Mom and baby are doing fine."

"It's amazing, isn't it?" Beth's eyes shone.

"It sure is." Any new life was a miracle, but having a personal connection made it extra special. "Thanks for letting me come in. You, the baby..." With her free hand, Molly rubbed at her eyes.

Although she loved medical research, she missed working with patients. Yet, she'd been so focused on one path she hadn't let herself consider other options. Could she work somewhere else and develop her career in a different way? Ideas flooded through her like the spring melt from the mountains that filled the creeks and rivers here.

"I'll give you two a minute." Lynn stepped away.

"Sorry." Molly sniffed and grabbed a tissue from a nearby box.

"No need to apologize. From TV commercials with cute baby animals to when Kristi gave me a free chocolate chip cookie, I cry at almost everything these days. I can only imagine what I'll be like when I see our baby for the first time." Beth paused. "I wanted to ask you… I already talked to Zach and he's okay with it. Would you be with us for my labor and delivery? We'd both be more relaxed having you there."

"I'd be honored." Molly reached for Beth and hugged her. She could think about those new and surprising career ideas later. Right now, she wanted to soak in this special moment she was privileged to share.

"Before Zach and I got married, I didn't have a sister, but now with you I have the one I always wanted." Beth's voice was choked. "Thank you."

"I should be the one thanking you." Molly's voice cracked. "I never had a sister either but now I do."

Out of all the moments in Molly's life so far, this one was among the happiest. And she'd keep it in her heart to treasure forever.

"Take care of yourself, bro." As Pete finished packing his computer bag in the Bitterroot ranch house's living room later the same day, he patted Troy's shoulder.

"You as well." Troy returned the gesture. "Say hi to Tina and the kids for me."

"Sure. The kids will love the board game you bought them. We'll play it as a family over the holidays." Pete stuffed a charge cord into the top of the bag.

"Send me some pictures."

Pete seemed like he wanted to say something else, but busied himself with his bag. Except for when they'd gone into town for lunch at the Bluebunch and shopping at the craft center, Troy and Pete had spent their time together working. However, after bumping into Molly, Troy hadn't missed his friend's barely suppressed curiosity and sideways looks. "Okay, spit it out. I know you want to."

"What?" Pete knelt to put the board game into his overnight bag.

"You know exactly what." Troy sat on the edge of his new sofa still covered in plastic since being delivered two days before.

"Okay." Pete drew out the word. "I figured it was your business."

"It is, but you're my oldest friend." And Troy needed somebody to talk to who wasn't from High Valley and could be objective. "What do you think?"

"About Molly?"

"No, the cattle out there in the pasture. Of course Molly."

"She seems great." Pete took his luggage into the hall, grabbed his jacket from the hook by the front door and slipped into his boots. "She's smart, kind and beautiful. The whole deal."

"But?" Troy followed his friend and shrugged into his own coat and boots. "There's a 'but' there."

"Maybe." Pete opened the front door and cold air rushed in. "She lives in Atlanta for a start. Fantastic city but you haven't mentioned moving there."

No, but what if he did? Troy could rent out the ranch or use it as a vacation property. Let Cathy and her boys live here. Her house in town was too small for the three of them. Or he could offer her the bungalow if his folks didn't want it. He stepped onto the porch and inhaled a lungful of fresh, crisp winter air.

"As long as there's an internet connection, I can work from anywhere." His gaze took in the gracious two-story white clapboard ranch house with its wraparound porch, surrounded by snow-covered fields that stretched into a blue haze. *His* house. *His* fields. And *his* cattle grazing in them. Land he didn't work himself right now but planned to one day and pass it on to children, grandchildren and great-grandchildren. A legacy like the Carter family had. Which took him back to Molly, the only Carter who'd made a life somewhere else.

"But do you want to work anywhere?" Pete gestured to the ranch. "That only makes sense if you like the place you're working from. You haven't lived here long, but the Bitterroot is home, right?"

"Yeah." Troy wanted to grow old here with a family around him. He followed Pete down the porch steps to his friend's rental car parked in front of Cathy's vehicle.

"Back in college, you mentioned a girl from Montana a few times. It sounded like she was important to you. Was that Molly?" Pete put his bags in the trunk of the car.

"It was." Troy wanted to leave that history behind, but it kept rearing up to intrude into the present. "We dated when Molly was eighteen and I was twenty. But we're adults now, and we've both changed."

"I'm also guessing she dumped you back then which is why you never said much about her to me." Pete snorted like Troy's dad did when he thought one of his kids had done something unwise.

"Yes, but—"

"When it comes down to it, you're still the same guy I met in college. Hardworking, devoted to your family, supersmart and loyal. And if somebody breaks your trust, you might give them another chance but I'm not certain you ever fully forgive them."

"Of course I do." Unease itched at Troy like a mosquito bite in summer. Was Pete right?

"What about when Dean shared that idea of yours with a competitor? Did you forgive him?" Pete shut the trunk and turned back to Troy.

"Professional misconduct's different, but I didn't fire him." Still, had he truly accepted his employee had made an honest mistake?

"No, but you watched over him so closely Dean left anyway." Pete shook his head. "All I'm saying is whatever went down between you and Molly, you need to be sure you're being honest with each other."

Troy *had* been honest with her, but had she been honest with him? He scooped up a handful of snow and made a snowball. With the temperature around freezing, it was perfect snowball-making weather. "How do you and Tina make it work? It takes a special kind of woman to be with guys like us."

"You mean a guy like you." Pete scooped up some snow as well. "Thanks to Tina, I have a life beyond work."

"So do I." Troy had spent more time with Molly recently and less on work. They were behind on a couple of projects and a new business pitch was also delayed, but those things would likely have happened anyway.

Pete tossed the snowball in Troy's direction. "Go with the flow for a change. As for Molly, I like her but make sure she likes you for you. With Tina, I know she does because we met in college. Back then, a fancy date was takeout food and a picnic blanket under the stars. Actually, that's still a great date."

Troy had simple tastes, and from what he'd seen Molly still did too, but how could he be sure? "Hey." Snow cascaded over him.

He threw his snowball at Pete, who returned another snow volley, the two of them pelting each other like kids.

"Hang on." Pete roared with laughter. "Do you remember the snowball fight—"

"That work term we spent in Boston. I sure do." Troy gathered more snow as a truck rumbled up the lane. Probably the fuel delivery he expected. "Do you give up?"

"No way." Pete stopped laughing and lobbed another snowball as Troy darted behind Cathy's car.

"Missed me." Crouched by the vehicle, Troy took aim at Pete as several cows in the nearby pasture came closer to investigate.

"Uh, Troy?" Pete's voice was muffled.

"What?" He sent another snowball over and this time, instead of Pete's deeper voice, there was a feminine shriek followed by a dog barking.

He scrambled to his feet and put a gloved hand to his mouth as heat rushed to his face. "I'm so sorry. Molly...are you okay?"

She stood beside Pete and brushed snow off her hat and coat as Cole's dog, Blue, let out a cacophony of howls from a Tall Grass ranch pickup.

"I'm fine." Her eyes narrowed. "But it's two against one, Clayton, and as a pitcher, I led the High Valley senior girls' softball team to the divisional championships two years in a row."

"I... You..." Pete glanced between them. "I have to get to the airport."

"Stand back. This won't take long." Molly's gaze didn't waver as she shaped snow into a ball and launched it toward Troy.

He ducked but the snowball still hit him face on. He sputtered and then laughed as a cow mooed and a ranch hand came out of the barn to see what was going on.

"Truce?" Molly joined Troy and brushed wet snow off his face with one end of her scarf.

"Yeah." At the tenderness in her eyes, his laughter stopped. And as they stared at each other, it was as if the past had been wiped out, like fresh snow had covered the muddy pasture and made everything new again.

He was as vulnerable as he'd ever been with anyone, and in that instant, Troy knew he'd truly forgiven her. The past was the past, and all he wanted was to think about the future—with her.

# CHAPTER SIXTEEN

"I LOVE YOU, Daisy-May." Molly patted the Appaloosa's neck. As they came over a rise and into open pastureland alongside the highway, she urged the horse into a trot. Two days after she'd dropped by the Bitterroot to deliver paperwork for Cole and ended up in a snowball fight with Troy, warmer weather and wind had cleared the snow away and today winter seemed like a distant memory.

The breeze whistled past Molly's ears beneath her riding helmet, and she urged Daisy-May to go faster. "Atta girl." She laughed, at one with the horse and the big landscape like she'd been that day with Troy and Cara. Here, though, she was on a familiar horse and riding across land she'd known from birth. Land that was part of her family's heritage, and she hoped would continue to be worked by Carters and their descendants beyond her own lifetime.

"Do you want to slow down? I keep forgetting

you're a senior lady now." Daisy-May had been born at the ranch, back when Molly's whole world had been her family and this place.

Daisy-May tossed her head and kept up the pace as if she, like Molly, relished the rare chance to run free.

"Okay, let's go." Before she gave the horse her head, she waved at a van passing on the highway, the logo on the side panel telling her it belonged to the Bluebunch Café. If Kristi wasn't driving, it would be one of her staff, all of whom Molly had gotten to know. In some ways, she'd slipped back into life here as if she'd never been away, but she'd also met new people who could become friends.

"Easy, girl." As they approached hillier, more uneven ground, she slowed Daisy-May to a trot, then a walk and to a stop while she checked her phone. There was a text from Hannah rescheduling that monthly dinner with high school friends, and another from Brooke, William's mom, organizing a time to visit the ranch and asking if Molly would like to meet up for coffee sometime.

As she typed quick replies, horse's hooves thundered, and a bay horse appeared at the top of another rise.

Molly shaded her eyes against the sun to take a closer look. Was it Cara? The rider waved, and Molly waved back. In town and out here, she greeted people she might not know personally but who would undoubtedly have people in common with her. Montana was largely rural and dotted with tight-knit towns like High Valley, so friendliness was a way of life. While as a woman riding by herself she'd stayed near the road and within cell phone coverage, she'd never had a reason to be afraid anywhere.

Horse and rider galloped toward her as several more vehicles passed on the highway, and Molly waved again, this time at Shane who, given the direction he was heading, was undoubtedly on his way to Squirrel Tail. It hadn't taken long for her to be immersed in her neighbors' lives again. However, that interest in other people, which at first she'd tried to dismiss as nosiness, was genuine caring and concern.

"Hey, Molly." Troy drew Cara to a stop beside her.

"Hey." Since that snowball fight, something had changed between them, and as they'd said goodbye to Pete, for a moment it had felt as if she and Troy were a couple. Had he sensed that new closeness too? "You decided to buy Cara, then?"

"Yep. Picked her up from the rescue yesterday."

As Troy rubbed Cara's ears, Molly's stomach flipped. Beneath his gloves, his hands were strong but gentle and when he held her close, she… *Stop it.* She mentally berated herself. "How's she settling in?"

"Making herself at home like she's always been at the Bitterroot." He shook his head and he put a hand to his chest. "I give her a week until she's ruling the roost, or should I say the barn."

"Only if you let her. Remind her who's the boss. You don't want a diva," she teased him, and gathered up Daisy-May's reins.

"You're right." Troy's smile was wide as he patted Cara. "I've had enough divas in my life. I don't need another one, even if she's a horse."

Past girlfriends? Troy had never talked about any of his other relationships and neither had Molly, but maybe it was time. "A guy I dated for a about a month last year was sure a diva. Everything was a big drama, and he always had to be the center of attention no matter what."

"So why did you go out with him?" Without needing to exchange any words, they walked Cara and Daisy-May side by side, as comfortable together as if their years apart didn't matter.

"A friend at work set us up. Joel seemed fun at first." And she'd been dazzled by his good looks, fancy car and what had seemed to her to be his urban sophistication. "It wasn't serious, and when I found out what he was really like I ended it."

"Did he take it badly?" There was an edge to Troy's voice that might have been jealousy.

"No, I think he was relieved." She chuckled. "We had completely different ideas about family, money, food preferences, pretty much everything. He also said horses smelled, although he'd never been closer to one than watching a parade."

"Big mistake." Troy's laughter rang out. Then his tone became more careful. "Have you dated a lot?"

"No and only one guy seriously. I went out with him my junior year of college. We're still friends but it didn't work out. I guess I haven't met the right guy." Maybe because nobody could ever match Molly's memories of Troy. "What about you?" She studied the distant mountain range as if absorbed in the scenery.

"Like you, I've dated, but the relationships never seemed right. I'm still friends with one of them. She's married now." Troy also gazed into the distance. "Along with my mom, Pete and his wife used to try to set me up with women, but I asked them to stop. Work keeps me busy, and maybe I'm one of those lone wolves who's better on his own." He shrugged, but his stiff posture atop Cara and the tightness in his jaw belied his attempt at casual indifference.

Molly opened and closed her mouth as she struggled to find the right words. "I always pictured you with a family. From what I remember from a school project about wolves, most of them live in packs." The careful crayon drawing she'd made of a mom, dad and several wolf pups popped into her mind.

"You don't always get what you want, do you?" A cloud drifted across the sun, shadowing Troy's face.

"No, but you could still have a family." She could have one as well, and if she applied for a job at the county hospital or another local health clinic, maybe that family could even be with Troy. Her heart thudded. They could start over, and if they were honest about what was going on between them, they could have another chance.

As Troy turned Cara around, the sun came out again and bathed him in light. "I should get going but…" He hesitated and then drew the horse closer to Molly and Daisy-May. "I'm going to Calgary for two days later this week. There's a livestock auction there I want to check out. I'll keep my eyes open for any cattle Cole might be interested in."

"Great, yes." Molly blinked at the change of subject. "Have a good trip."

"Thanks. When I'm back, the town's holiday parade sounds like it could be fun. If you don't have any other plans, I wondered if you'd like to go with me?"

"Sure. It would be fun. That parade has always been a big event. The ranch usually has a float, but not this year because of the weddings."

"Great." Troy's smile lit up his face.

"It's a date then." Molly's high voice didn't sound like hers.

Daisy-May pawed the ground and nickered, and Cara joined in.

"I think our horses are saying I need to kiss you."

"Yes." Molly leaned toward him, and as his lips met hers, a soul-deep rightness washed over and through her.

She wanted to stay here and be close to her family and old friends. And most of all, to be near this man who completed her in ways she hadn't known she needed—and the only guy she'd ever been truly serious about.

And one day soon, she'd find the courage to swallow her pride and admit to her family she wanted to change her life.

OVER BREAKFAST IN the hotel's restaurant in downtown Calgary, Troy glanced from the snow-covered street back to his phone to check his email. There were two messages from Pete, several from customers, a couple from Cole and one from Molly.

Ignoring the others, he opened Molly's first. While he hadn't admitted it to himself until afterward, he'd ridden in the direction of the Tall Grass Ranch the other day in case Molly might be out riding at the same time. And when he'd spotted her, his heart had filled with something that felt a whole lot like love.

He chuckled at the joke she'd sent him and typed a quick reply telling her about the livestock auction and heifers he'd bought. While he could have bid over the phone, he'd wanted to see the animals in person and talk to some of the stock contractors.

What about having dinner at Ruby's Place after the parade?

He added to his text. He'd give her the bear paw pendant then and think of something else for a Christmas gift. Maybe one of those hot chocolate gift boxes Kristi had at the café, along with a candle in one of the pottery holders she'd helped Pete choose for Tina.

"Troy?"

He looked up from his phone. "Cassidy?" He stood out of courtesy and before he realized what she intended, she'd pulled him into an embrace and kissed him on both cheeks.

"I thought it was you." Without waiting for an invitation, she sat across from him. "It's been years. What are you doing here?"

Under the guise of checking for toast crumbs, Troy used a napkin to brush at his face and remove any lipstick marks she might have left behind. It was only eight in the morning, but she was immaculately put together in a tailored charcoal business suit and cream blouse, subtle eye makeup and red lipstick, her dark hair pulled into a sleek bun.

"I'm here on business, heading home today. How about you?"

He'd gone out with Cassidy several times soon after he finished college and moved to California. He remembered her as smart, ambitious and pretty. He also remembered that over dinner at a cute and cozy diner he'd hoped she'd like as much as he did, she'd said he wasn't her type.

"It's too bad you won't be in Calgary longer." She waved down a server. "A coffee, and get me whatever your fruit bowl special is. And make it quick." Her eyes narrowed, and she pursed her lips.

Troy blinked. If one of his employees had spoken to anyone like Cassidy had done, Troy would have had a word with them. In life, as well as business, he didn't have time for rude people.

"Thanks." He gave the server a sympathetic smile as the teenager filled Cassidy's mug and then topped up Troy's coffee.

"I heard you're doing well." The server forgotten, Cassidy gave Troy a sunny smile and reached for his hand.

He drew away to pick up his cutlery. Although the food was good, breakfast was all of a sudden a lot less appealing. "I'm getting by."

"Don't be so modest. That's not what Darius says." That was odd. Darius was the friend of a friend who'd introduced them, and Troy was no longer in touch with him. "I also read that article about you." She mentioned a business magazine that had featured Troy and Pete on the cover about a year ago. Cassidy eyed him over the rim of her coffee cup. Had her brown eyes always been so cold? "How did they describe you? An entrepreneur who makes money and an impact, wasn't it? And those photos." She leaned across the table toward him, and Troy leaned back. "You should wear a suit more often, but there's also something about a cowboy." Her gaze dropped to his checked Western shirt.

"I want to give back. Lots of people are the same."

Troy focused on his omelet. He still felt uncomfortable whenever he thought of that article and the photoshoot. The magazine had sent a big city stylist to work with him and Pete, and while the guy on the cover might look like him, it was in no way the "real" him. It was only after the shoot was over and he'd gotten out of the borrowed designer suit and shoes that he truly felt like himself again.

"What are you up to these days?" He could make polite conversation for a few more minutes.

"I'm still in technical sales." Several heavy bracelets clanked against her coffee cup as Cassidy set it on the table. "I'm here on business. My company has a couple of clients in Calgary. Can't you stay longer? We could—"

"No, I can't." Troy picked at his savory home fries without tasting them. Just then, the server returned with Cassidy's order.

"I said a fruit bowl. I didn't mean with yogurt," she barked at the server, whose face reddened to his ears.

"Don't worry about it. I'll take that fruit and yogurt in a container to go. I can have it later. I planned to grab some from the buffet anyway on my way out." He tried to reassure the poor kid. He'd leave him an excellent tip and speak to the restaurant manager before leaving the hotel. Cassidy was the problem, not the server.

She reached for his hand again, but Troy kept a firm grip on his cutlery. "Why did you decide to bury yourself in rural Montana?"

"How do you know I live in Montana?" When he'd been interviewed for that article, he still lived in San Francisco. He'd never told the journalist he was looking at Montana ranches either. Bumping into Cassidy here was undoubtedly a coincidence, but had she kept tabs on him all these years? His muscles quivered, and he pushed the remaining food around his plate.

"I don't remember." She made a vague gesture and avoided his gaze.

"Oh, really?" Troy kept his private life private and his friend group small. He raised his eyebrows.

"Someone must have mentioned it to me." Her laugh tinkled. "How much land do you have?" Her brown eyes glittered, and this time there was no mistake. She wasn't interested in him. She was only interested in his money. "I imagine you're redoing your house. If you need an interior decorator, I could hire someone for you and oversee their work."

"I have enough land to keep me busy. As for the house, it's a work in progress, but I've already hired someone." Cathy wasn't an interior decorator, but she was handy with a paintbrush and that was all he needed right now.

The server reappeared and slid Cassidy's replacement fruit bowl in front of her like a rabbit trying to avoid a fox. Then he handed a takeout container to Troy for the fruit and yogurt bowl. Troy took it as his cue to leave. "I need to check out and—"

She made a moue with her lips. "But you haven't finished your meal." She pointed to his plate.

He ate the last of his home fries and drained his coffee mug. "There, done." He tried not to grimace.

"I'm still in San Francisco. The next time you're in town we'll have to get together. There's a wonderful new restaurant near Fisherman's Wharf. The chef's from France and is getting lots of publicity for his unusual food combinations and dramatic presentation. You could take me there." She toyed with a piece of melon and gazed at him from under her eyelashes.

Troy cleared his throat. "I'm not into fancy restaurants, remember? Good, home-style food is more my style." Like Kristi served at the Bluebunch. Although Kristi's fiancé, Alex, the chef at Ruby's Place, had also worked in France, he relied on simplicity instead of drama or the unusual to create a special meal.

"You're missing out." Cassidy flicked her gaze upward and let out a heavy sigh. Some men would likely find her appealing, but to him she seemed both manipulative and deceitful.

*Unlike Molly.* Her windblown hair and rosy cheeks flashed into his mind, along with the memory of kissing her. And when she hugged him, it felt right, honest and good. Everything the embrace Cassidy had forced on him didn't.

"I seem to remember you saying I wasn't your type." He couldn't keep amusement out of his voice.

"We didn't really have a chance to get to know each other." When her smug smile appeared, he knew their conversation was well and truly over.

"As I also remember, that was because of you, not me." Troy got to his feet and picked up the take-out container. Breakfast was included with his room, so he didn't have to wait for the check, and the food Cassidy had rejected was included in the buffet that was free for all guests. "Enjoy your stay. Take care." He wouldn't lie and say it was great to see her again or offer any other meaningless platitude.

"But…" Her mouth gaped open, and if she'd been one of his cows, she'd have bellowed in anger.

Troy grinned and held back a laugh as he

made his way to the front of the restaurant to find the server and then the restaurant manager.

Cassidy might have fooled him once, but he wouldn't be taken in by someone like her again.

He wondered what he'd ever seen in her, although he supposed that back then she'd seemed friendly and sincere. Ambitious, sure, but there was nothing wrong with being career-oriented. He'd liked that she had goals and was driven like him.

But had she dropped him because he wasn't successful enough for her? As he stopped at the end of the line for the host stand, the aftertaste of the excellent coffee was acrid in his mouth. Had Cassidy changed or had his judgment been flawed?

Deep down, in a place he usually kept hidden even from himself, he was still the kid whose family had lost their ranch and had to depend on the food bank. And an adult who, despite his outward success, still carried the self-doubt he'd had as a kid.

The first time, he'd rushed into a relationship with Molly. They both had, and when they were together, anything had seemed possible. It still did. Molly wasn't anything like Cassidy, but how could he be certain she truly liked him—all of him—and not only the man he'd let her see?

# CHAPTER SEVENTEEN

SLEIGH BELLS JINGLED, and Molly waved at her mom and Shane where they perched atop the light wagon that was usually stored in one of the Tall Grass Ranch barns. She stood on tiptoe to speak into Troy's ear, so he'd hear her over the excited crowd. "They weren't going to enter a float this year, but the kids were so disappointed not to be in the holiday parade, Zach and Cole put something together at the last minute. Isn't it a fun surprise? Both horses are so calm and don't get distracted. They've taken part in lots of town events."

Pulled by Daisy-May and Zach's horse, Scout, the vintage wagon had wheels decorated with white lights, while the bed featured red-and-white fabric candy canes, an inflatable snowman and a green plywood Christmas tree. Paisley, Cam and Skylar each kept hold of one of the family dogs, kids and canines both wearing Santa hats. With the softly falling snow, it was simple but magical, like a holiday card come to life.

Troy nodded, but his smile didn't reach his eyes. He'd been distant when she'd picked him up at the Bitterroot to come to the parade, but he was likely tired from his trip.

"Daisy-May's well trained and she's still fit enough to pull that wagon, especially with another horse helping. It's special for me to see her do it. My mom made those candy canes and the tree years ago." Molly gave the kids a thumbs-up. "The red fabric came from a dress I had in second grade. I remember Zach helping her to make the tree, and we all painted it with some of Paul's leftover paint."

"My mom does stuff like that." This time, Troy's smile was warmer and more natural.

Molly let out a relieved breath as the next float, decorated like a gingerbread house, came into view. "Oh, wow. That's amazing, isn't it?" She nudged Troy's elbow and pointed. "The O'Reillys own a construction company. If you're looking for someone to work on your place, you should call them."

"Is there something wrong with my house?" Troy's voice had an unexpected sharp edge.

"I haven't been inside so how would I know?" Molly stared at him trying to work out what was wrong. Troy would invite her to see his place when he was ready. He'd mentioned Cathy was doing some painting. Maybe he wanted everything to be finished before he had visitors apart from his family and Pete. "All I meant is houses often need things done to them and you work hard. You might not have time to take care of certain things yourself." She hesitated but Troy looked at the float, not her. "Like if there's a storm and you need to have shingles replaced, or you want to put in a new bathroom or kitchen. The O'Reillys are working on my mom and Shane's new house."

Troy's tense expression eased. "My mom did say the kitchen needed an upgrade. Sorry, I have a lot on my mind." He squeezed her mittened hand. "As for seeing my house, I want to give you a tour, but it's been a mess and I still have stuff everywhere." He bit his lip. "I want it to look nice for you."

"It's fine." But was it? If they were in a real relationship, wouldn't he talk to her about what was on his mind? Even if she couldn't help, she could listen. And why would he think she'd care about the state of his house? He'd only moved in recently, so it wasn't surprising he was still settling in. "Why don't I get us some hot chocolate and a bag of Kristi's mini sugar cookies?" She gestured to the pop-up food stand down the block from them at the Bluebunch Café. "That wind feels like it's coming from the North Pole, and the snow's getting heavier—"

"Molly?" Zach tugged at her parka sleeve. "Come quick. It's Beth. She…she can't be having the baby now, right? But she says she might be, and Ellie's calling an ambulance, and I don't know what to do." He rubbed his face and his voice shook.

"Beth's not due for two weeks yet but let me take a look." She turned to Troy. "Take my keys and get the first-aid kit from my trunk."

"Sure." Troy took the keys and left at a jog as Molly and Zach ran along the block to the corner near Rosa's craft center.

"Hey, Beth." Molly sat beside her sister-in-law who huddled on the curb and clutched her belly. "What's going on?"

"I don't know." Beth's face was pale, and her eyes were wide and frightened. "I'm having these pains, and the ambulance can't…" She jerked her chin at Ellie and then doubled over, letting out a low moan.

"There's construction so the bridge is out between here and the county hospital and ambulance service." Ellie's voice was steady, but her lips trembled as she glanced at Beth. "The dispatcher said they'll go around the other way, but it will take longer and with the snow…" She gulped.

"Why don't you come with us, Ellie?" Nina and Werner appeared out of the crowd. "We'll get you a snack while Molly talks to Beth."

"Good idea." From what Molly had seen so far, Beth indeed looked like she was in real labor. "Let's get you indoors and warmed up. The craft center's open." She got Beth to her feet. "Zach?"

"Is she… It'll be fine, Beth. Hang on until the ambulance gets here." Zach took his wife's other arm and between the two of them they guided Beth into the building.

"Hang on?" Beth's voice came out in a shriek, and she doubled over again.

"Sorry, I didn't mean…" Zach's gaze met Molly's over Beth's head. "Should I boil water or something?"

"Boil water?" Beth gritted her teeth. "I'm supposed to be in a nice, clean hospital where everything's already sterilized. My hospital bag's at home, and I can't…" She moaned and leaned against Molly.

"People boil water in movies." Zach's face was ashen, the tendons in his neck stood out and his usually measured voice was shrill. "Should I get Mom?"

"Yeah." Molly rubbed Beth's back. "Let's go into Rosa's workroom, honey. It's more private and I need to examine you." Her always stoic and calm and controlled big brother was an incoherent and panicky mess, but right now Zach was the least of her worries.

"Yes, and go get your mom." Beth waved in her husband's general direction. "Oh." Her voice echoed in a long-drawn out wail. "My water hasn't even broken."

"That doesn't necessarily mean anything." Molly glanced at Rosa, who'd followed them in. "Do you have any old sheets and something Beth could lie on?"

"In my studio office. I'll find clean towels as well." Rosa patted Beth's arm. "We're here for you. Between the two of us, Joy and I have had ten kids of our own, and Molly's a great nurse who's delivered lots of babies."

As Beth gasped for breath, she tried to give them a shaky smile.

Molly didn't consider several rotations on a maternity ward as delivering lots of babies, especially because she'd always assisted an experienced ob-gyn, but she'd do the best she could. Beth and the baby were depending on her. As Rosa returned with sheets, towels and a yoga mat, Molly helped Beth lie down and lowered her voice. "Is there anyone on call at the town's medical clinic?"

"No, we rely on the county hospital for after-hours care." Rosa glanced at Beth and then back at Molly with a worried frown. "The only doctor I can think of who lives nearby is on the other side of that bridge."

"I'm sure the ambulance will be here soon." Molly spoke in her normal voice as Beth gripped her hand tight. She wasn't actually sure of anything except that it looked like she'd be on her own with Rosa and Joy. Melissa was at a conference this weekend, and Carrie, who'd taken an advanced first-aid course, was on her honeymoon with Bryce.

Between them, Molly and Rosa got Beth out of her parka, boots and maternity jeans.

Rosa grabbed a blanket from the workroom table, a multicolored pictorial tree design, and covered Beth.

"That's beautiful and things might get, you know, messy." Again, Molly spoke in an undertone.

"It doesn't matter." Rosa tucked the blanket around Beth. "If ever one of my 'Tree of Life' designs was appropriate, it's now."

"Give me a minute to wash my hands, and then I'll examine you. I know it's hard but try to relax." Molly had to think of Beth as any other patient. If she let this situation feel personal, she'd be in the same state as Zach.

After using the sink in the corner of the workroom, she did a quick exam and then scooted up to crouch by Beth's face. "You're definitely in labor. Even if the bridge wasn't out, I doubt you'd make it to the hospital. You're going to have your baby here. Everything will be fine." She made her voice sound strong and confident. "It's fast, but everything's progressing normally."

There was a rustle at the workroom door and Zach poked his head inside. "I'm back with Mom and your first-aid kit. Troy's outside if you need anything else. He put the Closed sign on the craft center door."

"Come in." From the yoga mat Rosa and Molly had covered with sheets, Beth gave Zach a pained smile. "This baby obviously has a mind of its own. Not surprising, given what the two of us are like. I didn't plan on this kind of birth, but I guess I don't have a choice."

She didn't, and if Molly's instincts were right, this baby was coming within the next half hour, maybe sooner. "Zach, sit by Beth's head, hold her hand and coach her with her breathing like you practiced in your class. Rosa, I need you to time Beth's contractions. Use my phone." Molly unlocked it and passed it to her. "Beth, is it okay with you if Mom helps me?"

"Of course." Beth's initial terror had passed, and now her face held both determination and bravery. "Is Ellie staying with Nina and Werner? I need to—"

"You don't need to do anything except focus on yourself and the baby." Although Zach's face was still gray, he now seemed, if not calmer, at least like he'd gotten himself and his emotions more under control. "Cole took Ellie and the other kids back to the ranch with him. I just spoke to Ellie. She's worried for you but she's safe."

"Good." Beth panted and sweat trickled down her face.

"Tell me what you need." Her mom's voice shook but she straightened her shoulders, took off her winter coat and rolled up her sleeves. As Molly rummaged in the first-aid kit for surgical gloves and other supplies, her mom leaned closer and to Molly alone whispered, "You've got this, Jellybean."

Molly gave her mom a wobbly smile. She and the others were here for her, Beth and this newest Carter baby.

Beth screamed as another contraction hit, and Molly focused on what she had to do. Nothing had ever been more important.

"IT'S BEEN HOURS. What's taking so long?" Outside the craft center, Troy paced. The holiday parade had ended, and somehow the news had made its way around town that Beth was in labor. A small group had now gathered on High Valley Avenue.

"It's only been about twenty minutes." Nina patted Troy's back. "With my first baby, I was in labor for almost a day."

Troy shuddered. He wasn't the baby's dad, and he was barely keeping himself together. How had his parents gone through this experience twice? From outside the closed workroom door, where he lingered in case anything else was needed, he heard Beth's anguished cries. He also heard Molly's calm expertise in what, although he had no medical knowledge, was clearly a crisis situation.

"Why don't you come over to the Bluebunch with us, son?" Werner's voice was fatherly. "Kristi's opened the café so we can wait in the warmth and have a hot drink and something to eat. All today's baking is gone, but she's got a pot of chicken soup on the stove, and Alex brought leftover chili from Ruby's Place."

Troy shook his head. "You two go on." Nina and Werner held hands, and Nina looked almost girlish while Werner had a protective, loving air that was new. "I'm fine."

He wanted to stick around for the Carter family like they'd been there for him that summer when he'd been desperate for a job. He wanted to be there for Molly. Not that he could do anything practical, but he wanted to be here, as close to her as possible and not across the street in the café.

"Call or text us as soon as you hear any news." Nina hugged him before she, Werner and several others headed to the café. Both that building, and the other side of the town's wide main street were almost obscured by snow which now, fueled by a gusty wind, fell like a thick, white curtain.

Troy stamped his booted feet to get the circulation going again and shook snow off his parka hood. He wasn't used to standing around doing nothing. "Come on." He gestured to the few who remained, including a guy he recognized. "Mike, right? Hannah's husband? We met at the tree lighting."

"Yeah." Mike nodded and drew closer. "My dad owns the hardware store. If the ambulance has trouble getting through, Dad has snow chains and other stuff so we're sticking around in case we're needed." He introduced his friends. "We all played football together back in the day so we can offer muscle."

"If your dad has extra shovels, we can start clearing a path." The snow was so heavy that any path might have drifted in as soon as they'd cleared it, but Troy had to do something.

"Good idea. Dad's gone on his snowmobile to pick up a bag of baby and hospital things Hannah's putting together for Beth, but I've got a key."

At Mike's friendly smile, some of Troy's tension eased. When the two of them went into the hardware store to find and distribute snow shovels to the impromptu work crew, he reminded himself that unlike Cassidy, people here *were* genuine. As soon as the words were out of his mouth, he'd regretted speaking so sharply to Molly earlier when she mentioned making repairs to his house. He'd apologize to her as soon as he could, but right now he'd support her in the only way he could think of.

"Ready, guys?" He held up a shiny aluminum shovel before scooping it full of snow. "I'm guessing the ambulance will need to park here." He indicated a partially drifted space in front of the craft center.

"Ready." Mike and the guys were in a football huddle, and he gestured to Troy to join them.

Although he'd never played football, as part of that huddle Troy had a new sense of belonging, not only in himself but High Valley. These people didn't care about how much money he had. He was just one of the guys lending a hand to support a friend and neighbor in need.

And as he cleared wet snow and bantered with the other men, and Kristi, Nina and a few others came from the café with takeout cups of soup, hot cocoa and coffee, a sense of warmth enveloped Troy. It didn't only come from the hearty nourishment and backbreaking physical work but also from his heart, soul and this place.

"Anybody else hear that?" Half an hour later, Mike raised a hand, and an ambulance siren wailed in the distance.

A cheer went up, and Troy and the others leaned on their shovels, watching as a plow mounted on the front of a pickup truck cleared the western length of High Valley Avenue for the ambulance to follow.

"Good job." Mike exchanged a high five with Troy. "You'll have to join us for burgers on our next guys' night out. I owe you a beer."

"Sounds like a plan, but we all need a beer." Troy texted Werner and stood with the others as the ambulance pulled up and parked, and two paramedics got out and went inside the craft center carrying a stretcher.

Less than a minute later, Mike's dad arrived on a snowmobile with a small suitcase strapped to the back.

"I keep thinking about Beth and Zach." Mike wiped his ice-encrusted brow with a gloved hand. "I can only imagine what they're going through. It was hard enough for us when Hannah had our first and that was in the hospital."

"Yeah." Clearing snow had momentarily distracted Troy, but now worry flooded back. "Look. Is that Zach?" He peered through the window.

"He's with Rosa and Joy." Mike joined Troy at the window. The crowd around them grew as people in the café, including Nina and Werner, returned to wait outside. "The paramedics must be taking over. No, here one of them comes."

Although Troy now had his nose flattened against the window, he couldn't see Molly, Beth or a baby. But Zach wouldn't be standing there talking to Rosa and Joy if things weren't okay.

The crowd fell silent as one of the paramedics returned. "Clear a space, folks. We're bringing mom and baby out. They're both doing fine, but we're taking them to the hospital to be checked there."

"A baby." The words echoed around the snowy street as everyone moved back, and the paramedic went back inside, this time carrying the suitcase from Mike's dad.

Troy's legs went weak with relief, and he gripped the handle of his snow shovel to stay upright.

"Beth did amazing, and our baby's a girl." Zach stepped out of the craft center and spoke to the crowd. "As for my sister? I don't know how to tell you everything Molly did for us."

A cheer went up, and as Zach stood in the open doorway, he brushed tears from his cheeks.

"Here they come. Hip, hip, hooray." Werner's voice rang out, and then everyone joined in as the two paramedics carried Beth out to the ambulance on the stretcher as Zach walked by her side and held her hand.

"There's Molly." Mike nudged Troy's ribs and gave him a knowing smile. "Looks like she's got the baby."

Following behind Zach and Beth, Molly carried the small, precious bundle wrapped in a blanket. Troy's heart punched against his chest, and for a moment he struggled to breathe.

"Zach and Beth must have asked her to carry their girl. If I'd gone through what Zach has, I'd be afraid of dropping my kid. It's one of those times you're grateful there's an expert around to take charge." Mike shook his head and led another cheer for Molly.

As Molly waited outside the ambulance while Beth got settled inside, she scanned the crowd. Was she looking for him?

Troy made his shaky feet move toward her, and then she spotted him and smiled.

He tried to smile back, but tears burned at the backs of his eyes. *You're incredible.* He mouthed the words, and she scrunched up her face like she didn't understand.

He'd tell her later, but as he held her gaze for an instant that felt like a lifetime, he knew that what he felt for her wasn't fleeting or superficial but rather a deep and forever love.

She cradled her newborn niece and adjusted the blanket around the baby's tiny face with tenderness and maternal care. What would it be like seeing her hold their own newborn baby one day?

"You okay?" At his side, Mike took Troy's elbow.

"Yeah. It's a miracle." Troy didn't have any words beyond that.

To him, Molly was as big a miracle as the baby. But even as love and awe enveloped him, stronger than anything he'd ever experienced, he forced himself to be logical.

He loved Molly, but how could he ask her to stay in High Valley? Even if she was sincere, and he finally knew in his heart that she was and he could trust her with everything he had, today had also shown him she was destined for bigger and better things.

Troy would never hold her back or want her to give up her big city life and career for him.

# CHAPTER EIGHTEEN

"THERE YOU GO, GIRL." Back at the Tall Grass Ranch, Molly latched Daisy-May's stall after stabling the horse for the night. "It was a big day for us."

Daisy-May gave a soft nicker, and Molly rubbed her nose.

With Beth giving birth in Rosa's craft center, it had been a bigger day for Molly than Daisy-May, but the horse had done her bit in the parade and represented the Carter family well. "I'm proud of you, girl. 'Night, 'night, sleep tight." She chuckled as she repeated the bedtime rhyme her dad used to say to her.

As she left the barn, her boots sank deep into fresh snow, but the storm had passed to leave a crisp and clear December night. Montana weather often changed fast and never more so than today. She leaned her elbows atop the pasture fence and stared at the starlit sky.

Beth and her new baby were staying at the hospital overnight, so Zach was with them, and Ellie was having a sleepover at Cole and Melissa's. While Cole had taken Ellie, Skylar, Paisley and Cam home with him, her mom would head back to Carrie's farmhouse after she finished checking on the chickens in their coop. So apart from the hands, Molly would be alone at the ranch. She wasn't lonely, though. Instead, and for the first time in months, she felt at peace.

Her thoughts drifted back to holding her new, still unnamed niece by the ambulance. As she'd lifted her gaze from the baby's sweet face, it was as if she saw everything, and everyone, anew. And then, when she'd spotted Troy, it was like it was only the two of them. In that moment, and despite how she'd tried to deny her feelings, she'd known she loved him with every part of herself, now and forever.

She scanned the sky, trying to pick out constellations she remembered from her dad's astronomy book, which still sat on the shelf in the family room. There was so much artificial light where she lived in Atlanta she rarely saw stars, or even thought to look for them. Here, she drank in the overhead vista.

There was something about the winter silence, and that big familiar sky, that quieted and unsnarled her tangled thinking.

Footsteps crunched on the snow, and she turned. "Hey, Mom. Are you heading home?"

"Nope." Her mom's smile was wistful. "I called Shane and told him I wanted to stay here tonight with you. Carrie's house is great, but in a lot of ways, this ranch house is still home for me." Her mom stood beside Molly at the fence, her dogs Jess and Gus sniffing around their feet. "It's such a pretty night, but I'm restless."

"I always thought you were the most settled and steady person I know." Molly stared at her mom.

"Maybe on the surface but not always underneath." Her mom chuckled. "Inside, I often feel about sixteen, but here I am a grandma once again."

"And an inspiration to us all." Molly patted one of her mom's mittened hands.

"Thanks, honey, but today you were the inspiration. The way you delivered the baby." She sucked in a quick breath and shook her head slowly. "It seems like yesterday you were a baby yourself. Your dad would be so proud of you. I sure am."

"At first, I was scared." Her heart had raced, and for a few minutes she'd hardly been able to control her shaky limbs. But then she'd moved beyond the fear and found a sense of purpose, made a plan and had mentally talked herself through what she had to do to keep Beth and the baby safe.

"We were all scared, Zach most of all, but you were a pro. Today will go down in the history of High Valley and you were a big part of it." Her mom wrapped her hand around Molly's. "Folks are calling you a hero."

"I hope that doesn't last long." Molly gave a mock shudder. "You know me, I don't like being the center of attention."

"True, but sometimes I don't know if I *do* know you." Her mom's blue eyes were troubled.

"For the last while, I haven't known myself either." She bent to pat the dogs, and Jess leaned against Molly's leg.

"And now?"

"I'm still figuring parts out, but I…" Molly took a deep breath. "I've been lost for months, maybe even a few years, but I need a place to belong, and I want it to be here in High Valley."

"You'll always belong here, no matter where you live, but I—"

"Wait, I need to tell you the truth. All of it." If she didn't, Molly might lose her courage. "I want to be here to see my new niece and the other kids grow up. I want to be a real part of their lives and someone they can count on."

"What about your job? Nursing is what you always wanted."

"It still is, but today showed me I want to be a nurse here. I want to care for local children and their families and be part of this community. Someone like me is needed, and I hear the county hospital's hiring." After she talked to Troy, she'd call Kendra and ask her to put in that "good word" the other woman had offered. "If I'm a local hero, that should help me get a job, don't you think?" She tried to joke but her voice quavered.

"Oh, my dear." Her mom's arms came around Molly in a hug both loving and fierce.

"You aren't disappointed in me?"

"Why would I be?" Her mom cupped Molly's chin and looked into her eyes.

"Because you…my brothers, the whole family, you sacrificed a lot for me to go to college. I don't want you to think I'm a failure if I choose a career as a rural nurse over a city research job." She pushed the words out, afraid of what she'd see in her mom's face.

"All I ever wanted, all me and any of us still want, is for you to be happy." Her mom kissed Molly's cheek. "Changing your mind doesn't mean you're a 'failure.' It means you've grown and changed like we all do."

Molly had been so afraid and embarrassed to admit the truth to anyone, let alone herself, but now, with only a few words, her mom had made everything okay.

"The only failure would be living a life that no longer fits, and the rest of the family will feel the same." Her mom's voice was firm. "If anyone else asks nosy questions or judges you, who cares? That's their problem, and whatever they think isn't important."

"I guess so." Molly had been focused on one way of thinking for so long, it was hard to all of a sudden see herself and her choices through someone else's eyes. "I know I can be happy here."

"And we'll be happy to have you, me most of all." Her mom rested her hands on Molly's shoulders. "Maybe it's because you've been away that you know where you want to be. If you hadn't spread your wings, your roots wouldn't have called you home."

"You always did have a way of putting things." Molly laughed and then sobered as her mom tilted her head to one side and gazed at her with an expectant air. "What?"

"You can tell me it's none of my business, but I have to ask. Does Troy have anything to do with you being happy here?"

She could deflect her mom's question, but what was the point? Unlike her change of career direction, she wasn't embarrassed about her feelings for Troy. "I love him, Mom. I thought what we had was casual but it's not. It's serious, at least for me. But I'm not staying in High Valley because of him." She rushed on. "I don't know if he feels like I do, but if he does, I want to give our relationship a real chance."

However, there had been something in Troy's expression as their eyes met while she waited by the ambulance that had given Molly hope he might love her like she loved him.

"And if he doesn't share your feelings?"

In the distance, a coyote howled, and Molly shivered. "It'll hurt, but I'll pick myself up and move on. I won't run away because of Troy or any man." Yet, as Molly had cradled Zach and Beth's baby, she'd imagined her and Troy raising their own children here one day.

"All of us will be here for you, no matter what. We're your family." Her mom hugged Molly again, and in that embrace she knew she'd finally found her way home to stay.

They walked back to the ranch house with the dogs, the home that had sheltered Molly's family for several generations. She also knew that after being honest with herself and her mom, she now needed to be honest with Troy.

AT SEVEN IN the morning, the day after High Valley's holiday parade, Troy checked the email from Pete again, hoping the problem wasn't as bad as it had seemed the night before. Studying the attached document, he zeroed in on a column of figures.

The mistake was obvious, and he should have caught and corrected it a few weeks ago. Now it was too late and would cost them. Not only money, which was bad enough, but this kind of situation could also damage their professional reputation. They'd built their business on honesty, trust and care. If someone messed up, the responsibility ultimately rested with the guys at the top—in this case, him.

He stared out his home office window at the snowy fields and cattle grazing in a winter pasture. His heartbeat sped up, and a tingling sensation flooded the back of his neck and across his face. He couldn't avoid the truth any longer. He'd paid less attention to work because of Molly, and this problem was the result. Cause and effect, like he'd learned from his folks long before any school classroom.

*I'm sorry, son. You can't play hockey because we can't afford the equipment this year.*

*That microscope kit's expensive. What about putting this mini kit on your Christmas wish list instead?*

*We'll manage somehow. Don't worry. Go out and play.*

The voices of his mom and dad came back to him across the years. They'd sacrificed for Troy and his sister, likely more than he knew. And sacrifice had become a way of life he hadn't questioned. His folks had done the best they could, and so Troy did his best as well. He still did.

He rubbed a hand across his neck before picking up his phone to call Pete.

"I'm sorry." His hands were clammy, and a headache pounded behind his temples. "This is my fault."

"How could it be your fault?" Pete's voice cut through Troy's whirling thoughts. "Tim and his team made the mistake, not you."

"Tim reports to me. When he sent the draft document, I should have spotted there was a problem." Troy kept his voice low and controlled, and he turned away from the computer so he didn't have to face the evidence. "You and I also know Tim's not as meticulous as he could be."

"So? Mistakes happen. As for Tim, he's a good guy, and nobody's as meticulous as you."

"I took my eyes off the ball." And Troy couldn't forgive himself.

"You're human." Pete exhaled. "But knowing you, nothing I say is going to make you see things differently."

"I wasn't doing my job." Troy resisted the temptation to put his head on the desk and close his eyes, hoping that when he woke up all his problems would have magically disappeared.

He'd tossed and turned the whole night thinking about work, Molly and what he needed to do. The problem was that he was unsettled, unsure of where he and Molly stood, what they wanted, what kind of future they could have. He could focus on work if they were both committed to their relationship and all that that entailed. But he wanted to be here, in High Valley, and that had never been Molly's dream. If she didn't resent him now for asking her to stay here and give up her exciting city job, she would in a few years. He couldn't do that to her—or himself. If they built a life together and she left again, he might not survive the pain.

*You can run your business from anywhere.* The insistent voice in his head grew louder with the words he'd said to others and himself. But the issue was bigger than geography. With Molly by his side, he could find a way to be happy in Atlanta. But he'd begun to find the roots here he'd longed for. Just as he worried she'd resent him if she stayed, would he resent her if he left High Valley? Perhaps the truth was that he couldn't let a personal relationship distract him from work at all. He'd committed to that idea for years and it had served him well. This crisis could be contained. The next time, he might not be so lucky, and he couldn't risk losing the financial security he'd worked so hard to achieve.

Pete was still trying to convince him that this wasn't the end of the world. "We'll fix the problem and absorb the financial loss. It'll be fine. We have enough free cash."

True, but losing these funds could also impact Troy's personal investment in Cole's business. "I'm on it. I'll send you a new proposal later today."

As he ended the call, he dropped his face into his hands. First, he had to make sure Cole and his business would be okay. Then he had to see Molly. His stomach rolled as he considered what he had to say and how to say it. Even if it didn't feel so now, it was for the best for both of them.

He focused on the computer screen, opened a new document and input different combinations of numbers, trying to lose himself and his heartache in financial projections. He'd always liked math because numbers didn't lie. He also knew where he stood with a spreadsheet. And once he made a plan, he stuck with it until he reached his goal. He tapped the computer keys and didn't let himself think about Molly.

Several hours later, he let out a long breath

as he found a solution. It wasn't perfect, but he'd handled it as best he could without hurting their employees or investors. He'd also absorb the personal financial loss so there was no risk to Cole's business.

At his side in her bed, Acorn whined as if she sensed Troy's distress.

"It's okay, sweetheart." He picked the dog up and rested his face against her soft head. "I know what I'm doing."

Acorn nosed his cheek, and Troy swallowed the tsunami of emotions that threatened to overwhelm him.

The sooner he saw and spoke to Molly the better. Before he lost his nerve, he grabbed his phone and sent her a brief text.

She replied in seconds.

I'm at the Tall Grass. Not leaving for the hospital until around two this afternoon. See you in twenty minutes.

She ended the message with smiley face and heart emojis.

Troy's chest hurt, and he made himself take several deep breaths. As he gathered up his keys and put Acorn back in her bed, his gaze caught the small box from the Medicine Wheel Craft Center covered in shiny green paper and tied with a curly silver bow. It held the bear paw pendant with the blue stone he'd intended to give Molly over dinner after the parade.

For an agonizing instant he stared at it and remembered what it represented—the fun, the laughter and the love. Then he opened the bottom desk drawer, took the box and put it at the back behind old project files.

What he was doing was for the best for both he and Molly. Before he left the house, he also messaged Pete.

Found a solution. All good.

It would be good, if not right now, then in the future. All he had to do was convince Molly. And then himself.

# CHAPTER NINETEEN

"I WASN'T EXPECTING to see you today. What's up?" As they walked away from the Tall Grass ranch house along the snow-covered path to the creek, Molly slid her arm through Troy's. "I'm always happy to see you, but you look rough. Bad night?"

He looked worse than rough. He looked haggard, as if he'd aged years overnight. He was still handsome, though, and she imagined what he'd look like as they grew older. Was now the right time to tell him she loved him and wanted to make a future together? No, she'd better wait to hear what he had to say first.

"I didn't sleep well. Work stuff." His arm beneath hers was stiff and although they stood close, there was nevertheless a distance between them that so far Molly hadn't been able to bridge.

"Would it help to talk to me about it? I could listen, and as an outsider I might have a new perspective." Unease curled from Molly's stomach to lodge in her throat. Her instinct told her whatever was bothering Troy was more than something to do with work. Yesterday at the parade he hadn't been himself, and before Beth had gone into labor Molly had wanted to talk to him about it.

"There was a problem that bothered me all night, but I found a solution this morning." Troy took his arm away to dig in his jacket pocket for a pair of sunglasses.

"Oh, well, that's good, then." Molly found her own glasses. The sunlight against the snow was bright and made her squint, but not being able to see Troy's eyes also made her wary.

"Molly, I…" Troy stopped by the edge of the creek. "There's no easy way to tell you this."

"Tell me what?" Her stomach lurched.

"It's not you. It's me." Despite the dark glasses, his anguished expression was clear.

"What do you mean?" Except, she already knew. He was breaking up with her. They'd never even made their relationship official, so how could it be over?

"Getting involved with each other, even though we kept it casual, was a mistake. I can't give you what you need and deserve. The kind of lifetime love your brothers and their wives have.

Like your folks had and now your mom has with Shane."

"I don't understand." Tears stung behind her eyes, but by sheer force of will she held them back. "We're good together and—"

"We were but it won't work." Troy paced along the bank of the half-frozen creek where water still trickled in the middle. "I have a lot going on with my business and I don't have time for a relationship, especially a long-distance one."

"What if I disagree? You haven't given us a chance, not really. And…" Molly gulped. "I only decided for sure last night, but I'm going to stay in High Valley. I'm applying for a job at the county hospital. If I'm here, we can—"

"No, we can't. And you shouldn't stay here because of me or because you think we have a future together."

Molly took several steps back. "I'm not choosing to stay here just because of you." Although, given the pain she felt now, she'd underestimated how hard it would be to see Troy around town. And how, in only a short time, his life and hers had gotten intertwined.

Troy turned to face her. "I care about you, Molly, but it's over." His voice cracked. "It's for the best. You'll see. Nothing will change with my investment in Cole's stock contracting business, and we can still be friends."

"*Friends?* I don't think so. I don't understand. I thought we had something special."

"We did and…" He continued pacing and dug a narrow path in the snow with his boots. "You have a great job in Atlanta. I won't let you give it up for me."

"Shouldn't it be *me* who makes that decision?" Anger mixed with hurt made her voice shrill. "Is this because I ended our relationship before, and you want to get back at me?" She'd never thought Troy was mean or vindictive, but had she misjudged him? The night before she'd been so sure he loved her, but this man was a stranger.

"Of course not. The past is done. I'm talking about now. The Atlanta job is what you've been working toward for years. Apart from family, what's here for you?"

"How can you say *apart* from family? I love my family, I always have, but the past while has shown me how important that bond is. I need to be part of their lives in a way I can't on occasional visits. I need them to be part of my life as well." She sucked in a breath as Troy stared at her, his lips pressed tight together. "I also have a community here and sense of belonging I've never found anywhere else. I can get a job here that would make me an even bigger part of High Valley. Yes, I'd be giving up a job in

Atlanta, but I'd gain a lot more. Things I can't put a price on." Molly put her trembling hands into her jacket pockets and clenched her fists. "Maybe for you, life's about work and money, but it's not for me."

"My work's important to me and the money gives me security but…" Troy's face went red. "I want you to be happy. I'm doing this for you."

"If you truly wanted me to be happy, you'd listen to what I'm saying, and you wouldn't throw away what we could have together. You're making excuses. And you're breaking up with me because you think it's somehow better for me, but I think it's really for you because you're too afraid to take a chance in life." Her voice rose higher. "You're right, Cole's business is between the two of you, and this shouldn't affect it. As for the rest? I'm staying here and if that's a problem, sell the Bitterroot and go live somewhere else. If all you think about is work, it shouldn't matter where you live." She whirled around and started back along the path to the ranch house.

"Molly, wait I…"

"What?" She turned and pressed one hand to her heaving chest.

"These past weeks have meant a lot to me."

"If that were true, you wouldn't say we were a mistake." She hesitated for a few seconds in case he realized what he was giving up, but he stared at his boots. "Have a good life, Troy. I hope money gives you enough of that security."

With one last look at his bent head and hunched shoulders, she turned around again and started for home, walking as fast as she could before breaking into a run. When she reached the barnyard fence, she veered toward the house and stumbled in snowy tractor ruts. Half-blinded by tears, she took off her sunglasses and shoved them in her pocket. If she could only make it inside the house and upstairs to her bedroom before—

"Molly? If you have a second, I… Hey, what's wrong?" A pair of strong arms came around her, and then she was pressed against Cole's broad chest. "Are you hurt? Did someone hurt you?"

"I'm not hurt." At least not physically. "But…" She buried her face in her brother's jacket and choked back sobs. "I thought you went into town."

"I started to, but I came back because… It doesn't matter. Is it Troy?"

Molly nodded and cried harder as Cole half carried her the rest of the way.

"I'll return the money he invested. I can pay him back over time. I won't be beholden to anyone who's hurt you." He guided Molly up the stairs to the back deck and then into the ranch house kitchen.

"What on earth?" Her mom's voice penetrated Molly's sobs.

"You need that money. Besides, Troy said…" Molly hiccupped. "He said it wouldn't make a difference to his investment. I said the stock contracting business was between the two of you. It's okay. I'm okay."

"You're not okay, and I'm not okay taking money from Troy. It's tainted." Cole pulled out one of the kitchen chairs and Molly almost fell into it. "Besides, I'm going to be a successful stock contractor, and why should a guy like him benefit?"

Her mom knelt to take off Molly's boots and then unzipped her parka. "You're freezing, honey. Let's get you a blanket and a mug of tea. I just made a pot for myself."

"Here's a blanket." Shane hovered in front of Molly between her mom and Cole. "I'll be in the barn office if anyone needs me."

"What did Troy do?" Cole thumped around the kitchen in his sock feet.

"Nothing." *Everything.* "I thought there was something special between us, but he…whatever it is…was, it's over." She huddled in the chair and curled her hands around the mug of tea her mom gave her. Despite the warmth of both it and the blanket, she shivered so hard her teeth chattered.

"I want to stay here but how can I? I'll always be worrying about bumping into Troy around town." She pulled a handful of tissues from the box her mom had set on the kitchen table and mopped her eyes. "I'm so embarrassed."

"It's Troy who should be embarrassed, not you." Cole stopped by Molly's chair and crouched in front of her. "Do you want me to talk to him?"

"No." Molly gave him a wobbly smile. "I'm too old to have my brothers fighting my battles."

"But you're never too old to have your family in your corner." Molly's mom pulled out another chair, sat and tucked the ends of the blanket around Molly's trembling shoulders. "There's no reason for you to leave because of Troy. How about this—why not go back to Atlanta for a few months and take the time you need to find a suitable job here? It doesn't have to be right in High Valley."

Molly nodded and sipped the hot tea. Her mom's suggestion was good, and it would give her time and space away from Troy and this heartbreak to clear her head and be ready for job interviews. "I do want to be in Montana. That hasn't changed. And I want to be in or close to High Valley so I can visit you often."

"Maybe Troy will leave. Once folks find out

how he treated you, it won't be comfortable around here for him." There was a determination in Cole's voice that told Molly he was keen to be the source of that discomfort.

"No." Molly put a hand on her brother's arm. "This thing is between Troy, me and our family, nobody else. I won't be the subject of town gossip." If people talked about her or she became an object of pity, she couldn't live here, ever. And although she'd told Troy he could sell the Bitterroot and move somewhere else, would he? Owning that ranch was his dream come true.

"Okay, but if I ever bump into the guy behind a barn, I'll have a thing or two to say to him." Cole stood and paced around the kitchen again.

"You won't do any such thing." Molly's mom's voice was soft but firm. "It isn't your fight to take on. If you want to give Troy his investment back, fine, but that's it. Understood?" She eyed her son with an expression Molly remembered from childhood.

"Yeah." Cole gave a short laugh. "It doesn't mean I can't think about what I'd like to say and do to him, though."

"Make sure you stick to thinking. That goes for Zach and Bryce as well." Molly's mom was almost a foot shorter than Cole, but she didn't stand for any nonsense. She never had. "Don't you have something to do outside or in one of the barns?"

"I can take a hint, Mom." Cole gave her a curt nod.

"Good." She turned to Molly again as Cole put his outdoor clothing back on. "I have my homemade chicken noodle soup and your favorite ice cream in the freezer, and there are chips and cookies in the pantry. We can snack and binge-watch old movies."

Those were her mom's feel-better remedies for everything from a head cold to heartbreak. "Don't you and Shane need to go home?" Molly blew her nose and tried to pull herself together. "I was planning to go to the hospital to visit Beth and the baby, but I…" She couldn't face Zach and Beth's happiness right now.

"Zach texted. Beth and the baby are being kept in for another day or two, but he's on his way back here to pick up some things for them." Her mom stroked Molly's hair. "If you want, I can make up a care package, and you can come stay with Shane and me for a few days. It'll be quiet, and you can take the time you need to figure out next steps."

"I'd like that." Molly straightened. She'd gotten over Troy once before so she could do it again.

And in the meantime, no matter where she

was, she'd find happiness in the life she had and would build, and not let herself imagine what might have been.

"YOU GUYS HAVE worked a bunch of extra hours lately." In the barnyard at the Bitterroot, Troy spoke to his foreman and ranch hands. "Leave early and go spend time with your families or do holiday shopping. You too, Wyatt." Cathy's son was smart, ambitious and reminded Troy a lot of himself at that age. "I'll finish up here."

"Thanks, boss." Wyatt grinned. "I can go home with my mom now instead of her having to come back for me."

"How many times have I told you not to call me boss? It's Troy, remember?" If he ever had a son, he'd like one like Wyatt.

"Yeah… Troy." Wyatt's grin widened, and he ran to the house to find Cathy as the others murmured their thanks and left.

Although it was only midafternoon, daylight was already fading. Day or night didn't matter, though. Troy felt like he'd been living life in a permanent state of gloom ever since he'd ended things with Molly. That would pass. He had to give it time. In the meantime, there was no better remedy for his misery than keeping busy.

He waved at Cathy and Wyatt as they came out of the ranch house and got into Cathy's car, and then he went into the barn. "You'd like to spend time outside, wouldn't you, girl?" He unlatched Cara's stall and led her out, setting his phone on a nearby shelf so it wouldn't fall out of his pocket while he did chores. Then he led Winnie out as well. "You two can keep each other company."

He tried not to think about the irony of them being more sociable than him. He had friends in San Francisco, but apart from Pete, how many true friends did Troy really have? Werner and Mike had the potential to be friends, but building a lasting friendship meant spending time together. In the past week, he'd turned down a dinner invitation from Werner and Nina, and Mike and the guys for beer and pizza while watching hockey and playing pool. He'd had work calls both nights, but could he have rescheduled those to do something fun instead?

Outside the barn, he opened the pasture gate and removed the lead ropes and halters from both horses. "There you go. I won't be long, but you can enjoy some fresh air."

After patting Winnie, who was as friendly as Cara, he let the gate swing shut behind him as his thoughts swirled. He'd spotted Cole in town earlier, but although he'd waved, Cole hadn't returned his greeting. And last night, Troy had found an envelope from Cole in the mailbox at the end of the lane. It had contained a check for part of the money Troy had invested in Cole's stock contracting business, along with a note outlining a repayment schedule for the rest. So far, Cole hadn't replied to Troy's voicemail messages and texts.

On his way back to the barn, he saw a ladder propped against the outside wall to the left of the barn door. It reminded him that he'd asked one of the hands to fix the roof where water had leaked into the tack room. He hadn't followed up on whether the job had been done, and it would only take a minute for him to check it now. He moved the ladder into position by the corner, made sure it was steady and then climbed its metal rungs.

If not for the situation with Molly, Cole could have been a friend as well. And Bryce and Zach. For a while there, Troy had almost felt like part of the Carter family.

Reaching the top of the ladder, he checked the seal. The hand had done a good job. Was that another hole farther along the roof as well?

He missed Molly and her family but...

As he leaned forward, the ladder wobbled, Troy's right foot slipped, and when he grabbed for the ladder, it flew backward through the air, taking him with it.

Troy waved his arms and shouted before he

hit the snowy ground with a thud. Pain shot through him, and when he tried to sit up, he gasped and fell back.

"Molly." Something wet trickled along Troy's cheek, and then there was only darkness.

# CHAPTER TWENTY

MOLLY AND COLE drove along the highway from
High Valley to the ranch. Molly turned off the
radio. Her life was hard enough right now without a sappy song about loving and losing reminding her of her troubles.

In only a few days, it seemed as if she'd eaten
almost her body weight in ice cream, cookies,
chips and chicken noodle soup. She didn't know
how she'd make it through Christmas without
falling apart.

"I appreciate you coming with me." When
Cole glanced at Molly, his face wore the same
perpetually worried expression as everyone else
in their family. "Thanks to you, for the first time
ever I'm finished my holiday shopping before
Christmas Eve."

"No problem." She'd wanted to get out of the
house, and when Cole had gone to his physical
therapy appointment, she'd hung out with Kristi
in the kitchen at the Bluebunch. Since Kristi

didn't know what had happened with Troy, she'd treated Molly like she always did. More than anything, that "ordinariness" had soothed the ache in Molly's heart. "Mom's going to love that spa gift card and framed family picture you got for her."

"I hope so." Cole's anxious expression eased. "Like you said, she doesn't need 'stuff.' When Melissa suggested we all wear holiday sweaters and have our picture taken, I thought it sounded fun."

"It's adorable." After she'd helped Cole choose a frame, Molly's eyes had filled with tears as she looked at the sweet photo of the smiling family of three and their dog. She was happy for her brother, but seeing his contentment with Melissa and Skylar was a reminder of what she'd let herself imagine having with Troy.

She looked out the passenger window, afraid Cole would try to comfort her. Although her family was kind, if they kept fussing over her, she'd never be able to move on. Outside the truck, the rolling snow-covered landscape stretched out in an endless vista, and gray clouds scudded close to the horizon. "Looks like another storm coming in."

"Yeah." Cole slowed the vehicle. "Hang on, what are those horses doing running loose?"

"Where? Oh, no." Molly swiveled to see. "That's

Cara, Troy's new horse. The other Morgan must be his as well."

Cole pulled over onto the shoulder. "No halters or lead ropes. They must have gotten out. I have a couple of rope halters in back."

"Pull into the laneway," Molly said, gesturing to a wider area with space to park. "While you try to get the horses to trust you, I'll look for a grain bucket and hay or feed." When it came to catching horses, there was nobody better than Cole. "The place looks deserted." Although worried about the animals, Molly let out a sigh of relief at that. She didn't want to bump into their owner.

"I saw Troy in town on my way back to meet you at the Bluebunch." As he drove the truck halfway up the lane, a flush crept across Cole's face. "He waved but I pretended I didn't see him. I couldn't face talking to him and not saying something, since I promised you and Mom I wouldn't."

"I'm glad you avoided him. I'd have done the same." Hopefully by the time Molly had to see Troy again, she could be if not friendly, at least civil. She wrapped her scarf more firmly around her neck, pulled on her hat and mittens and was out of the truck as soon as Cole parked it. "I'll be back in a few minutes."

As she ran up the rest of the lane, she glanced

at the horses again. Catching them and getting them to shelter before the storm broke was all that mattered. Most ranchers kept extra buckets near the barn, and there would likely be a feed trough in a nearby pasture.

In her haste, Molly skidded on a patch of ice, staggered but kept her balance. The barn was to her left and the house to her right. No lights shone from any windows, but Troy's truck was parked near the front porch.

"Troy?" Molly shouted into the howling wind, but even if he'd been around it was doubtful he'd have heard her.

In the growing darkness, she walked around the pasture fence where an open gate caught in a snowdrift showed her how Cara and the other horse had escaped.

As she moved forward, an automatic light outside the barn came on to illuminate the barnyard, and Molly gasped. Why was the barn door open? While it would make her job easier because she'd find an ample supply of grain and buckets inside, no rancher or hand would leave without closing up.

"Troy?" she called again, and glanced around. Inside her mittens, she curled her fingers into her clammy palms. Cole was only in the lane. If horse thieves or cattle rustlers were around, she or her brother would have seen people and at least one other vehicle.

Molly took out her phone and found the emergency call key. Maybe she was being paranoid and there was nothing to be afraid of, but it was better to be prepared. She reached the barn door in a few strides but before going inside scanned her surroundings once more.

In the overhead light, something silver gleamed on the ground around the corner, and the snow was dotted with bright reddish patches. Her heart raced as she hurried to the side of the barn to investigate further.

"Oh, no," she gasped, and with shaking hands used her phone to call an ambulance. She managed to give her location.

Six feet or more beyond the ladder, Troy lay sprawled in deep snow. His right foot was twisted beneath him, and blood trickled from a cut on his head.

"Troy." She touched his cheek, and his eyes flickered open.

"Molly?" His gaze was unfocused, and when he tried to reach out a hand to her, he winced.

"Don't move. An ambulance is on the way." She pulled off her scarf and pressed it to his head while also checking for other injuries. From the angle of his foot, she suspected his ankle was broken and that was only what she could see.

"Oh, Molly." Troy rested his head against her knee. "The ladder…the last thing I remember is slipping. Flying."

"Cole's rounding up the horses." And she was supposed to help him. With the hand that wasn't holding her scarf against Troy's head, she called her brother to tell him what had happened. "He's bringing blankets from his truck." She took off her parka and covered Troy with it, all the while murmuring reassuring words.

He was conscious but only barely, and while she focused on basic, makeshift first aid, she tried not to let herself think about any other possibilities.

"What horses?" Troy's voice was slurred. "I put Cara and Winnie in the pasture. I let everyone go home early." He moaned as she touched his chest around his ribs. "You're my angel."

"No, I'm not. I'm a nurse and you're going to be fine." He likely had some broken ribs, along with his ankle, but right now she was most concerned about what was going on internally and any injuries she couldn't see.

"It was a mistake. A big mistake." He tried to raise himself up and then fell back with a groan. "Tim. I fixed it. Cole can't know. That I love… Don't tell…my mom."

He was clearly mixing up his words. "You can call your mom later. I know you love her and your dad and Sara. Right now you have to stay still."

"But I love...oh, Molly. It was bad."

Troy wasn't making any sense. Had he only cut his head, or did he have a traumatic brain injury? She patted his hand, and it convulsed beneath hers before he muttered something else unintelligible.

"Here." Cole appeared at her side with several blankets and leading Cara and the other horse.

"How did you get them both?" Molly stared at him open-mouthed as she tucked the blankets around Troy, and Cole gave her his own parka.

"Piece of cake. I was a rodeo cowboy, remember? Rounding up horses is all in a day's work." His feeble attempt at joking couldn't mask his clenched fists, tight jaw or the sallowness of his skin. "How bad is it?"

"He'll be okay." *Bad enough.* A person couldn't fall off a ladder and expect to come through unscathed.

"I was there when Dad..." Cole's voice was choked. "He was fine one minute and then the next...the tractor rolled and..."

"I remember." Over the intervening years, Molly had managed to think about her dad without bringing to mind how he'd died, but even before Cole had mentioned the accident, it had come flooding back as she knelt over Troy.

An emergency siren echoed, and she let out a breath. Lights flashing, an ambulance came up the lane and parked, and two paramedics raced toward them.

"I'll see to the horses. If you hadn't…" Cole's face worked as if he held back tears.

"If *we* hadn't." Molly stood and squeezed her brother's arm before greeting the EMTs and giving them a brief rundown of what she thought had happened.

Yet, as she watched them load Troy into the ambulance, she felt stomach-churning fear along with her love for him.

He'd done her a favor by ending their relationship. This kind of accident was why she'd vowed long ago never to marry a rancher, cowboy or any other man who made his living on the land. It was dangerous work, and she didn't need to look any further than her dad to know you could lose someone you loved in an instant.

She'd get over Troy in time. It was for the best that he didn't love her back.

"THERE YOU GO." Two days after his accident, Cathy set a tray with Troy's lunch on the table by the recliner Werner had insisted he borrow. "Are you sure you don't need anything else before I come back at dinner? I still think you'd be better having someone around overnight. The boys and I would be happy to stay here as long as you need us to." She shook her head and frowned. "You look bad."

He *felt* bad, but he could manage the physical injuries and they'd heal in time. The ache in his heart was the bigger problem. "I'll be fine." He tried to smile but even that hurt.

"It's okay to ask for help, you know." Cathy rearranged a quilt that Rosa had made and sent to him over Troy's legs. "Everybody's worried and wants to pitch in to help you. And your mom called me again last night. Your folks want to come here now."

"The ranch hands are looking out for me and Acorn." He didn't want his mom and dad to see him like this. Since he couldn't travel to San Francisco, it would be hard enough having them here for Christmas—and asking about Molly. He patted the dog curled up on his lap. Since he'd gotten home from the hospital, Acorn had hardly left his side. "If I need you or anyone else, I can call." He indicated his phone on the table.

"From now on, keep your phone with you." Cathy gave him a mock glare. "If Molly and Cole hadn't happened along, you'd have frozen to death out there. When the hospital called me, at first I couldn't make sense of what that doctor was saying."

Troy hadn't wanted to worry his folks or Pete, but what did it say about him that the only person he could think of to ask the doctor to call was someone who worked for him? "You've been great, Cathy. Truly. I don't know what I'd do without you. Now go get your boys and take them to their dental appointments."

Cathy picked up her purse and car keys from a table near the living room door. "If you can't reach me, call Werner or Nina. They make such a sweet couple. We're all thrilled for them."

The older couple *were* sweet, but seeing their later-in-life happiness was a poignant reminder of Troy's solitary state.

"I'm surprised Molly hasn't been by. None of the Carters have called either. Joy's usually one of the first to rally around whenever someone's in need." Cathy's eyes narrowed. "Is there something going on I should know about?"

"Molly and I…it's a business relationship. Like with Cole." Troy rubbed Acorn's ears.

"Right." Cathy's laugh was short. "If that's what you want to call it, fine. You can lie to yourself but don't lie to me."

"I don't want to talk about it." Helpless in the snow, fearing he was going to die, he'd faced more than a few hard truths. He loved Molly and he always would, but he'd made a mess of everything. And when she'd appeared at his side, like the angel he needed, he'd been desperate to tell her how he felt but hadn't been able to find the words.

"You don't need to talk to me about it." Cathy put on her winter coat and boots. "You need to talk to her."

"I do, but how?" Abandoning any pretense of hiding his real feelings, Troy picked at the foil cover on the food he had no interest in eating.

"Since you can't go to her, ask her to come here." Cathy's tone was soothing. "I expect one of those brothers of hers would give you a hand. From what I hear, all three of them made their own mistakes with the women they love."

"I do love Molly." There, he'd said it out loud and it felt good. And somehow he had to win her back.

"I thought so." Cathy nodded. "You're a smart guy, but in love, that can be a disadvantage."

"How so?"

"You're making decisions with your brain instead of your heart. In business you also pay attention to your intuition, right?" She pulled on her fleece hat and mittens.

"Yes, but…" Troy had analyzed the situation from every angle. He'd assembled evidence and made the most logical decision based on the facts. He put a hand to his head as the pieces of a puzzle clicked into place. "You're right." And he was wrong, so wrong, and now he had to fix it.

"If I were you, I'd call Bryce. Cole can be hotheaded. He speaks and acts before he thinks. And since Beth and the baby have only come home from the hospital, Zach's naturally caught up in their new family. But Bryce is level-headed. Besides, he's just back from his honeymoon. He'll likely be sympathetic to a lovelorn guy in need." Cathy's smile was teasing. "And it's almost Christmas, and that's the season of miracles."

He needed a miracle, that was for sure. "Thanks, Cathy. I owe you." For things no amount of money could repay her for.

She waved a dismissive hand. "What else are friends for? You'd do the same for me."

"Yeah." He'd been so sure making money was the key to security that he hadn't understood what real security meant. It was everything Molly had talked about. Family, friends and a community you could count on. "Go on, I'll be okay."

"You will. Good luck."

As Cathy opened the front door, a gust of cold air came in but instead of making him cold, and despite his bandaged head, it seemed to blow away the last of the cobwebs that had muddled Troy's thinking for weeks.

His lunch could wait. Instead, he picked up his phone and scrolled to Bryce's number.

"Troy? What's up?" When he answered, Bryce's voice was cool.

Molly's brother had only said a few words, and Troy was already sweating. "It's…" He'd learned in business that with certain people it was best to be direct. Bryce seemed like one of them, and Troy sensed the guy didn't like having his time wasted. "It's about Molly. I need to talk to her and—"

"Why do you think my sister will want to talk to you?" Although Bryce was polite, he cut straight to the point too.

"She probably won't but…I love her, and I made a big mistake. I need to explain but I'm stuck at my house. I have a fractured ankle and a couple of broken ribs, stitches in my head and bruises all over. I can't drive." He could barely make it to the bathroom without help. But he didn't have a brain injury or paralysis and he was still alive. All things considered, he had to look on the bright side. "I won't hurt her again, I promise." His voice cracked, and Troy tried to cover it with a cough. Which was a mistake because it hurt his ribs.

Bryce exhaled and silence hung between them for several seconds. "I want Molly to be happy and despite everything, you seem like a good guy. So, okay. What do you need?"

"If you can get Molly to my place, I'll do the rest."

It wouldn't be fancy, but it would be honest and heartfelt. Troy could only hope that would be enough.

# *CHAPTER TWENTY-ONE*

"I'LL BE BACK in ten minutes. Promise you won't leave? And if I don't come back, you'll come in and get me?" Standing outside Troy's front door, Molly glanced at her brother who'd parked his truck at the foot of the porch steps. "This whole thing also stays between the two of us, right?" She'd gotten herself somewhat back together and didn't need the rest of the family chipping in to console her or even worse, offer advice.

"I promise, and of course I won't tell anyone. Not even Carrie." Bryce leaned across the truck to speak to Molly through the half-open window. "For what it's worth, Troy sounded really sincere."

He'd sounded sincere before he'd broken up with her. He was also a business whiz. He must be used to telling people what they wanted to hear. Molly took a deep breath and went into the house through the unlocked door.

"Molly? Is that you?" Troy's voice reached her from a room off the main hall.

"Yes." She took off her winter boots but left her coat on so she could make a quick getaway. "Why did you want to see me? And why couldn't you say whatever you need to over the phone?" Molly hovered inside what turned out to be the living room door, keeping a good fifteen feet between her and Troy, who sat in one corner in a dark brown recliner with Acorn on his lap.

His face was pale and from the cast that covered most of his right foot to the surgical dressing on his head, he must be battered, bruised and in pain. But he was still the man she'd foolishly fallen in love with. The nurse in her wanted to assess his condition and comfort and care. The woman, however, tried to harden her heart.

"You could hang up on me on the phone." His smile was awkward, and he flinched as if even that minor movement hurt. "As for wanting to see you? I've missed you, Molly, and I had to apologize in person."

"Apologize?" Her stomach rolled and her breath quivered.

"Yes. Won't you sit down?" He gestured to a cozy armchair upholstered in a cheerful red plaid near the fireplace. "Or take the sofa. You picked it out with me. I guess we should have bought a recliner too. Since I can't make it upstairs to my bedroom, this chair is on loan from Werner."

Molly sat on the edge of the chair. If she'd had a real relationship with Troy, she'd have visited his house before. Instead, she was seeing it as a stranger. The living room was welcoming, though, and from the basket of red and white flowers on a shelf by the window to the comfortable furniture and Western-themed art, it felt homey.

From Troy's lap, Acorn's soft, brown eyes were solemn as she stared at Molly.

"As you can see, I'm not very mobile."

"Yes." She clasped her hands so he wouldn't see them shake.

"Before I say anything else, I want to thank you. You and Cole saved my life." Troy's voice was low and husky with an intimacy that made her pulse race.

"Anyone would have done the same." The trembling in her hands increased. Even if she and Troy weren't together, Molly didn't want to think about a world without him in it.

"Maybe, but when you showed up, at first I assumed I'd imagined you. I thought you were an angel." He pulled at the collar of his shirt, which was a dark blue flannel one Molly hadn't seen before.

"So you said." She kept her voice neutral. He'd said a lot of other things lying in the snow by the barn as well, but since none of them had made sense, she hadn't let herself dwell on them.

"You see, the thing is…" He hesitated and patted Acorn who snuggled closer into the curve of his arm. "Even before I fell off that ladder, I wasn't happy, but I couldn't figure out why. Now I know it's because I sent you away. I tossed away what we had like it didn't matter when it mattered more than anything, at least to me. I'm sorry for that and a bunch of other things."

Molly stilled and pressed her lips together.

He shifted on the recliner, and she resisted the urge to go over to him and rearrange the pillows that propped up his hurt ankle. "Because of how I grew up, I've always needed to feel secure. Making money gave me that security so that's why I focused on it. But in the last few days, what with the accident, and now being stuck here hardly able to do anything for myself, it's shown me that real security isn't found in making money at all."

"Oh?" Her heart raced, and her insides felt like a washing machine on the spin cycle.

"No, what's truly important is everything you said by the creek that day I…we… Anyway, it's being part of a close-knit community. Being supported by family and friends who are there for you because they care and don't expect to be paid. And…" He hesitated again, and in the depths of his eyes Molly saw something she thought she'd lost forever. "It's love. I love you, Molly. I did before and I do now. Even when we were apart, I tried to move on, but my heart never forgot you. The love and security I really need are with you."

"I… You…" She brushed away unexpected tears. "I need that with you. I love you too, but—"

"Wait. I have more to say, and I…you might not love me after I tell you." His mouth twisted.

"Go on." Molly waited and time slowed, making her hyperaware of the warmth that flooded through her body. All she wanted was to go to Troy, wrap her arms around him and say nothing else mattered. Whatever was troubling him, they'd figure it out together. However, a sixth sense told her he needed to be on his own right now.

"I made another mistake. Not with you but it could have hurt you, or rather Cole and his business. I fixed it, and I didn't want to tell you, but you need to know." A red flush spread across Troy's cheeks. "A project Pete and I are currently backing… I didn't check something as thoroughly as I should have and so Pete and I lost money I'd counted on earning for Cole's investment. I took responsibility and the financial hit personally. Pete wasn't mad at me, but I was sure mad at myself." He gulped. "I hadn't been paying as much attention to work as I should have been, and at the time I thought it was because of my relationship with you. That's why I said we couldn't be together. I thought I couldn't let myself be distracted by you or anyone else or I'd lose that security money gave me." He bent his head, and his voice shook. "I was wrong, Molly, and I hope you can forgive me."

"Of course, I can. You made a mistake. That makes you human." She couldn't sit on the other side of the room any longer, so she went to his side and knelt by his chair. "I love you and part of loving someone is being there for them in good times and bad. It's loving every part of them and recognizing we're all imperfect."

"I don't deserve you." He reached for her, and Molly eased carefully into his open arms. For the first time ever, she saw the real Troy, faults and all, and it only made her love him more.

"Well, that could be a problem because I'm not going anywhere." She laughed through her tears. "I doubted you and I was wrong. You're a good man and sincere." The kind she needed in her life for always.

"But your job…you can't sacrifice your career for me. I won't let you." He moved back and winced. "My ribs, I…"

"You poor thing." Molly gave his arm a gentle pat as she extricated herself from his embrace. "You've been honest with me, so now I need to be honest with you." As she looked into Troy's eyes, she saw all the love and trust she'd ever need but, as he'd done, she had to take this last step alone—before what she hoped would be a lifetime together.

"Okay." He patted Acorn, and she put one hand over his. "I love you and that won't ever change but..." She took a deep breath.

This was it. No more secrets between them, ever.

TROY STUDIED MOLLY'S bent head. He'd never known or even imagined having a love like the one he had for her, and he wanted to spend the rest of his life showing her how much she meant to him. She'd accepted him, all of him, and in her he'd found a partner who'd be with him for himself, not what he could buy her.

"It's okay, whatever you want to tell me." He clasped her cold hand, giving the unspoken acceptance and reassurance she'd given him.

She finally raised her head, and he wanted to see those loving blue eyes looking at him until he took his last breath. As if he was the most important person in her world, and she trusted him with her heart and soul. In that moment,

he promised himself he'd never take that trust
for granted or do anything to make this woman
who was his world ever think any less of him.

"I'll start with my job." She sat on a nearby
footstool and gave him the ghost of a smile. "I
love nursing, and I always thought my goal was
a research position in a big city. But the truth
is, I'm tired of it. I want to live and work here.
That's for me, not you or us." She raised a hand
when Troy would have interrupted. "Even if you
weren't in my life, I'd decided I was only going
to go back to Atlanta temporarily while I looked
for the right job in Montana. I enjoy medical
research, but I miss working one-on-one with
patients." She shook her head. "I'd have come
home to stay before now if I hadn't been too
proud to admit my goals had changed. It turns
out my High Valley roots are a lot stronger than
I thought."

"You mean you won't miss Atlanta?" Adrenaline rushed through Troy, and if he could have
gotten out of the recliner to jump around the
room he would have. As it was, he had to settle
for a wide grin.

"I'll miss some things, sure, but I…*we*…"
Molly grinned back. "We can go there on vacation. I was confused about a lot of things, but it
feels like for the first time in my life, I'm truly
seeing myself and what I want. I loved my time

A RANCHER'S RETURN

in Atlanta, but I'll love being home even more because I went away."

"And?" As he eased closer to Molly, Acorn hopped off Troy's lap to sit on the rug beside them.

"You know me well." Her smile slipped. She twirled a strand of hair. "When I broke up with you before, I—"

"That's in the past. We don't have to ever talk about it again." He pressed a finger to the sweet curve of her lips. There was nothing she could say that would make him love her less.

"Not after today, but there's something I have to tell you. I can't live with myself—or see where our relationship goes—until I do."

Troy knew exactly where their relationship was going. As soon as he was up and about again, he'd ask Molly to marry him. If she accepted, and he was certain she would, they'd be planning a wedding and invite their families, friends and the whole town if that's what she wanted. But before that, he'd ask Cathy to get that box with the bear paw moonstone pendant out of his upstairs desk drawer. He wanted to give it to Molly as soon as he could as a symbol of their past, present and future.

Troy nodded, hardly able to contain his excitement. After losing what had felt like everything, all the dreams he hadn't let himself dream were on the brink of coming true.

"I broke up with you mostly because I was afraid." Her voice cracked, and she swallowed. "If we'd stayed together, yes, I was afraid I'd end up like my mom and not earn my degree or have a career. But I was even more scared of losing a man I loved in a farm accident like my mom lost my dad."

"And now?" He leaned as close as his fractured ribs allowed and breathed in her sweet jasmine scent. "Ranching's important to me, but not so much that I wouldn't give it up for you."

"No, despite everything, I love ranch life." She gulped and composed herself. "When I found you after you'd fallen off that ladder, I tried to tell myself it was good we'd broken up because I couldn't face losing you. Then, only a few minutes after the ambulance pulled away, I realized I could lose you or anyone else in lots of ways. You could be in your office and well... I've worked in an ER. I don't need to give you a list."

"Thanks." Troy chuckled.

"I said you were scared to take a risk, but I was so afraid of risk I couldn't do anything that wasn't part of the plan I set out for myself when I was a kid. Leave the ranch and get my nursing degree. Leave Montana, work in a city, marry someone who lived in that city and had what I thought was a 'safe' job." She closed the distance between them until her face was only inches from his. "Now I realize I have lots of choices, but my love for you will always be bigger than anything else."

"We were both afraid of risk, but we can take the risks that are right for us together. I love you, Molly, and that will never change."

"I love you too." She tilted her head, and he read the invitation in her face.

And as their lips met in a kiss he never wanted to end, he knew he was exactly where he was supposed to be.

Acorn barked, someone cleared their throat and Troy raised his head.

"It's been a lot longer than ten minutes, and Molly asked me to…" Bryce poked his head into the living room with an amused smile. "I take it you two worked everything out?"

"Yes." Molly's face was pink as she dragged her gaze away from Troy to look at her brother. "Sorry I kept you waiting."

"I'm not in any hurry." Bryce's smile broadened. "I'll go check out Troy's horse pasture. It looks like you two might need some privacy."

"Thanks, bro," Troy said, and as the front door shut behind the man Troy hoped he'd soon be able to call "brother" for real, he bent his head to Molly's again. "I'll never stop being grateful I came home to Montana."

"Me too. It's home." Then she kissed him once more. Home, family and all the love Troy ever needed were right there in the only woman he wanted to hold, now and always.

# EPILOGUE

*The Bitterroot Ranch,*
*July, almost five years later*

"GREAT JOB, DENNY." From outside the fence, Molly clapped as her small son sat atop the placid pony that Troy led around the paddock.

"I wanna get off and have lunch, Daddy." At three and a half, Denny was in perpetual motion and reminded Molly of his uncle Cole.

"Here you go, kiddo." Troy lifted Denny off, removed his riding helmet and ruffled the boy's hair. "Everyone's on the deck." He left the pony with a ranch hand, joined Molly and slipped an arm around her shoulders as they followed Denny to the house. "You're sure it's not too hot out here for you?"

"I'm fine." Molly fingered her moonstone bear paw pendant, which, apart from her engagement and wedding rings, was the most precious piece of jewelry she owned. She smiled at her husband. She loved Troy more with each passing year, and she also loved the life they'd made together. The wish she'd made on that star so long ago—the same one he had made, as it turned out—had come true beyond her wildest dreams. "This baby's a live wire, though. Even more than Denny was." She patted her pregnant belly. "Carrie says I've got a future barrel racer in here."

"She should know since she and Bryce are raising their own. Emma and Lucy can't wait to be old enough to compete and follow in Paisley's footsteps." Troy laughed as they reached the deck where the extended Carter family had gathered to celebrate Zach and Ellie's birthdays. "Between your brothers' kids and ours, we could be building a family rodeo dynasty."

"Maybe, but I'd rather build a close family who are there for each other no matter what." As they stepped onto the deck, she nodded toward Paisley, Skylar and Cam in the middle of a group of smaller cousins that now included Denny. As they took turns hugging Ellie, currently a college student who'd returned from Helena the day before, Molly's heart felt full. "Ellie's a big sister to all of them, isn't she?"

"She sure is." Troy nodded approval as Zane and Zoë, Cole and Melissa's twins, stood on either side of Denny and held the younger boy's hands.

"Lunch is almost ready. All you have to do is sit and enjoy." Wearing a pink gingham bib apron, her mom guided Molly to a folding chair by a table shaded by a big patio umbrella. "Between your job and running around after Denny, you need to put your feet up more, honey."

"Thanks, Mom." Living here had blessed Molly's life in so many ways, but having her mom nearby was one of the biggest.

As Troy went to check in with Shane and her brothers at the barbecue, Molly sank into the chair and poured herself a glass of lemonade from an ice-filled pitcher. In late pregnancy, Molly wasn't working on a hospital ward but spent all her time on the other half of her job, heading up a satellite pediatric research project linked with the Atlanta hospital where she'd once worked. Over the past few years, she'd found the best of both worlds—patient-facing nursing mixed with interesting clinical studies that stemmed from work she'd done for her master's program.

"Your dad and Paul would be so proud of you. *All* of you." Her mom sat across from Molly and gestured to the assembled family, which also included Troy's parents, who spent summers in High Valley. "And your little Denny helps keep their legacy alive."

Molly covered her mom's hand with hers as

she watched her son, Dennis Paul, play with his cousins. "Dad and Paul would be proud of you too. I don't say it enough, but I love you, Mom, and I'm so grateful for you and the family you and Dad began for us. Even if we're not all linked by blood, we're connected by love."

"Aww, honey." Her mom held Molly's hand tight. "That means so much."

"Auntie Molly?" Zach and Beth's daughter, Holly Rosa Joy Carter, nudged Molly's arm.

"Yes, sweetheart?" This precious niece, who Molly had helped bring into the world on that snowy December evening, had an extra special place in her heart.

"Daddy just said Mommy's his happy-ever-after. What does that mean?" Holly stared at her with the solemn brown eyes that made Rosa call her an "old soul."

"It means…" Molly paused and looked around the family group. "What we all have here. We're happy for the rest of our lives because we have each other."

"Happy-ever-after is nice." Holly grinned before darting off.

"And you're *my* happy-ever-after." Troy returned to Molly's side and wrapped his arms around her.

"Like you're mine." Molly looked into his eyes, knowing the love they shared would go on not only through their own lives, but those of their children, grandchildren and beyond.

A legacy that would extend across the years, no matter what the future might bring.

\* \* \* \* \*

*For more great romances in the miniseries, visit www.Harlequin.com today!*

front porch,
backlighted from the howling wind